MINE TO GUARD

PROTECTION SERIES BOOK 3

KENNEDY L. MITCHELL

© 2021 Kennedy L. Mitchell

All rights reserved. This book or any portion thereof may not be reproduced or used in any manner whatsoever without the express written permission of the publisher except for the use of brief quotations in a book review.

This book is a work of fiction. Any references to historical events, real people, or real places are used fictitiously. Other names, characters, places and events are products of the author's imagination, and any resemblances to actual events or places or persons, living or dead, is entirely coincidental.

Cover Design: Bookin It Designs

Editing: Hot Tree Editing

Proofreading: All Encompassing Books

❦ Created with Vellum

ABOUT THE AUTHOR

Kennedy L. Mitchell lives outside Dallas with her husband, son and two very large goldendoodles. She began writing in 2016 after a fight with her husband (You can read the fight almost verbatim in Falling for the Chance) and has no plans of stopping.

She would love to hear from you via any of the platforms below or her website www.kennedylmitchell.com You can also stay up to date on future releases through her newsletter or by joining her Facebook readers group - Kennedy's Book Boyfriend Support Group.

Thank you for reading.

PROLOGUE

A gust of scorching wind whipped down the narrow alley, applying another layer of West Texas dust to his sticky cheeks and neck. The stench of piss, sewage, and rotten food infiltrated his dry nose, but he paid it no attention. Those smells were more familiar to him than anything else in this world. But the dust—he dug his cracked nails into the back of his neck, scratching at the irritated surface—was annoying as hell.

Everything itched. His skin, his blood, his mind. This insistent urge to claw beneath his skin, to soothe whatever lay beneath, had been a part of him for as long as he could remember. The itch that irritated his very existence was one of his constant companions. Either from the relentless dry and dusty air, the need to remove the feel of another's cruel touch, or the demand for a fix, he didn't give a damn why. Only one thing mattered to him.

Revenge.

And soon, he'd have it. The game of cat and mouse grew boring years ago. Time to catch his prey and end it all.

Beneath jagged nails, bloodred lines marked his naturally fair skin with each frantic scrape to his wrist, dipping beneath the cuff of the faded dark sweatshirt to scratch his forearm. Scars of varying shapes and sizes stayed hidden beneath the long sleeves—not that anyone paid close enough attention to him for them to notice, even if exposed. The only scars he couldn't conceal were the faint row of slim lines stacking along the column of his neck.

Those scars were his other constant companion, or rather the memories they invoked anytime he caught his reflection.

He rubbed one cracked lip against the other as he stalked from the shadows, waiting.

It ended tonight. She'd lived her lie of a life long enough. Now came the time for her to pay for ruining his. Soon she'd feel the same pain he endured, be lost in the darkness of hopelessness.

Crooked, black-spotted teeth showed as a sinister smile stretched across his face. Leaning back, he rested against the brick wall. He couldn't wait to watch her pain, cause her torment. The one thing he was good at, what kept him alive and employed this long.

Removing a fresh joint and lighter from his baggy jeans, he sealed the twisted end of the paper between his lips and lit the opposite end.

He held the lungful of laced smoke, hoping whatever concoction Bradley put in this batch would kick in faster and calm his eager nerves. Desperate for oxygen, he slowly released the toxic smoke through pursed lips, watching as it quickly vanished into the late evening night sky.

The chatter and high-pitched laughter of a passing group of women had him tucking the joint behind him as he slunk deeper into the shadows. The five women passed the alleyway none the wiser of the evil and danger lurking within.

Again, he smiled and took another hit.

Maybe tonight, to celebrate, he'd find some junkie desperate enough to fuck him for a hit. There were always a few who knew his unique preferences and would answer his call. The thought grew in his now calm mind, the drug's effects already kicking in. His hands casually hung by his side, no longer attempting to dig beneath his skin.

Relief. His lids drooped, the restaurant across the street he'd been watching for over three hours now only a sliver in his vision. Yes, tonight was the night. It was a long time coming for the cunt who ruined his life, but the minor hiccup in his plans ten years ago kept him from fulfilling his sinister ambitions.

Nothing stood in his way now.

A flash of light across the street diverted his attention from the glowing ember at the end of his joint and pulled his confusing thoughts back to the task at hand. The gray sidewalk brightened as the door swung open, chasing away the night's darkness with glowing lights and filling the quiet with muted laughter and chatter pouring out from inside the restaurant.

Having done this stalking business many times before, he slunk deeper into the shadows but kept his eye on the figure that emerged from the downtown restaurant and stepped onto the empty sidewalk. Heat from the brick seeped through his sweatshirt where he sealed his knobby spine against it.

Even before the person turned, he knew who it was.

He clenched both hands into tight fists, the still-smoldering joint crushed between his fingers. His breaths came faster, the earlier calm brought on by the chemical additive gone.

Every Tuesday was the same, and tonight was no different.

Her long dark ponytail swept from side to side as she stepped toward the curb, her fingers slipping from the door's edge. It slowly closed behind her. Jeans, a basic white T-shirt, and completely alone. This was her routine. The clothes, the timing, the lack of friends or company always the same since he began watching her after his release.

Relaxing his fists, his fingers twitched at his side, the desperation for more weed making his mind and nerves dance.

The rough brick snagged the threadbare cotton of his sweatshirt as he slid along the building. With each step he grew closer to her, his heart raced faster.

This was it. Maybe finally he'd have peace once the score evened, the imbalance in his life righted. It wouldn't take away the nightmares, the memories, or change his future, but it would calm the beat of rage that tormented him since that day he'd learned how she ruined his life.

Tall, thick in the hips and shoulders, she wasn't the weak addict he'd grown accustomed to ending, but he'd make do. He might have been scrawny as fuck, but he could hold his own.

From the corner of the building, he observed as she wandered down the sidewalk toward the late-model Ford Taurus he knew waited around the corner in the restaurant's parking lot.

Now was his chance.

He stepped forward, half his body illuminated in the streetlamp's glow, only for him to dash back around when the restaurant door swung open once again. He narrowed his eyes, frustrated at the intrusion. A man stepped out, hand in the air, calling her name.

A growl rumbled in his chest as he watched the man chase after her.

The woman paused and turned but didn't rush away in fear. Instead, she stayed rooted directly beneath a soft glow of light.

He waited, cheek now resting along the brick as he watched their short exchange.

Then it happened.

Even with the shadows covering her face, her wide smile at something the interrupting fucker said was clear as fucking day.

A smile.

Indignation and hate boiled in his veins, making more sweat collect along his hairline and slip down his temples. He sneered, his broken and chipped nails clawing into the brick to hold him back from launching himself across the street and ending this shit out in the open.

Her irritating voice whipped down the street, her words too muffled for him to understand. He watched the two talk, the man stepping closer to her with casual, slow steps.

This would not do.

His molars ground together as he sawed his jaw back and forth.

Maybe....

An idea rolled around in his rapid-fire thoughts, building with each second the two spoke. The plan fully formed, he relaxed his fingers, the stiffness painful, and eased his shoulders away from his ears. Yes, this would teach her a fresh lesson.

An additional emotional torment and pain before the physical torture he would soon inflict. It had been a while since she felt loss. Time for a reminder of what happened to those she befriended or loved. The fact that the bitch hadn't learned her lesson from the past spoke to her lack of intelligence.

The conversation between the two lasted only a couple minutes, but long enough to seal the fucker's fate. With a raised hand, she disappeared around the corner. Seconds later, a familiar brown Ford Taurus eased out of the gravel parking lot onto the empty downtown streets.

With his original target gone, his stony gaze focused on the man still standing on the sidewalk. Hands shoved into the front pockets of his jeans, the man turned, finally facing his hiding spot. Anger flared at the amiable smile on his perfect fucking face.

The man tilted his face up to the night sky, that smile growing wider.

Fuck. That.

No one deserved happiness or love but rather horrors and darkness like his.

That drove his rage, his hatred for every person he encountered.

Was he born or made into this burning ball of hate, death, and evil? Fuck if he knew. But it didn't matter. He dealt with it all the same.

As the man moved down the sidewalk, he followed, sticking to the shadows. This was his favorite part, stalking the prey. Their fate in his vile hands.

Ten feet ahead, a broken streetlamp cast a six-foot area in darkness.

Perfect.

Shifting from one shadow to the other, he weaved his way across the street, his prey none the wiser that a predator lingered hot on his heels. Just the way he liked it.

This man would endure his wrath for disrupting his plan. Maybe he'd draw it out, make him suffer for not only making the cunt smile but for postponing his ultimate plan. Yes, he'd use the man to practice what he envisioned with his blade, insuring each slice inflicted the most pain on her creamy flesh.

A thrill stirred in his gut, the anticipation rising with each new cruel thought. He'd have fun with this one, then leave the body for her, an omen of what would come.

Rae Chapin would die by his brutal hand soon.

Very soon.

1

RAE

I might puke.
 The crappy police station sludge they called coffee plus the herd of elephants stomping inside my brain made the nausea unbearable. A loud grumble erupted in my gut, in desperate need of greasy food and something bubbly. But not champagne. Bile rose in my throat at the mere thought of ingesting another ounce of alcohol.

Why did I open that third bottle? Or was it a fourth?

Groaning, I pitched forward. "Fuck me," I whispered, my lips brushing against the cool metal table, not caring who watched from the other side of the two-way mirror. Eyes closed and pressed into my forearm, I fought against the urge to eradicate my stomach of the wine and popcorn I consumed for dinner the night before.

I knew better than to open the damn shoebox that worked as a time capsule for the past while listening to Delilah reruns on the radio. Yet I did, again. It'd been a while since I broke down, allowing the hurtful memories to overwhelm every thought. I blamed it on that damn article in the local paper, triggering the emotional over-drinking, snack food fest, and self-torture by reading through our old handwritten notes.

Not only did I know better than to open that third bottle of cheap white wine, but I also knew better than to allow myself to fall into the memories and dwell on disappointment in the life I wanted but never had. Even the simple action of reading his name sparked a swell of emotions I'd long forgotten about, or at least tried to.

Alec Bronson, now Texas Ranger Alec Bronson, the man I once loved and then hated, and now... well, that was complicated. Then that picture of him didn't help at all with yesterday's downward spiral. All that prompted the tiny stalking mission where I dug up everything I could about him via Google.

I was a damn mess over that man. Ever since he walked out with a simple "Dear John" note left in my locker, I'd been a pining fool.

Not that everything terrible in my life was his fault.

No. That bitch fate dealt my life's horrific events.

Fate drove me to the minimal existence I now lived. Trapped in a cycle of monotony, making every day my personal hell. Work, home, drink, and repeat. No friends, no family, 100 percent alone in every way.

I saved lives this way.

I didn't become the local recluse and hide any glimpse of happy away for my well-being. No, I did it for others. A curse surrounded me, one that left those I loved or who befriended me dead. Since that day I morphed into a shell of my former self, no one had died because of me.

Before those first murders, I was happy, friendly to anyone who needed a smiling face. But now I'm this. A lonely, drunken mid-thirties woman who deep down still pined for the boy who broke her heart in high school.

Pathetic.

And that wasn't the worst part of my sad existence.

The worst part was the reason I now sat in an interrogation room instead of at work.

A faint click sent me bolting upright. The door swung open, bringing with it muffled shouts and laughter from other areas of the police station. My lids slid open and shut several times to clear away the dryness blurring my vision. As my surroundings sharpened, a heavyset man in a cheap brown suit waddled into the interrogation room, his accusing glower locked on me.

If I didn't think it would hurt, I would've rolled my eyes at his attempt at the intimidating stance and glare. It wouldn't work considering I was innocent of whatever they wanted to accuse me of today. Not succumbing to standard interrogation tactics must have been in my extensive file, right?

A low hum vibrated in his thick throat, like he'd just figured something out about me. Metal legs scraped along the tile as he dragged the only other chair in the room out from under the table and plopped down. I kept my dark eyes on him, matching his intensity even though all my bravado was fake.

My attention slipped to the buttons straining to hold his dingy white dress shirt together. Each of his wheezing breaths threatened to pop one off and assault me. A laugh bubbled in my chest at that thought, but I kept the practiced blank mask in place.

He cleared his throat and slapped a manila folder onto the table between us, its contents at least an inch thick.

"Rae Chapin," the detective said, his voice gravelly, probably from years of smoking based on the thick scent that followed him into the tiny room.

"That's me," I huffed, crossing my arms over my chest, tugging the edges of my black cardigan closer. It was freezing in here, a small win for my hungover state.

"Welcome back," he mocked.

Oh, this ass has jokes.

Shifting on the hard metal seat, I failed to stop my wince. In their typical "sweat them out" tactic, I'd sat in this chair for an hour now. Half my wide ass was now numb from the uncomfortable seat and lack of movement.

"Funny. What happened?" I asked, straight to the point.

After being dragged out of the library by two uniformed officers plus the killer hangover, I wasn't in the mood to beat around the bush with this guy. I knew how all this would go down considering this routine wasn't new for me, unfortunately.

His bushy dark brows rose along his forehead. "You tell me, Rae. What happened?"

This guy is a joke.

Instead of responding, I interlaced my fingers and rested both hands back on the table. The cool surface soothed my warm skin and offered a smidge of relief to the rolling in my stomach. My calm facade was just that. Inside, my rattled nerves made sweat build beneath my armpits and collect down my spine, while my breaths grew quicker with each passing second the detective stared down his long thin nose with that condemning sneer.

I hated this. Every time it was the same, which was why I asked what happened. Because all this—dragging me from work, interrogation room, salty detective—meant one thing.

Something bad happened, and they thought I did it. Which I didn't. Unless they wanted to arrest me for being a pathetic human who drank too much and loved listening to sappy eighties' love songs. That I would be guilty of.

Nothing like being assumed guilty of heinous crimes to make a woman with already low self-esteem feel special.

When I didn't respond in the timeframe of his liking, he leaned forward, placing an elbow on the table. "Not feeling very chatty today, Rae?" he asked.

"Can I get a Coke or maybe a few Twinkies?" I deadpanned. If he asked stupid questions and avoided answering me, then I would do the same. Plus a Coke sounded glorious. I licked my dry lips just thinking about the miracle concoction that would settle my stomach and give me a boost to help survive this interrogation.

A deep red flush sprouted along his sagging cheeks. "This isn't a game, girl." *Girl? Really?* "You know why you're here."

"Really, I don't, but please enlighten me. What happened?"

"Tell us what we need to know and I'll tell the DA you cooperated." I sealed my lips together to stop myself from mouthing off. That only pissed him off more. "You say you don't know why you're here, but you automatically assumed something happened. Why?"

Chapter 1

An agonizing groan of metal vibrated through the room as the detective leaned back in the chair and balanced on the two rear legs.

"Why? Seriously? This isn't the first time I've been in this room. You've seen my file," I said with a flick of my wrist toward the manila folder. "Every time I'm in here it's because someone died and you guys seem to think I'm involved."

"It is an extensive file." He patted the top of the folder. "The suspicions surrounding you—"

"With no proof," I snapped, interrupting him. "Five times now you or some other detective has dragged me to the station because of circumstantial evidence. Each time it's been for nothing. You could've spent your time searching for the actual suspect instead of trying to pin me with a crime I didn't commit."

His humorless laugh grated on my frayed nerves. "Those are some big words, Rae. Seems someone has been reading too much in the reference section at the library."

My fingers curled into tight fists, my short nails digging into my callus-free palms. "I've read every damn book, article, document, and archive in that damn building. It's not like I have anything else to do." I hoped he didn't notice the way my voice hitched with the swell of emotion those truthful words spurred.

"Rae, I'll let you in on a little secret." He leaned in close, sending a heavy waft of stale smoke my way. "You're no smarter than us, and this time we caught you red-handed."

I arched a dark brow, which only made his anger-fueled flush deepen. "No you haven't, because I haven't done a damn thing wrong. I've told you guys this every time you've dragged me down here. It's not me. It's never been me. I'm cursed," I whispered, knowing full well those words might get me tossed into the looney bin. "Want to test my theory? Be my friend. Hang out with me a few times, make me laugh or smile. I give you two weeks' tops before you're dead too, and not by my hands."

"Is that why you killed him?"

"Killed who?" I shouted, wincing when the echo sliced through my ears into my pounding head.

"Gregory Basin." The damn bastard had shifted from angry to smug, like he caught me in something.

Annoyance flooded my veins, wiping away any semblance of patience I had left. This had gone on long enough. It was time for me to get out of here and go home.

To no one.

"Listen here, jackwagon. I'll tell you this again. I have hurt no one—ever. Hell, I even brake for squirrels. I don't even know a Gregory Basin, so why would I kill him?"

The weight of those words hit me in the chest. I didn't even know a Gregory Basin. I didn't have any friends or family left, so why would they suspect me of killing some guy I'd never met?

Unease grew, making my heart race.

Ignoring my demand for answers, again, he rapped his fingertips along the top of the folder. "Where were you last night?"

"The same place I am every Tuesday night. Jones's downtown," I grumbled, wrapping my arms around my chest in a motion the detective noted with a raise of both bushy brows.

Tuesday nights were the one night I allowed myself to go out. To sit in the same back corner booth and watch the world go on without me. I never interacted with anyone other than the server, and even those conversations remained brief and impersonal. Keeping to myself ensured those around me stayed safe. Which was why I continued to turn that one guy's advances down.

The same guy who followed me out....

My eyes widened in realization. A clammy palm slapped to my lips to cover my gaping mouth.

The detective let out an incredulous chuckle. "I see you've realized your mistake, considering that was the last place anyone saw Mr. Basin. In fact, we have several witnesses stating they saw you two leave together." I shook my head, my hand still firmly sealed over my mouth. "Which means you were the last person to see him before he disappeared."

Disappeared.

A hefty breath whooshed from my burning lungs as my hand fell to the table. Disappeared, not dead. Maybe there was still time to save him.

Guilt clawed in my chest, making each inhale painful. He was harmless, so damn young and innocent. A man who didn't deserve this because he wanted to buy me a drink, to cheer up a lonely woman.

I squeezed both eyes shut to prevent the tears from spilling over. He'd approached my booth for the past few weeks, each time with a lame pickup line and a smile. Last Tuesday night, he broke through my solid walls somehow, catching me in a weak moment that allowed him to talk for a few minutes before I made him leave.

Too many times I told him I was no good for him, that he should just leave me alone, but he never stopped, never let up on his onslaught of kindness and charm.

"Find him," I whispered.

"That's what I'm trying to do, Rae. It's why you're here."

I shook my head, the tip of my ponytail swishing from side to side with the quick movement. "I don't know where he is. When I drove off, he stood outside Jones's. It wasn't me. It's never me." Panic added a high pitch to my rising voice. "Someone is doing this to me. Someone has to be following me. It's happening again," I half cried, half demanded.

"Sticking with the same story, I see." His disappointed sigh filled the room. "Tell us where he is, Rae. We won't let you out of here until we find him. It'll go a long way with the DA if you cooperate."

I flung my hands out wide, fingers spread. "How can I cooperate when I know nothing? I didn't do this." I searched his hard gaze. "You can't keep me here without charging me."

The detective's lips curled in a knowing smile. "True, but since you were the last person to see Mr. Basin, we can hold you for forty-eight hours. Maybe two days in holding will make you more compliant." His gaze slipped lower. "What happened, Rae? Did he not return your advances? The bar owner said you two spoke several times before Tuesday night. Did you kill him like the others because this time he turned you down?" His eyes continued their once-over. "I can see why he would. Based on his driver's license, you would've smothered the poor boy."

My shoulders rounded in an attempt to curl into myself. My heavier weight, full curves, and tall frame were my biggest self-esteem triggers. And this asshole just struck a low blow, knowing full well it would knock me off-kilter.

This was bad. Never had they threatened to hold me as a suspect. Snagging the tip of my ponytail I nervously brushed the end along my dry lips. Prison? I was too soft; I'd be someone's bitch in no time. Plus, I didn't know how to make a shank, didn't have anyone in my life who would come talk to me through that plastic window, offering a small reprieve from the horrors of day-to-day prison life.

The scrape of the chair legs snapped me out of my dark, strange downward spiral. Frantically I stood, mirroring the detective. Fingers hooked into the waistband of his pants, he hiked his belt higher.

"We've got you this time, Rae. Soon you'll be behind bars, unable to hurt anyone else."

A smidge of truth hid in that statement. If I were in the slammer, I couldn't hurt anyone else just by my association. I thought this was over, the death. Over ten years with no one dying around me. And now this happened.

"Believe me," I pleaded. "I didn't do this. Someone is out there doing this to me, to them."

Without another word, he shook his head and turned for the door. Panic slammed through me, and my thoughts turned more erratic. Searching the small room, I racked my brain for anything that could help, anything that would get me out of this shit situation.

The only answer to this predicament was simple, yet not.

"Wait," I shouted just before the door shut, sealing my fate. This was the dumbest idea I'd ever had, but it was my only option. It had to work or I was screwed. This guy could only see what he wanted to with this case. I needed to look out for myself since no one else would.

"Ready to confess?" the detective asked, not bothering to turn from the hallway.

I waited for him to give me his full attention before I responded.

"No, Detective. I won't confess to something I didn't do to make your job easier. But I want one thing."

"And what's that?" he sneered.

Palms to the metal table, I leaned forward, attempting an intimidating stance as I met his glare.

"My one fucking phone call."

2

ALEC

The weighted bag swung with each punch, absorbing the rage that had blanketed me in bitterness since arriving home two days prior. Left, left, right, right. For thirty minutes now I repeated the same sequence, tossing in a few uppercuts here and there. Each time my bare knuckles slammed into the red leather, I relished the burn of my now exhausted muscles.

Rivers of sweat slipped down my exposed back, dipping beneath the gym shorts hung low on my hips. In my private in-home gym, I wasn't embarrassed to go shirtless. Here I could run around butt-ass naked if I wanted—and had once or twice before—without a single side-eye stare or question about the array of scars lining my back and upper thighs. With as much money as Mom left me, I could afford to have the scars removed, but I never would.

The crisscross patterns, long stripes of scarred flesh, tugged each time I moved, which served as a reminder of the monster lurking just beneath my skin—of the man I would become. Today, however, those scars dragged me down a dark memory lane, threatening to swallow me whole.

My roar drowned out the blaring music as I slammed one fist and then the other into the punching bag with as much force as I could muster, imagining my bastard of a father's face instead of the swinging leather bag.

Fatigue tightened my muscles, slowing my swings and force. A weak punch sent my split and raw knuckles skimming over the sweat-slick covering. I stumbled forward with the missed impact, throwing off my stability. The smack of skin popped in my ear as my shoulder slammed into the bag, stopping me before I fell face-first to the sweat-dotted mat.

Chest heaving from physical and emotional exhaustion, I hugged the bag like a long-lost friend, allowing my trembling muscles a momentary reprieve. Minutes ticked by with me frozen in place, eyes shut as I struggled to forget. Forget my childhood, my loneliness, and the past several months in Orin.

They sentenced that bastard from Orin last week. The cult was disbanded, the gates locked. Everything worked out in the end. We offered those who were afraid, who needed to disappear, the option to do so. I helped them move, offered witness protection to those who testified against their leader, which gained them hate from those still loyal to that bastard. Even my spitfire friend Ellie found her happy ending with Peters.

So why was I so damn angry? Why couldn't I get over the churning in my gut urging me to release my frustrations on anyone within arm's reach? It'd been a long while since I let myself sink into this dark hole of self-pity, allowing it to tug my actions and thoughts into the dark too.

The few women and kids we liberated, their bruises, old and new wounds, and blank stares could have triggered this demanding relapse.

With an annoyed grunt at no one other than myself, I pushed off the bag and stalked out of the gym, snagging a fresh white towel off the shelf as I did. Bare feet slapped the polished dark hardwood floors, leaving sweaty footprints as I marched toward the kitchen. The soft cotton wicked up the sweat as I scrubbed it along my forehead and face. A grumble seemed to echo down the hall, my stomach telling me it was time to replenish all the calories I just beat out of my system.

The floor-to-ceiling windows greeted me as I entered the large kitchen, dining, and living area. I paused, giving myself a second to appreciate the acres of nothing except mesquite trees, rocks, and dirt. The sun burned through the windows, its harsh afternoon rays causing me to squint even with the tinted glass.

"Beautiful day." I tore my unseeing gaze from the landscape to look over my shoulder toward the kind voice. Sherry smiled, her hands clasped in front of her crisp apron. That smile slipped a fraction when she took in the droplets of sweat littered along the floor.

Sherry had been with me for years now acting as my live-in cook, housekeeper, friend, mother hen—anything I needed. And sometimes exactly what I didn't.

I grimaced and bent forward, swiping the damp towel along the floor to clean up the mess. "Sorry, Sher Sher," I said. Apparently living with Agent Peters for a couple weeks and a few more on my own in that damn creepy religious rental turned me into a slob. "I'll do a better job cleaning it up." My stomach chose that moment to gurgle with hunger. "After a snack," I said with a grin.

"You mean meal number four for the day," she corrected with a smile of her own as she bustled about the kitchen. She loved my vivacious appetite for her cooking. "What will it be?"

"Any pasta?" My stomach growled at her confirming nod. "And to add on to our conversation earlier, I wasn't out saving the world."

"It was the world to those you saved." I tracked her movements around the kitchen as she removed food from the fridge before bustling about selecting plates, silverware, and a cloth napkin. After placing a damp paper towel on top of the food, she slid the plate into the microwave and pressed a few buttons. "Never discredit what you do because you're quick to dismiss the impact of your actions. There were kids in that hellhole. You saved them and those women who couldn't have gotten free on their own. You did that, Alec Bronson. You." For emphasis, she pointed the dinner knife at me.

I held up both hands in surrender. "I had a lot of help, Sher Sher." She rolled her eyes at my term of endearment. She hated it, which was why I kept using it. "The FBI, Marshals, and...." I paused, my lips pressed in a thin line. "Wait a second. How do you know those details? I haven't told you any specifics regarding the case."

"The media loves a fanfare, you know that. A cult in the heart of our state was the biggest story of the year. They covered everything from the time you arrested that man till the end of his trial." Her blonde brows rose. "You really didn't know?"

Hard calluses scraped my forehead and cheeks as I tried to scrub the annoyance off my face. I should've known it would've been a media sensation, but considering I worked thirteen-hour days the last six months, I hadn't noticed.

My nostrils flared as I inhaled deep, filling my lungs with the savory scents now heavy in the kitchen. A hum of excitement vibrated in my chest. No one should get this excited about food, but I always had. Being a bigger-than-normal guy came with the constant need to eat. The microwave's high-pitched beep signaled the food was ready, causing saliva to collect in my mouth.

"What about those hours you put in helping move those who testified?" Sherry questioned as she pulled the steaming plate from the microwave and deposited it on the placemat. "How are they doing?"

"Ah hell," I snapped, annoyance overpowering my hunger. "Is there nothing those vultures won't cover? I moved them for their protection. If anyone finds out where...." I closed my eyes and took a calming breath. "Did they give details?"

"Calm down before you give yourself a stroke. They didn't say who or where, just that Texas Ranger Alec Bronson led the charge on relocating those who feared for their lives after testifying against the leader. One article also stated you put a male cult member in the hospital for going after one kid." Peeking up from the sink where she stood washing the dirty container, she wore a knowing smile. "Which I'm sure was completely exaggerated."

"Sounds suspicious," I said, humor lifting my tone. Whether it was her presence, the knowledge that my belly would soon be full, or the impromptu workout doing its job, I felt lighter than I had in days.

Chapter 2

As much as I wanted to believe Sherry, I was far from the man she thought I was. A hero didn't have a rage-filled monster lurking inside him, fighting every day for a way out. The curved edges of the fork pressed into my palm under my tightening grip.

"That's for eating, not bending."

Teeth clenched, I forced a smile and relaxed my grip, turning my attention back to the food. Each savory spice combined with the heat soothed the remaining jagged edges of my temper, easing the tension from my shoulders and neck.

"Damn, I missed you," I said, my tone and features soft with adoration.

Sherry scoffed and popped the edge of a hand towel toward me. "You missed my cooking."

"I can miss you both equally."

"I know which you favor," she said, wiping along the counter. "So what's next? You back on the road soon?"

The fork rattled onto the now empty plate. I stared at the remaining sauce, debating licking it clean, but she stole it away, deciding for me. I hummed in approval and leaned back in the chair, hand absentmindedly rubbing my stomach.

Sherry watched with joy radiating in her dark eyes and wide smile. For a brief second, I allowed myself to remember another woman with the same bursting happiness about her. A girl I hadn't seen in over two decades but thought about every now and again. She was my sunshine during those dark years with my father, my only channel of hope and good in the world.

"I'm taking a few days off," I said, finally responding to Sherry. Taking the napkin, I wiped the corners of my mouth and tossed it to the placemat. "That case was...." I struggled to find the right words to depict how the cult case and incident involving Ellie affected me. "It got to me. I need some time to myself to shake off what's lingering before I can move on." Heels of both hands on the counter, I pushed back and stepped away from the bar. "I'll be in my office if you need me."

Now that Rae's innocent, smiling face had flashed through my mind, it was all I could think about. Remembering the way she smelled, her soft skin, and kissable full lips. I hadn't thought about my high school sweetheart—the only woman I ever really allowed myself to love—in years. The familiar ache of leaving her without an explanation crept into my chest.

I was finally losing my mind, the stress of it all finally taking its toll. Why else would the mere memory of Rae's sparkling eyes and honest smile make my heart clench? Me losing my mind over the memory of a girl who probably moved on the day I left, unlike me, made sense.

For years I wanted to reach out to her, see if she missed me like I did her, but I couldn't. I left for a reason: to keep her safe.

That reason still stood today.

Interlacing my fingers behind my head, I tilted my face up to the ceiling, looking for answers there. The only one was a waft of male stench. My stench. Turning my nose, I gave a tentative sniff and gagged.

Instead of heading into my office as planned, I turned into my master suite. Hooking both thumbs into the elastic waistband of my shorts, I gave a hard tug. Not missing a step, I let them fall to the floor and continued on to the large en suite bathroom. Cool slate stone tile greeted my bare feet, sending a shock up my legs at the sensation. My reflection flashed in the two mirrors hanging over the dual sinks as I marched for the freestanding shower.

I turned the chrome handle just enough to get the water flowing to the rainfall showerhead and then stepped under the freezing stream. The full spray battered against my skin, washing away the sweat, but it did nothing to the thoughts of Rae running on a loop through my mind.

Forearms to the tilted wall, I relaxed my neck as the water beat against my back. Only after all the sweat had rinsed down the drain and my dick and balls were nearly shriveled to the size of a newborns did I twist the handle. Hot water pelleted my chilled skin, soothing the tension in my muscles before slipping down the drain along with the suds from my shampoo and soap.

Chapter 2

I shut off the water after a quick wash and stepped from the smooth river rock shower floor onto the tile. I gave a haphazard scrub of the towel over my longer hair—I really needed to schedule a haircut now that I'd decided to stay home for a while—and down my chest before the shrill of the office phone reached my ears. Water continued to stream down my legs as I wrapped the towel around my waist and hurried toward the office.

Stretching across the mahogany wood desk, I tapped the speaker button.

"Bronson," I said, my voice gruff. If a call came in through this line, something bad happened in my territory. Only the dispatcher used this number. Dread weighed in my chest as I padded around the desk and sank into the oversized leather chair, its wheels rolling with my weight.

"Hey there, Alec." I rolled my eyes at the sticky sweet voice. Pam didn't hide her attraction, even after many obvious rejections from me. "How are you today?"

Lifting my hips, I tugged the towel out from under me and began drying my legs. "As good as can be." Before I could tell her to get to the point, her chipper voice poured through the speaker once again.

"You know, I can always come out there and help you feel great." I shook my head, my lip curled in disgust. This got old a long time ago. "Your place is only a few hours from headquarters."

I rubbed the towel along my chest, down my abs, and then carefully dried my favorite body part. Even with me touching my cock, Pam's suggestion of coming over did nothing to stir my dick into action. The leather squeaked as I adjusted my damp ass along the seat.

"Was there a reason you called, Pam?" I asked, putting some bite into my tone to shut down her advances. Again.

"A woman called for you." I chose to not comment on the annoyance now filling her tone.

Sitting up straight, I looped the towel around my shoulders and held on to each end, my focus on the phone's speaker. "One of the women we relocated?" I gave them my cell number; why would they call the station? "Are they okay? Did something happen?"

Pam's huff filled the office, making me bite my tongue to not snap at her to hurry the fuck up. "No, this is a new one. She called asking for you specifically and won't get off the line until we connect you to her. Desperate if you ask me." She mumbled the last few words.

Towel forgotten, I gripped the edge of the desk and stood, towering over the phone. Teeth clenched, I somehow got out "Put her through, Pam."

"Say please," she retorted.

"Pam, if you don't do it right the fuck now, I'll report you for hindering Ranger business." My temper flared with the rising annoyance and dread. Inhaling through my nose, I pushed it out slowly, hoping to keep from saying something that could get me reported.

The line went silent for a moment, signaling the call transfer. Seconds later, shouts filled my office, pouring through the speaker along with soft mumbled ramblings and curses.

I stared at the phone, curiosity now pushing the flare of anger aside.

"Ranger Bronson here," I said, my voice booming so the caller could hear me over whatever ruckus continued in the background. "You asked for me?"

A sharp inhale indicated the caller heard me. "Alec?" said the unsure female voice. Intrigued, I leaned closer to the speaker, afraid the caller's words would get lost in the noise. "Alec Bronson?"

"That's me."

A throat cleared, snapping my attention to the doorway. Sherry stood there with her lips in a tight line, holding a mop in one hand while the other rested on her hip. "Sorry," I mouthed while snatching a folder to cover my dangling cock. That woman needed a raise to deal with my lazy ass, at least until I became house-trained again.

She waved me off and went back to cleaning up my trail of water from the shower.

"Are you there?" said the woman. "Alec?"

That inflection, the way she said my name, felt familiar. "I'm still here. Who is this?"

"You might not remember me. Actually, I'm pretty sure you wouldn't. I mean, it's been years. Decades," the woman rambled. "And we were just kids. Well, not really. We were almost legal," she said around an awkward laugh.

My heart thundered in my chest. I knew this person, but I couldn't pinpoint how. Whoever she was, my heart knew her.

"It's, um… me," she finished.

I smiled at the phone, not hiding my amusement even though I could feel Sherry's fiery gaze no doubt curious about this strange interaction.

"And who would 'me' be?" I prodded. "I've known a lot of 'mes'."

"I'm sure you have," she grumbled. "You always were the popular one. Hot to boot." A smack of skin against skin made me chuckle. "Shit, I did not mean to say that."

"Who is this?"

"Rae. Rae, um, with an *e*, not a *y*, Chapin. Chapin with a *Ch*, not a… well, I guess that's the only way you'd spell it."

A lead ball plummeted in my stomach. I opened my mouth to say something, but nothing came out.

"Alec?" Her voice sounded panicked. "Shit, did you hang up?"

"I remember you, Rae." A crash of metal and following shouts sent my heart leaping up my throat. Both hands tightened into fists, desperate to protect her from whatever shit show was happening around her. "Where are you? Are you in danger? Why are you calling?"

"I knew this was a long shot, but I just had to try." Her long pause amped up my nervous anticipation. "I'm in trouble, Alec." My gut twisted, turning the previous delicious meal sour. "I need… I need your help."

My raw knuckles dug against the hard desk, sending pain traveling up my fingers into my hands, but I didn't give it a second thought. My only focus was Rae.

"Where are you?" I internally begged her not to say our hometown. Anywhere but there. I hadn't been back since the day I packed my belongings and left.

"Sweetcreek," she whispered. My lids shuttered closed. *Fuck.* "Please, Alec. You're the only one who can help me."

Slowly, I opened my eyes. I had no choice. This was Rae. I'd do anything for her, even if that meant going back to the town where my nightmares were created. I could do this for her.

Determination straightened my spine and shoved away my concerns.

"I can be there in three hours," I said, keeping my voice steady. Her relieved sigh blew over the mouthpiece. "Now tell me exactly where you are and I'll find you."

What she said next left me speechless.

"Great. That's great, Alec. Thank you. And, um, where am I exactly?" I could almost hear her cringe. "Well, that's a funny story. You were my one phone call. I'm at the Sweetcreek police station."

What the actual fuck?

3

RAE

The leather soles of my ballet slippers scuffed along the cement floor as I shuffled down the long white-walled hall. At my back, the officer assigned to escort me to holding maintained a mere few inches between us, so close that each pop and smack of his gum sounded like a firework exploding in my ear. My shoulders inched up closer to my ears, trying to muffle the annoying sound.

Two minutes into our walk, I couldn't take it anymore. "Is that gum as good as it sounds?" I snapped over my shoulder. "Anyone ever teach you to chew with your mouth closed?"

"Shut the fuck up," he barked and prodded my lower back with his baton.

Why he thought he needed that bemused me. It wasn't like I might be a flight risk. His next prod sent me stumbling forward. My hand to the cement brick wall caught me before I could fall face-first.

At the end of the hall, I paused in front of a gray metal door. Based on the small barred window in the middle, the door was at least two inches thick. I swallowed hard, my fingers trembled with nervous energy. My hangover pains were long gone, my body realizing we had worse shit to worry about.

The officer scanned his badge over a card reader, and a loud buzz vibrated, tickling the hairs along my arm and the back of my neck. Thin, pale fingers reached around, brushing against my waist, and grasped the steel handle.

"Get inside," he said. I cringed away from his crowding and maneuvered under his arm to slip through the door without having to touch him. The moment I crossed the threshold into the holding area, fear took root, freezing me in place. "Come on, move your fat ass."

That snapped me out of my fear-locked stupor. When I was two steps into the room, a hand lashed out from between the bars, dirty fingernails stretching for my arm. I jumped with a shriek, my shoulder colliding with the wall in my attempt to evade the attack.

"Cut it out," the officer yelled and whacked the baton against the metal bars. The hand immediately retracted. I didn't dare look into the cell to see the person or persons inside. Forcing my legs to work, I stumbled forward, keeping half my body sealed to the wall to avoid another attack.

Keys jingled behind me as we approached the last cell. I swallowed hard, terrified about the women I'd be confined with until Alec arrived and could work some magic to set me free.

Hopefully.

I wasn't sure how he would react when he found out why I sat in the police station. I conveniently left that part out of our phone call earlier. Telling someone the police suspected you of murder seemed like an in-person conversation.

The cell door's metal hinges groaned and screeched in protest as it swung open. Halfway through the small opening on my own efforts, something hard jabbed into my lower spine. My steps faltered as I pitched forward. A silent cry whispered past my lips as I tumbled, turning into a hiss when both knees and palms slammed to the unforgiving floor. My teeth clattered together, nipping at my tongue with the jarring movement.

Breathing hard, I gave myself half a second to reorient my vision and thoughts before sending a death glare over my shoulder. I sucked in a breath, a new flicker of unease igniting within me at finding the officer blatantly staring at my upturned ass. Instantly, I flipped over and crawled backward on my throbbing palms until my upper back hit the opposite wall.

The officer narrowed his beady eyes and snorted. "Don't flatter yourself, heifer. I don't fuck women who outweigh me." Which, by the looks of him, had to be most women. I wasn't overweight by any means, but wide hips, a plump backside, and broad shoulders meant I resided on the bigger side of the normal-sized woman.

Those uncaring eyes slid to the only other woman in the cell. "Now, Penny." The woman's dead gaze lifted from her chipped nail polish to him. Well, maybe to him. The way her eyes were glazed over, who knew what she actually saw. "If you want to get out of here sooner than normal, you know what you need to do."

Disgust had my nausea roaring back in full force, but I choked back the bile. "Get out." The words burned in my raw throat. Palms to the cold wall, I crawled up to stand, not wanting to be at a disadvantage with him towering over me. "You disgusting pig. Leave." My finger trembled but not from fear as I pointed in the exit's direction.

He huffed and slammed the cell door shut. The clang rang like a death toll, sealing me to my sad little fate. Only knowing Alec answered my plea for help kept me from falling to my knees and crumbling into the fetal position.

"It's fine," I whispered while gnawing on the end of my ponytail. "It'll be fine. I did nothing wrong."

"Keep telling yourself that, honey," a scratchy voice said.

Slowly I turned to face the disheveled woman who swayed on the only bench in the cell. Pink hot pants hugged her bony thighs, and a black crop top covered little of her flat chest, exposing the clear impression of her sternum. Track marks dotted the insides of both rail-thin arms. I pursed my lips, not in disgust but pity and anger. Anger at the drug that had taken over our town over the past several years, converting innocent citizens into crazed meth heads.

Absentmindedly, she scratched short jagged nails along the opposite forearm, leaving long red marks in their wake.

"You okay?" I asked. Leaning against the wall, I massaged one throbbing palm with the thumb of the other hand.

Instead of responding, she shifted that zoned-out gaze to the floor once again.

Right. She didn't want to be friends, and that was okay. A conversation, a distant memory floated into my head of Alec telling me not everyone deserved my friendship. He'd told me that when one of the mean girls turned on me again, attempting to comfort and chastise me in the same breath.

A smile tugged at my lips. Typical Alec. Wanting to comfort yet protect, even from your own dumb mistakes. We became friends in third grade, which grew into more until we became the oddest couple in middle school. Once we were in high school, everyone assumed Alec would dump the poor fat girl.

I guess, in a way, he did.

Except not in the way anyone expected. Certainly not me.

We were in love. Actual head-over-heels, innocent love. I was, at least. His touch set my skin on fire. Our conversations continued until late in the night, talking about everything and nothing, and his smile melted my heart the rare times it peeked through.

Then he left.

Leaning against the wall, I rested my head back and closed my eyes. With the initial shock of the situation wearing off, the full weight of the call I made slammed into my heart, making my breath catch. Pitching forward, I placed both hands on my knees.

Oh shit, I called Alec Bronson for help.

The man I hated and yet fantasized about at night with my vibrator.

What would he think when he saw me? Did he remember leaving, breaking my heart with his disappearing act? Heat swelled along my cheeks as I fought back tears. This was all too much. Suspected of a crime and having to call my ex-boyfriend for help all in one day was a lot to ask of anyone.

Young me dreamed Alec would come back for me during those couple years in foster care, then after when trying to figure out life

Chapter 3

with just a high school education and no family, saving me from it all.

But he never did.

Now he was headed back to Sweetcreek because I called, not because he wanted to see me. I counted on that protective spirit of his when I made the call. Even if he didn't care about me, the guardian side of him wouldn't allow him to *not* come to my aid.

Cheap shot? Sure. But so was leaving a note in my locker telling me goodbye the day after we made plans for our future. Days after our innocent relationship took a passionate turn. His hands between my thighs, the flood of desire and passion he pulled from me those few times we were alone haunted my dreams. I wanted more then, told him as much, desperate to return the favor but he simply smirked with a shake of his head.

I shook my head, dislodging all thoughts of Alec. What the hell was wrong with me? Focusing on Alec when I was in jail and an innocent man was missing. One thing was for certain: the person who haunted my life, killing everyone I loved, was back. After everything I did to keep others at arm's length, the sicko following me still sliced into my heart without ever touching me.

Grief could do that to you, could hurt worse than physical pain, and I went through it with my parents, two ex-boyfriends, and best friend. All ripped from my life violently and without warning, leaving me utterly alone in every way.

When would this end? Would only my death stop the death of others?

Or could Alec maybe jump into the case and find the actual person responsible? If he stuck around long enough to hear my side of the story after he sprang me from the pen, that was.

A pitiful whimper broke through my wandering thoughts, directing my attention to my cellmate. I moved across the small cell and knelt in front of the woman. Goose bumps covered her bone-thin legs and arms. Without a second thought, I removed my three-quarter-length cardigan and draped it over her lap.

"Hey," I whispered. "You okay?"

Short, greasy blonde hair swung with the shake of her head. "I need money."

"Bail money?"

"No," she rasped, finally looking up from her lap. "I need... I need more."

I pressed my lips into a thin line. There wasn't a question what she needed more of. Meth had taken mothers, sisters, fathers, and brothers away from family, making them only care about one thing—their next hit. The dealers infected our town with the drug.

"I can't give you money," I said with a sigh. "But if you want to get clean, I can help."

A flash of desperation crossed her makeup-smeared face. "I don't want help. I want my next hit. Can you give me money? I need money." Her frail fingers reached out and grasped my arm. "I'll do anything."

Her weak grip slid away as I stood, my knees throbbing under my weight from the earlier fall. "I can't help you with that. But when you're ready, come by the library. I'm there most days and can help you get your life back on track."

Instead of responding, she shifted those glassy eyes back to her lap.

For a few seconds, I stared at the crown of her head, wishing she'd look back up and take me up on my offer. But she didn't. The thin charm bracelet on my left wrist tinkled as I rubbed both hands up and down my bare arms, its sound a reminder that I couldn't help those who didn't want it or just weren't ready.

Backing away until I stood in my original spot, I let out an anxious breath.

All I could do now was wait.

The growing flutter in my stomach and tightness in my chest told me calling Alec had set something new in motion. Inviting him back into my life, exposing him to what all had happened over the past two decades, had the potential to change my life forever.

For better or worse, only time would tell.

At least I knew I wouldn't have to wait too long to find out.

4

ALEC

The deep rumble of the diesel engine was silenced with the press of a button, cutting off the near arctic cold air that roared through the vents. Braided leather along the steering wheel pressed into my forearm as I leaned forward to peer out the windshield. The Sweetcreek police station was unremarkable, just a small square white-brick building, but it still invoked painful memories.

It looked smaller than I remembered it, more run-down too under its brown tint from layers of dust from the West Texas wind. I came here once as a child seeking help from our situation only be turned away, and bonus the assholes ratted me out to my father as to why I visited the police station. Several of the scars on my back were from that night when I got home. I learned a valuable lesson that day: no one in Sweetcreek would help us, including the police.

The temperature in the truck inched higher with the sizzling July temperatures and lack of AC the longer I stared at the glass front doors. July in Texas was as brutal as they come, chasing people from one air-conditioned building to the next in order to not melt into a puddle of sweat.

"Stop being a damn pussy, Bronson," I muttered to myself. The Dodge Ram's heavy door swung open without a sound, allowing a billow of sweltering heat to slick against my face. Sweat had already built along my neck and lower back. My boot heels stomped onto the blacktop. Leaning back into the cab, I secured my sidearm and clipped the Ranger badge to the front of my Wranglers—an obvious symbol of my authority anywhere in this great state, even if this wasn't my territory. One phone call to Ted, the Ranger over this area, letting him know I needed to help out a friend and my presence in Sweetcreek became sanctioned and welcomed.

A shout from inside the station paused my feet in front of the glass door, hand hovering over the ridged metal handle. Raising my Aviators, I squinted past the gold emblem and writing stuck to the door to see what the commotion was all about. A large man, almost the same size as me, shouted at the officer at the front desk before slamming a tight fist onto the wooden top.

Hot metal seared into my palm and fingers when I gripped the handle and tugged the door open. The loud shouts, words now clearer, continued as I stood just inside the door to gain additional understanding of the situation before moving toward the man.

"Find my wife," he bellowed, reaching across the desk and sending the skittish uniformed officer back several feet. "It's been five damn days. Do your fucking job."

Aggression laced his words, a clear sign this fuckhead wasn't afraid to turn this argument violent. Just as the thought popped into my head, the man lunged forward, grabbing for the cop's throat.

"I don't think so," I grunted and closed the two feet separating me and the idiot. Before he could wrap his hand around the kid's neck, I snatched it midair and pulled it back to our side of the desk. "Hands to yourself."

The fool's already flushed face turned purple with rage. "Let me the fuck go." His biceps and forearm bulged as he attempted to remove his hand from my grip.

He didn't.

Smirking, I tightened my hold on his hand, causing joints to pop. He cried out in pain.

"This is police brutality," he shouted, eyes frantically searching the now silent station. *Right, buddy, like any of them would side with you after what you just pulled.* "You all see this. It's against the law to—"

"Actually," I said casually, cutting off his rant, "you see *this*?" I tapped my middle finger on my shiny badge. "This says I'm a Texas Ranger. Do you know what that means?" Fury built behind the man's bloodshot eyes. "It means you can cry and whine and all you want, but the laws you're picking to uphold and spout mean nothing. Want to know why?"

When he didn't respond, I gave his fist another tight squeeze.

"Why?" he ground out.

"I am the damn law. Now get the hell out of here and come back when you've calmed down." I pivoted him toward the front doors and gave his back a hard shove. "I'll take your grievances and concerns when you do."

Not that I needed something tying me to this town, but surely Ted wouldn't mind me helping. Maybe a case of good whiskey was in order to keep things copasetic.

The violent fool flipped me off and stormed through the glass door. No doubt plotting my death as he climbed into his small red sports car and tore out of the parking lot.

After digging a card out of my wallet, I held it between two fingers extended toward the front desk officer. "Here. Call me when he comes back and I'll hear him out."

Trembling fingers carefully retrieved the card.

Remembering what the man shouted, I asked, "His wife is missing?"

"Yes, sir." The officer paused like he wanted to say more but stopped himself. I motioned for him to continue. "He's not the only one either." The kid's voice dropped several decibels. Instinctively, I leaned closer to hear his hushed words. "It started about five years ago. Wives, mothers, some kids, they all vanished."

Well, shit. What did I rope myself into? That case of whiskey might be for me instead of Ted.

"How many?" I asked.

"Maybe a couple a year. The most happened last year. Five women and two kids went missing."

I worked my jaw back and forth. That was a significant number, yet I hadn't heard anything about it. Sure, this was Ted's territory to cover, but all us Rangers talked, keeping each other abreast of pressing cases if we needed help or any crossover.

"I'll look into it. Now, the reason I'm here is to see a woman you're holding. Rae Chapin."

The officer nodded and hooked a thumb toward the side door. "The detective is expecting you. I'll buzz you through."

Detective? What the fuck did Rae get herself into?

We didn't have time earlier to discuss why she waited at the police station. I just assumed a DUI or, knowing Rae, maybe a UIP if her bladder was still the size of a walnut.

Buzzing vibrated through the lobby, followed by the distinct click of a lock disengaging. The door had barely shut behind me when a heavyset man in a cheap suit rounded the corner, a thick manila folder in his hand. I hitched my chin in acknowledgment, earning me a tight-lipped smile.

Hmm. Seems someone isn't happy I'm treading on his case.

"Ranger Bronson," he assumed and extended a hand between us. Our palms smacked as I sealed my hand against his and gave a hard shake. "I'm Detective Danny. Mind telling me how you know my suspect?"

"It's personal," I said evasively. I learned early on to keep everything closed off until I knew the full story. "That the case file?" I nodded toward the folder he was holding.

"It's *her* file." *Oh hell.* I kept my shock hidden behind an unemotional mask. "We've kept tabs on Miss Chapin for a while now."

Well, fuck. Could my sweet little sunshine be a hardened criminal now?

"Where is she?" I demanded. The sooner I got answers, the sooner we could both get out of here.

He held up the folder and narrowed his bushy brows. "You don't

Chapter 4

want to review this first? I listed the details of my current case and Miss Chapin's association in the front for you."

I shook my head. "I'd rather hear her version first. Now, where's holding?"

He grumbled something about arrogant Rangers, which I chose not to react to, and turned, motioning me to follow him with a swipe of a hand. The stench of piss, stale alcohol, and vomit cleaner assaulted me, filling my nose and burning my eyes as I walked into the holding area. Fist to my tight lips, I cleared my throat and switched to breathing through my mouth.

The first couple cells contained the men. I frowned at the idea of Rae being anywhere near them, even if a wall and bars separated the men's area from the women's. At the last cell, I scanned the area and froze.

The Rae I remembered wasn't in the cell.

No, the person leaning against the far wall was all woman. A beautiful woman. Tall, curves for days, and creamy fair skin. I saw the resemblance to the girl I once knew, but the woman now staring wide-eyed back at me was so much more, her petite face still just as beautiful as I remembered it with her almond-shaped eyes, pert little nose, full rosy lips, and small chin.

Perfection then and now.

I stepped closer to the bars and wrapped a hand around the steel.

There was a minor difference. Those dark, soulful eyes that once housed the only happiness and joy in my life were now cold and cautious.

The battling emotions clogged in my throat. "Rae?" The strength in my voice surprised me when just the sight of her nearly brought me to my knees.

"You came," she whispered. "You really came for me." Those long dark lashes fluttered as she blinked back the tears I saw welling along her lower lids. "Took you long enough."

I barked out a laugh.

"Same old Rae." I shook my head, keeping the smile tugging at the corners of my lips at bay. "You said you were in trouble, and now here I am." My eyes drifted to the prostitute sleeping on the bench. "If you want me to get you out of here, I need to know one thing. Did you do it, whatever they think you did?"

Her dark ponytail swished from side to side. "I didn't. I swear I didn't. They've always blamed me first ever since...."

"Since what?" My grip tightened on the bar, nearly bending the metal as I watched grief wash over her beautiful face. "Talk to me, Rae."

"You've been gone a long time, Alec. A lot has changed, but I swear I didn't do it. I'm innocent. I've always been innocent."

"Okay," I breathed. "I'll go talk to the detective and get you out of here. Then you and me, we talk. I need to know all the details of what you've dragged me into."

Her head bobbed in a frantic nod. "Great, yeah, sure. Whatever you need to get me out of here." She pointed toward the exposed single toilet. The shimmer of a silver charm bracelet glinted in the low florescent light with the movement. "I really need to pee, and I am not going in that."

Same old Rae, which I had to admit offered a rush of relief. Not only seeing her unharmed but unchanged released the fist of worry that had squeezed around my chest since her call.

I shoved off the bars. "Be right back." I shot her a smirk. "Don't go anywhere."

"Everyone's got jokes today."

I huffed a laugh and turned to find that damn detective. I didn't care what I had to do, Rae would get out of that cell—now.

THE TRUCK IDLED, vibrating my seat. Both hands gripped the leather steering wheel as I fought to not turn toward the passenger seat. Awkward silence filled the cab the moment we climbed into the truck.

Yep, we. Because apparently the dumbass detective believed Rae to be a flight risk and would only release her if I agreed to be her personal guard, ensuring she didn't leave town. So now until we cleared her name of whatever they thought she'd done, I couldn't leave her side. I hated not being in control, not having the full story, yet here I sat with no fucking clue because of the woman sitting beside me.

"I'm at a loss, Rae," I finally said, breaking the silence. Unbuttoning one cuff and then the other, I rolled both sleeves halfway up my forearms, hoping that would help the heat building beneath my skin. "What the hell is going on?"

Her resigned sigh filled the truck. "Listen, I appreciate you coming and busting me out of the slammer." I shook my head, smiling at the windshield. "But you don't have to stick around if you don't want to. Just drop me off at the library where my car is and we can go our separate ways. I hope those idiots locked up when they escorted me out of work."

The bite to her tone reminded me of childhood Rae. As friendly as she was, she also had a quick temper that got her into as much trouble as her kindness got her out of.

"You're stuck with me, Rae." I swiveled in the seat and leaned against the door. She did the same, her lips pressed into a tight line. "To get you out of there, I convinced that detective to reluctantly release you into my custody. That means where you go, I go, and vice versa until we get this figured out. You're under my control until further notice."

"What?" she squeaked.

"Yep, it's you and me, Sunshine." Her eyes flashed with something at the nickname I gave her in fourth grade. "So, now that you know the terms, out with it." I waved a hand over the console, giving her the floor. "What have you gotten yourself into?"

"Alec," she groaned. That sound sparked a fire in my pants, my body remembering other times she'd groaned and moaned under my ministrations. I shifted in the seat to calm my dick down. "This isn't a good idea. You'll end up getting hurt."

"Try me, Rae. Give me something."

"I guess it all started with my parents' murder," she said flatly as she stared at the dash.

"What?" I exclaimed, bolting up straight. "Your parents were...? When?"

"After you left. A lot has happened, Alec. I don't know where to start, and...." She bit her lip. "I can't do this on an empty stomach. I'm starving."

That made sense. Who knew how long they questioned her before she could call me, then the three hours it took for me to get here. My hands tightened on the steering wheel, hating the idea that she'd been hungry for a while.

"Okay," I said, shifting the truck into Reverse. "Is there still that Chili's—"

"No," she shouted, catching me off guard. "Nowhere public. It's not safe."

"Okay," I said slowly, not understanding. "Then where?" When she failed to respond, clearly lost in her thoughts, I reached over and gripped her chin between my thumb and finger, forcing her attention to me. "Give me something, Sunshine. Talk to me. You're the one who called me."

So much pain seeped through her brown eyes. "No one close to me is safe. After ten years, it's all happening again. And if you stay, I'm afraid you'll be next."

For the second time that day, I was speechless.

What the actual fuck have I gotten myself into?

5

RAE

Easy, Rae. Play it cool.

But with the sexy-as-sin Alec Bronson less than a foot away from where I sat, my mantra did little to slow my racing heart and erratic thoughts. I bounced from focusing on the imminent danger I put Alec in by being connected with me to wanting to lift his shirt to see if his abs were as lickable as they were in my dreams.

Who was I kidding? Of course they were.

Fucking look at him.

I cast a side-eye stare his way, cataloging his features. Some things were different, others the same. Those smoky gray eyes saw every move, catalogued every breath while giving nothing away to what went on inside his head. Long dark hair drifted past his ears, softening his masculine square jaw and deep-set eyes. A smooth forehead, neat dark brows, and nibble-able lips completed his attractive yet stern look. And those thick, tan, flexing forearms....

I licked my lips. Oh, I was so screwed.

Not only was there a man missing, meaning the person who killed everyone I loved was back, but now all my thoughts were lust-filled with Alec as the lead character.

He stole a look my way, catching me red-handed.

Whoops.

Playing with the end of my ponytail, I scrambled for something to say. We hadn't said a word since we left the police station parking lot. I hadn't even had the nerve to give him directions to my place, just pointed left, right, and straight like a damn fool.

I cleared my throat. "So. How have you been?" Lame. I was so lame. I'd like to blame it on the fact that I hadn't had a full conversation outside the library in nearly ten years, but I knew it was more than that. It was him.

Alec's rumbling laugh launched a horde of butterflies fluttering in my lower belly.

"Seriously, that's what you're going with?" I shrugged like I didn't have a clue as to what he meant. "Fine. I'll play along. I've been working my ass off, leaving zero time for everything else." His lips pressed together like he had something to add but stopped himself. "You want to know what I'm wondering?" I nodded. "Why?"

My heart galloped. "Why? Why what? I told you I didn't do it." Him not believing me hurt worse than those weight remarks from the detective and officer.

"Not that." I released a relieved breath. "Why me? After all this time, why reach out to me now?"

"Oh, right. That makes sense." Soft hairs brushed along my dry lips as I debated my response. "The short story. Wait, turn right here," I said while pointing to my street. The rhythmic tick of the blinker hiked up my growing nervousness about him entering my home. "I read the article in the paper about your involvement with the cult case outside Waco, and when all this happened today, I thought about you. I figured it was worth a shot even though it's been a while since...." *Since you left me.* I shook my head to not drag that hurtful memory out into the open. "Since high school. That cottage, the white one with navy shutters."

I gripped the door handle as we slowed to a stop along the curb in front of my house. My stomach twisted and sweat coated my palms as

Chapter 5

I stared at my tiny, dilapidated house. Navy shutters outlined the three front windows, one hanging slightly askew thanks to the straight-line windstorm last year. White paint peeled from the siding and porch, revealing weathered wood beneath. The best feature was the large oak tree in the front yard, offering shade to half the house with his full branches that desperately needed a trim.

It wasn't pretty, but it was home.

"Alec," I said between increasing quick breaths. "I...." How did you explain to someone that you were a paranoid freak of nature who hadn't had a single person enter her home in years?

"What?" he questioned. The sounds of him shifting in his seat reached my ears. "Something wrong?"

I tilted my head one way, then the other. "I don't have people over. No one goes into my house except me. So you, the idea of you entering my house, is nerve-racking. New."

"New," he repeated in a tone that spoke to his confusion.

"I've lived a very simple life since you left." Well, mostly, and all he'd ever find out about. "I have a rigid routine. No friends or dates, no family. I construct everything to keep others out and safe." Groaning, I leaned my head back against the headrest and stared at the cloth covering the roof. "And now you're here after years of nothing, and I haven't talked this much in a single day in I can't tell you how long and—"

He held up a hand, halting my rambling. "Is there a point to this?"

Was that a hint of humor in his tone?

Rolling my head, I turned my gaze to him. "The point is, I'm nervous. You're breaking my routine, and that makes me scared."

Those gray eyes searched mine. "Scared of what, Rae?"

"You," I admitted.

He flinched like I'd hit him.

Shit, that came out the wrong way. I wasn't afraid of him, just scared of what he could do to my heart.

"You called me, Rae, not the other way around. I don't even know what's going on, yet you say you're scared of me."

"I know, I know." Reaching across the dash, I gripped his thick forearm. "Scared is the wrong word. Damnit, Alec, I've had a shit day, okay? I'm intimidated, worried, freaked out, nervous, panicking. Nauseous." I released him and turned toward the door before I could spew any more of my emotions. "It's fine. I'm good. Let's go."

A billow of dust rose around my ankles before whisking away in the breeze when I leapt from the seat to the curb. The dark navy sky glittered with millions of bright stars and the nearly full moon, lighting the way down the concrete path to the house. If Alec cared about the state of my house, he didn't say a word as we walked side by side to the front door.

At the door I unlocked the first lock, then the next and the next.

The weight of Alec's stare had me swallowing hard. "I like my privacy."

When I'd unlocked the fourth and final bolt, I twisted the knob and stepped inside, holding the door wide enough for his broad shoulders as he followed. The moment we were both inside, I secured all the locks once again and pressed the nine-digit PIN into the alarm's keypad.

Leaning against the wall, I let out a relieved sigh. Finally home. Like Pavlov's dog, my skin itched with the need to remove all clothing the moment I deactivated the alarm, just like I did every day when I arrived home. But today was a different story. Peeking one eye open, I watched Alec survey the small living room, his powerful arms crossed over his chest, making the sleeves of his dress shirt pull at the seams.

That cataloging gaze zeroed in on something, making him smirk. I leaned forward to see what he found so amusing. Haphazardly dangling from the couch arm was the crimson bra I'd removed yesterday and tossed aside. I checked the rest of the living room, finding the remaining clothes flung randomly throughout, an empty popcorn bowl turned over on the floor, and three empty wine bottles staring back at me from the coffee table.

Embarrassment heated my cheeks. I pressed my fingers to my face to ease the growing warmth as I dashed around the room picking up the discarded clothes, snagging the bra first. Hopefully he didn't have time to notice the small cup size. My breasts never got the memo that I was a full woman and had stayed at a small size B since puberty.

"I thought you didn't date," Alec said, his voice deep, almost accusing.

Bent over, picking up my pants, I shot a look over my shoulder.

"I don't." After tossing the armful of clothes into my room and slamming the door, I checked the room again only to cringe when I saw the dreaded shoebox shoved beneath the coffee table. He could not see that. Then he'd know exactly how pitiful I really was.

Alec moved as I shouldered past him. "Then why are there clothes strewn about the room? Seems like someone tugged them off you in a damn hurry. You have a boyfriend you've conveniently left out along with the details regarding your incarceration?"

I snorted. "First, they never charged me, thank you very much. Second"—I looked up and held his gaze as I kicked the shoebox under the couch—"No boyfriend. The clothes, that was me." His head tilted in this cute little confusing way. "Regular clothes are...." I wiggled a little, as if the mention of them added another layer of itch to my skin. "When you have this much to cover, clothes are uncomfortable. I shed my work clothes the moment I walk through the door in exchange for my comfies."

A beat passed between us. The corner of his perfect lips twitched before tugging up into a smirk, making that damn dimple I'd forgotten about pop. How could I have forgotten that little tidbit about him? I used to love poking it whenever it made an appearance.

"Then what are you waiting for?" His voice was deeper, full of mischief. He slipped both hands into the front pocket of his jeans. "Strip and get comfortable. Don't let me hold you back."

"Um, no?"

"Nothing I haven't seen before, Rae." His straight white teeth gleamed with his wide smile. Those stormy gray eyes twinkled.

"Wow. Wow," I said, not having any other retort. "Stop right there. We are not going there." Even though my now throbbing center *so* wanted to go there. Every part of me remembered what his talented fingers could do.

He shrugged and stretched his arms high above his head, the curve of his knuckles hitting the ceiling. "Your choice."

I scoffed. Right, my choice. Like he'd want anything to do with me. He probably had women in the wing ready to fall on their knees with a simple acknowledgment. Was I jealous? Hell yeah. There was only so much pleasure you could wring from a battery-operated boyfriend. And pretty sure I passed that unfortunate threshold last year. Sure, it felt good, but I missed the feel of another's hands on my body, of riding high on lust, making me forget everything but the person in my arms.

An attention-grabbing cough turned me back to Alec, whose brows furrowed as he studied me.

"You need to eat, right? I know how you get when you're hungry."

A sinking feeling settled in my stomach at his words. I didn't want him to do that, to remember things he tossed away—that he left without a second glance back to the woman he said he loved.

Reluctantly, I followed him to the small galley-style kitchen while reinforcing the walls around my heart from this man.

"Whoa," he remarked as he scanned the contents of my fridge. "All there is in here are takeout boxes."

"Yeah, I don't cook. It's hard for one." I shrugged like admitting that out loud didn't rub salt in an old wound. "Let's order something. But first." I stepped around him and slid a bottle of red wine off the counter. "Remove work clothes, put on comfies, then wine. If I can't have the first two, I'll definitely need this." Good thing the stress of the day chased away the earlier hangover.

He shut the fridge door and came to stand behind me, leaning against the opposite counter while I twisted the metal cap off the bottle. Yep, high-class drinking for this girl. No corks, just twist tops. I withdrew a wineglass from the cabinet and filled it halfway.

"Want some?" I asked, my voice faltering with the intensity of having him so close.

"I'm on the job, remember? No drinking for me."

"Afraid I'll make a run for it?" I released a humorless laugh. "Pretty sure you could catch me if I somehow got around you. I'm not that fast. Plus, there's no way to sneak out of here. The locked windows have a protective coating, making them unbreakable. There are seven bolts on the back door, four on the front, and a highly sensitive alarm that's almost always set. Believe me, if I planned to escape your studious guarding, I wouldn't have brought you here."

I turned and leaned against the opposite Formica counter, then took a long sip.

His grip along the edge was so tight his knuckles were void of color. "Who are you protecting yourself from? Why all the security?"

"To keep me safe inside where I can't hurt anyone." I took another lengthy drink. "You're my last resort, Alec. I have no one left to help me figure this out."

"No one?" His hand loosened and reached forward, almost like he wanted to grab me and pull me close, but stopped.

"No one. Listen." I downed the remaining cool wine from the glass. "If we're going to do this, me hashing out everything that's happened over the last several years, explaining why I was at the station, and dealing with being stuck around you—" I blew out a breath, pushing the stray hairs away from my face. "—I need my pajamas, pizza, wine, and my couch."

Humor lit behind his soft gaze. Standing taller, he waved a gentlemanly hand toward the bedroom. "You change and I'll order the pizza. Then we talk. And, Sunshine?" He leaned in close, putting us nearly nose to nose. "I think you're stalling. Don't get too comfortable or drunk, because we won't be sleeping until I get the full story."

"Okay, you mean leaving, right? As in you leaving to stay at a hotel. You won't be *leaving* until you get the full story."

A few locks fell along his forehead as he shook his head. I fought the urge to brush my fingers along his skin and sweep them away. "Sleeping. I'm not going anywhere, Sunshine. You're mine to guard until further notice, which means I'm your new roommate too."

I licked my lips, dragging his intense gaze lower.

A sleepover with Alec Bronson.

Was I terrified or excited?

One thing was for certain: I didn't imagine the heat behind his eyes right now or the way he leaned closer than necessary.

This could get very interesting.

Hope I have enough wine.

6

RAE

"Where are your takeout menus?" Alec's voice rumbled from the other side of the closed—and locked—bedroom door. It still wasn't enough to keep his voice from doing funny things to my lower belly. Somehow he hadn't lost that effect over me in the two decades we were apart.

Awesome.

"In the takeout menu drawer," I shouted through the crack between the door and frame. "In the kitchen near the phone on the wall."

Yep, I still had a home phone. Old-school rotary dial with a long beige curly cord. Since I had no family and stayed friendless, there was no need for a cell phone like the rest of the world. The home phone did everything I needed it to do—make a call for food orders and be available for emergency purposes.

I never even received calls from my boss. The head librarian knew I hated my schedule messed with, so I'd worked the same days and times every week for the past six years.

Sighing at the reminder of my boring life, I removed the soft black crewneck tank and tossed it onto the growing pile of dirty laundry. After stripping everything else off, I walked past the full-length mirror without a glance to the dresser and removed a matching pair of loungewear.

I didn't spend what little money I made on the house's upkeep or on fancy work clothes. It all went to soft coordinating pajamas and sexy matching bra and panty sets—those were my vice.

And wine.

But the wine was cheap.

Speaking of which....

With the long neck of the wine bottle in my tight grasp, I brought it to my lips for a drink. I eyed the clean clothes, not loving the idea of putting them on with the feel and stench of the station lurking on my skin. Glancing at the door, I debated my next move. I really wanted a shower, but that would require going back out there with only a towel between Alec and me.

If something happened between us, knowing I wasn't stinky would be nice. At least I didn't have to worry about shaving considering I was always smooth; taking the time to shave was a time filler instead of the typical time suck for most women.

My life really was depressing.

The soft cotton towel wrinkled beneath my grip as I wrapped it around my chest. With a quick look in the mirror to make sure my lady bits were covered, I unlocked the door and cracked it open. Alec was nowhere in sight. Perfect. Opening the door a little wider, I poked my head all the way out.

"I'm going to take a quick shower," I shouted even though the house was small enough for me to whisper and him hear my every word. Except there was no response.

Easing through the door, I tiptoed a few feet to see every angle of the living room. Nothing. "Alec?" I called, the rising panic of not finding him making my voice shake. Had my curse already taken him from me? When I found him, would he be dead just like how I found Mom and Dad? "Alec!" I screamed in a full-on panic attack.

Heart slamming against my chest, I rushed to the kitchen, desperate to find him. My feet skidded to a halt at the narrow threshold. I placed a hand over my chest as relief flooded through me at the sight of him bent forward, searching the contents of the fridge with a cell phone pressed to his ear.

"Don't do that to me," I hissed. Grabbing the wine bottle cap off the counter, I chucked it at his back, hitting his ass instead.

He turned, both brows high on his forehead. "Yeah, two large supreme pizzas, two side salads with the house dressing, and a sweet tea." Those intense gray eyes swept down my nearly naked body, pausing on my legs. Clenching the towel tighter, I fought the urge to hide from him. "What do you want?"

Wait, does he mean food or...?

"For dinner." His lips quirked.

"Right, I knew that." I totally didn't. "That wasn't for both of us?"

He shook his head, that heated gaze locked on my long legs. Which I was fine with. As much as I critiqued the rest of my body, my legs were amazing. Long and lean from my early morning jogs. Even though I was a curvy woman, that didn't mean I wasn't fit too.

"Right, forgot how much you can eat. Order another one of everything you just ordered except for the tea. Make mine unsweet." I pointed to my lower half. "The sugar goes straight to my hips."

He ran the tip of his tongue along his lower lip. "And that's a bad thing?"

I sucked in a breath, preparing for him to launch across the kitchen and pin me to the wall, but he didn't. Instead, all heat and desire vanished from his face and a blank mask slipped into place. Before I could register his sudden swing of emotions, he slammed the fridge shut and turned, putting his back to me, and relayed my order to the person on the other end of the line.

One hundred percent confused and slightly hurt, I slipped from the kitchen and hurried to the bathroom. Only once I'd closed the door and sealed my back against it did I let out a long, slow breath, releasing the tension that had climbed each second I stayed in that kitchen.

Was that sexual tension? Or something else? He flirted, then pulled back, like he couldn't make up his damn mind. Maybe he'd turned into a natural flirt, and when he realized who he was flirting with, he shut it down.

That hurt.

I had to tell him to stop, to keep this professional. It was the only way I would make it out of this intact and survive when he left. But that look in the kitchen had ignited a spark between my thighs that still throbbed even though he shut down. Apparently my core didn't care if he was wishy-washy; it only wanted relief from the ache he started.

But I didn't need him to fix the uncomfortable situation he put me into. My toys were in the bedside drawer, which meant if I wanted relief, this would have to be a hands-on job. Damn that man for leaving me hanging and being so sexy that I was dripping wet just from his proximity and commanding, rough voice.

I released my death grip on the towel and it fluttered to the floor, puddling around my feet. Teeth digging into my lower lip, I brushed my fingertips along my collarbone, sweeping lower with each pass. Nipples tight, I pinched and twisted, biting back the moan desperate to escape from the spike of pleasure bolting through my veins. It wasn't my hands, my fingers I imagined caressing and pinching to the point of pain, no, it was his. Alec wouldn't be gentle; he'd take and take, demanding more of my pleasure with each tweak and tug. Keeping one hand in place, I stroked down my soft belly, fingers itching to slip into my drenched core.

Fuck, when was the last time I was this wet without extensive buildup from a racy romance novel and a toy in each hole?

A groan resounded in my chest when my fingers slipped between my slick folds, brushing over my swollen bundle of nerves. My head thumped against the door, causing it to rattle against its ancient hinges.

"Food will be here in forty minutes," Alec's voice said through the door. His very close-sounding voice. I leapt back, turning in the same movement, my heart now racing from surprise instead of lust. "You okay in there?"

"Great," I said, my voice pitched higher than normal. "I'll be right out." My shoulders sagged as I turned to the shower and twisted the hot and cold knobs. Fingers playing under the spray, I squeezed my thighs to ease the prominent throb. I would not let him cockblock me from my pleasure. Instead of depriving myself, I stepped into the shower to pick up where I left off.

Hopefully this would make being in the same room with him easier.

If he wanted to keep this professional, then so could I.

He was here to make sure I didn't run, not pick up where we left off all those years ago. Even if he wanted to, did I? Would my younger broken heart allow him back in with a simple look and smirk?

Yes. Yes, it would.

I was so screwed.

RELAXED, clean, and comfortable, I collapsed onto the worn love seat, keeping the wine bottle raised to prevent spillage from the jostling. Since I'd claimed the only actual seat in the living room, Alec stared at me, then the unsteady three-legged stool I'd picked up off the corner last spring, lips pressed in a tight line. Great, seemed his foul mood from earlier still lingered.

I tilted the wine bottle back, never dropping his stare, and patted the other lumpy cushion. "There's room for both of us. If you don't mind getting close, that is."

His nostrils flared at my words, but he still stood and stretched from side to side.

"Why aren't there more seats in here?" he grumbled, eyeing the area beside me like it might hurt him. Or maybe more worried about me. His jaw worked back and forth as he drew closer.

"No one comes inside, remember? No reason for seating when it's just me. And I only sit here when I'm reading."

Careful to not disturb me, he eased onto the love seat, almost sitting on the armrest instead of the cushion to keep any part of him from touching me. I frowned at the vacant space between us. *What a dick*. If he didn't want to rekindle what we had, fine, but he didn't have to act like I had the plague.

"I don't have cooties," I grumbled and then downed another swig straight from the bottle.

Ignoring my comment, he leaned forward, resting his elbows on his thighs and interlacing his fingers. "Enough stalling, Rae. Out with it. Every detail, anything and everything you think I should know about the mess I've fallen into. I need…." He flexed and tightened his hands. "I need to know everything."

"Still a control freak, I see."

Those gray eyes snapped to me and narrowed. "You have no idea."

"Where should I start?" Apprehension bloomed within my chest, making me regret ever calling Alec, even if it was a last resort.

"From the beginning. You mentioned someone murdered your parents. Start there. But first let me say I'm sorry you lost them. I know they meant the world to you and you to them. Can't imagine how hard it's been for you without them."

"Thanks," I whispered, the sincerity in his low tone releasing the flood of emotions I'd kept at bay for years. "They were amazing, the best parents." Curling my wrist, I held the nearly empty bottle of wine close to my chest like a security blanket. "Everything they did was for me. The tuition to our private school nearly broke them every year, but they figured out a way to make it work, sacrificing things they wanted for me to have the best of everything."

The warm glass rolled along my lower lip as I lost myself to the memories I never allowed to float to the surface. We were the perfect family. Not rich, not poor, but filled with love and laughter. That's what someone stole from me.

"Then one night, it was all taken away." I took a long gulp to chase away the unshed tears clinging to my throat.

"What do you remember?" he asked. Reaching over, he rested a hand on my knee and gave it a comforting squeeze before retreating like I really did have cooties.

"For you to get the full effect of how long this has been happening to me, I should start earlier than that night. Do you remember me having a dog in middle school?" His dark hair shifted with the shake of his head. "We rescued him from the animal shelter. Rocky, that was his name. And we were best friends until one day I found him dead in our back yard. It looked like an animal hopped over the fence and ripped him to pieces. My parents said it was a coyote, that some prowled around town, but it never felt right. I think it started then. It wasn't a coyote that killed Rocky. A someone, not an animal, hurt him."

"I don't understand how all this ties to why I came to save you from the police station today. That happened years ago."

"Saved me from peeing my pants, that's for sure." His head bobbed with a brief chuckle. "And I'll get there. You said to start from the beginning, so I am."

Alec simply shook his head and motioned for me to continue.

"The night of my parents' murder was like any other. I was seventeen. We ate dinner together, laughed. Mom even made me drink my full cup of milk before I could get up from the table. She said I'd get my growth spurt late, she just knew it, and my bones would need the calcium. Which I did. The summer I turned eighteen, I grew five inches to my now five-foot-ten self."

"I wondered when that happened. The little Rae of sunshine I remember barely came up to my waist."

"Disappointed?" I questioned.

His head tipped forward and hung between his wide shoulders. "Not in the least." The words were muffled, almost like he hated saying them out loud.

Confusion drew my brows together as I stared at his profile. "Anyway, that night I went to bed, and I never heard a sound. Later I found out they died in their sleep, so maybe there wasn't even a noise for me to hear. That next morning when I woke up, I stayed in bed until lunchtime since it was summer vacation. I ate a package of stashed powder donuts and watched reruns of *Saved by the Bell*. Since both my parents worked, I didn't think twice about them never coming in to say good morning."

My grip tightened on the nearly empty bottle. "That's why the detectives at the time suspected my involvement somehow."

"What?" Alec whipped his face my way. I sucked in a quick breath at the restrained anger in his eyes. "They suspected a seventeen-year-old girl for her parents' murder?"

"Oh, it gets better."

"Great," he grumbled and leaned forward to run both hands through those dark locks.

"As I was saying, they assumed I knew something, because who in their right mind would lie around in bed eating junk food, never checking on her parents? They assumed I knew what happened and was just buying time to call the police. It wasn't until lunch that I rolled out of bed. There was a strong smell, a strange, unique scent besides Mom's normal lavender plug-ins, but like any teenager, I ignored it and went about my day. They found my socked footprints with drops of their blood all over the house. I never noticed because of the dark maroon carpet."

"Why would you have looked for blood? It wasn't your fault."

Tugging on my ponytail, I brought it over my shoulder and brushed the ends over my lips. This next part would be the most difficult to relay, the part that still haunted my nightmares.

"It wasn't until they never came home for dinner that I thought something was wrong. That's when I noticed other things out of place. Their closed bedroom door, the back door slightly opened, the smell." My voice turned monotone. "I found them. Both in their bed, lying side by side. So much blood, but that didn't stop me from trying to shake them awake even though I knew."

Alec's large hand engulfed my own and dragged it to the space between us, interlacing our fingers.

"I'm so sorry, Rae."

"Have you ever smelled death?" I asked without expecting an answer. "It never leaves you. Like this dark stain sealed inside your nose, your mind. The smell stays attached to your soul almost no matter what you do."

"Fucking hell," Alec hissed. Hot skin pressed against the back of my neck, fingers carefully circling. With a gentle tug, he guided me across the small gap between us and urged my head against his chest. A heavy arm draped across my shoulder, securing me to his side. "I can't believe you had to go through that alone." The grief and sincerity in his gruff voice finally broke the dam holding my tears at bay. Streams of warmth trickled down my cheek before dripping onto his white dress shirt. "I didn't know. I would've... hell, I don't know what I would've done, but I would've done something."

I so wanted to believe that lie. That he would've come back, but the fact is he didn't. He wasn't there, and I had to endure the investigation, questions, funeral arrangements, everything on my own.

"Were you ever charged with accessory to your parents' murder?"

His heart raced beneath my ear. I pressed a palm to his solid pec, cherishing the strong steady beat. "No." Scooting closer, I tucked my knees to my chest and finagled half my body onto his wide lap. He always had a great lap to snuggle on, but now it felt like solid muscle. "There were assumptions, some kind of evidence that pointed to me, but nothing solid. There was no forced entry, the fact that I waited so long after their death to call the police, and other small things."

"What evidence?" His tone was all business.

"I don't know. They weren't that forthcoming on what they found to a traumatized girl who they thought had something to do with a brutal double murder." Sliding my cheek along his shirt, I tilted my face up to his. "Those assumptions made it difficult for them to find a foster home willing to take me."

"Foster care?" he whispered. Warm fingertips brushed along my forehead, shifting a piece of hair out of my eyes. "For how long?"

"A little less than a year before I turned eighteen. I had to move schools, to a completely opposite side of town. I ended up on the east side the longest."

"That was a rough part of town even before I left," he growled, clearly not liking the idea of me somewhere gang shootings happened on the regular.

"It's worse now. Around my senior year, meth swept through town like a sudden dust storm, addicting anyone in its path. It's still bad."

A deep line formed between his tight-knit brows. "Wonder if that's what's happening to all those missing women," he mused while twirling a few sections of hair around and around his fingers.

I bolted up, my palm pressed against his chest to stay upright. "What women?"

"At the station, I met a big fucker who came to see where they were on finding his missing wife. The officer up front said there were several missing women cases over the past several years. Makes me wonder if meth has something to do with it."

"Oh, yeah, wow." I bit my tongue to stop rambling. "That's terrible." I tipped the wine bottle that I'd hugged to my chest up for a drink, but nothing came out. "I'm going to get more wine for the next part."

"Next part?"

"Yeah, we're just on murders one and two. We have three more plus the disappearance of the guy last night to cover."

"Well, hell, Sunshine. Got any whiskey?"

7

ALEC

The coarse brown napkin scraped across my lips, soaking up the excess pizza grease with my slow swipe across my mouth. Like the other five, I crumpled it into a tight ball and tossed it into the empty pizza box. Groaning at the fullness in my gut, I leaned against the back of the small couch.

Rae had downed another bottle of wine and polished off most of her food by the time she wrapped up her horror story. Guilt rode me hard that I wasn't there for her, able to support her through everything she'd been through. But I didn't know. The day I packed up my shit and left for that military academy, I never looked back.

I couldn't risk it. Couldn't risk allowing my heart to pull me back to Sweetcreek, putting her back in danger. The night I realized what I'd become, who I would be exactly like, I left her. I left everything to save her, but hearing what she went through without me made me wonder if I made the right decision all those years ago.

But none of that changed anything. I could never have Rae, never be the man she deserved. Which was why I had to hold back. I needed to stop imagining what she looked like under those soft cotton pants and top. It was a constant battle to keep from touching her. It was the worst and best idea to pull her over to me on the couch earlier. She fit perfectly against me, almost like her on my lap was where she was meant to be—forever.

I wanted everything my sunshine would freely give, but I couldn't ever act on my desires for her. No, I had to hold tight to my control, keep away and leave when it came time.

I left her once for her own good, and I would do it again. But first I had to make sure she stayed safe and happy again.

A small smile tugged at one corner of her lips as she chewed her pizza. "Good, right?" she said.

I eyed the two empty wine bottles on the table.

"You always a two-bottle-a-night woman, or is me being here a special occasion?"

"Eh, a little here, a lot there." Her features turned pensive. "Never had a reason not to indulge. The nights get pretty lonely, and wine helps fill the void."

"I know." *Fucking hell, I did not mean to say that out loud.* I coughed into my hand and leaned forward. "One more question for you."

"Just one?" She laughed. "I tell you how the police have tried to pin several murders on me, that I might be on my way to being a lonely alcoholic, and all you have is one more question?"

"Touché. I have several, but this is about our food. Why are the boxes odd?" I couldn't put my finger on it, but the cardboard felt different, lighter than the normal pizza box too.

"Because all their boxes and packaging come from recycled products. I only order from places that use this type of box or at the very least to-go containers that are 100 percent recyclable."

I flicked the cardboard lid. "Rae Chapin became a tree hugger," I said jokingly.

"Conservationist. Get your labels right, Ranger." Humor lifted her tone, but she still didn't show that wide smile I remembered, the one that saw me through many bad days. In fact, I hadn't seen her really smile once. Maybe a smirk here or there, but no smile. "Now you're all caught up, know everything I know. What do I do now?"

There was no missing the hesitation or her choice of words. She fully expected to battle this on her own. I couldn't allow that. Not that she wasn't capable—obviously she survived this long without me—but fuck, I didn't want her to have to deal with it on her own. I wanted to be the one she leaned on, the one who held her, the one who caught the bad guy.

I'd never wanted to be anyone's hero until now.

"You're not doing this alone, Sunshine." Her dark eyes widened with a mix of hope, fear, and hesitation. *You and me both, Rae.* "From what you're telling me, you're being targeted. Someone is going to great lengths to position you alone and vulnerable while causing you extreme emotional pain at the same time." Standing, I grabbed glasses of water for her and myself from the kitchen. "Let me make sure I didn't miss anything."

Our fingers brushed when she took the tall pint glass from me. It wasn't the first time I touched her tonight, but this simple touch sent a spark of heat up my arm and into my chest. Returning to my seat, I relaxed and stretched my arm out along the back of the couch.

"There were your parents. Some evidence, but everything circumstantial. Then the boyfriend found dead in his car. What tied you to that case?"

A red blush sprouted along her fair cheeks. "The car they found him in, they also found some, um—" Rae looked everywhere other than toward me. "—DNA in the back seat."

"You conveniently left that out earlier," I grumbled. The muscle along my jaw twitched under the strain as I worked it back and forth.

"He was my first." That pert little nose crinkled in disgust. "In the back seat of his Impala. It was terrible and—"

I shot out a hand, stopping her. "I don't need to know the details. They found him in the car, where they also found your DNA."

"Right. That pointed them to me. Plus, our relationship was rocky. Add that in with the previous suspicions surrounding me from my parents' deaths and the police came knocking on my door before dragging me down to the station for questioning. Again, circumstantial evidence, so no charges were filed."

I nodded as I took mental notes about each of the cases. "Then the next, your best friend, Beth. They found her in her home, dead."

Sadness hung over Rae like a dark rain cloud. It took all my self-control to not reach over the coffee table and put her back on my lap where she belonged—where I could keep her safe.

"They found drugs in her house—"

"Drugs?" I exclaimed.

"Beth and I liked to partake in smoking every now and again. She said it helped with my borderline depressive state. They found pot along with, surprise, my fingerprints all over the house. So they dragged me down to the station and asked questions again."

I shook my head. "Did they ever have any actual suspects?"

Rae shrugged. "Dunno. Me and the Sweetcreek police are not on the best of terms. They seem to think I'm a psychopath, and, well, I know I'm not, so we fail to be on the same page time and time again."

With both thumbs, I massaged my temples, trying to ease the building headache. "And then the last one, another boyfriend found murdered."

She gave a slow nod. "I wouldn't really call him a boyfriend. We went on a few dates, nothing serious. That's when I realized I had to lock myself away. No one was safe around me anymore. I was afraid a stranger would die just because they smiled at me or I acknowledged them. I've been living this"—she waved a hand around the sparse room—"since then. Which worked until last night. I'd barely ever spoken to the guy."

"Where did they find the body?" I fought against the urge to ask more interrogative type questions. Rae was in trouble, but not with the police. Someone slowly zeroed in on her, and I needed to find out who before she ended up as the next victim.

"That's the thing. They haven't. Last night at a restaurant downtown, customers saw us leave together. Which means I was the last person to see him. That led to the interrogation today. They think I did it, think I'm holding him somewhere."

"Who's the guy?"

"Greg or Gregory something. I never even knew his name. He flirted for weeks before last night. All shallow one-liners before I told him to go away for his own good."

"How was last night different?"

"I talked to him," she whispered. Closing her eyes, she squeezed them shut. "I knew better, damnit, but I was lonely. He followed me out, we talked for a few minutes, and then I left. When I drove off, he stood outside the bar smiling."

The memory of how I found the living room flashed to the forefront of my mind. "Then why did it look like someone had a party in your living room last night? You sure he didn't come back here with you?" I hated accusing her of lying, but something wasn't adding up.

"Yes, I'm sure," she hissed and threw the pizza crust at my head. I dodged it easily and prepared for another projectile to come flying toward my face. "I had a pity party for one. Well, two if you count Delilah, but I don't since she never seems to talk back when I ask her questions about love and life."

Delilah. Delilah. Where have I heard that name before?

"The radio personality?" I barked a laugh at her slow nod, confirming my assumption. "You always had a thing for that sappy love radio shit."

"Don't do that, please." All the fight drained from her, leaving her features full of exhaustion and sadness.

"Don't do what?"

"Remind me of what we used to be. Bring stuff up that you shouldn't remember. It makes me think...." She shook her head and stood. "I've gotta pee."

I watched her run away from me, avoiding the conversation neither of us wanted to have. When the door shut, I stretched across the coffee table and snagged a piece of her pizza.

I leaned back, chewing slowly and processing everything revealed tonight. Five murders and Rae the prime suspect. Well, I assumed she was the prime suspect. Now that I knew the entire story from her side, I needed those case files. All of them. But I didn't trust that detective to give me everything. He would probably only include the evidence that pointed to Rae, which meant I needed help. And since I was shit with computers, I needed help from someone who could hack into the Sweetcreek database and retrieve all the documents surrounding each case.

And I had just the man for the job. Even if he annoyed the shit out of me with his easygoing personality and carefree attitude toward everything.

The bathroom door clicked open. "I need to make a call," I said to the room as I stood and dug the phone out of my front pocket. "I'll just step outside—"

"No," Rae exclaimed, throwing both hands up as if to stop me. "It's not safe now that you know me."

I scoffed. "Rae, if anyone should be scared, it's the fucker who's after you. I've got enough anger and pent-up hostility to take out anyone who tries anything."

"Who are you calling?" she asked nervously, running her fingers through her ponytail.

"A friend who can help us."

"Us?"

"Us. I told you I'm not going anywhere until we sort this out."

A full smile made her cheeks bunch. I sucked in a breath at the beauty radiating from her. "I always knew deep down you were a good guy. Just a bad boy to everyone else."

She wasn't wrong. I got in more fights than I could remember. Most of them revolving around something to do with Rae. The first fight I ever got in was in fourth grade. I punched Teddy in the nose for saying something negative about my sunshine. It only got worse from there.

I took her in, surveying the beautiful woman standing just feet from me. Those curves begged for me to run my hands over them, her soft fair skin meant to be kissed, her long dark hair perfect for wrapping around my fist to arch her neck back, allowing me to slowly fuck those full lips.

I groaned and stormed to the door. I couldn't think that way. This was business, that was it, and how it had to stay. Even if my hardening dick had other plans.

The door slammed shut behind me. I winced as the entire house shuddered with the force.

Note to self: this house is one hard wind gust away from collapsing to the ground.

After entering the phone number, I pressed the hard glass to my ear and paced the short porch.

"Ranger Bronson," the cocky-ass voice poured through the earpiece. "What do I owe the pleasure at—" A long pause. "—one in the morning."

"Hello, Charles." His hiss on the other end of the line told me he still hated when I used his given first name instead of the cooler nickname he preferred to go by. Special Agent Charlie Bekham was arrogant as fuck but had every right to be. Not only a computer whiz, but also amazing at piecing a puzzle together, making the random outliers make sense to the complete picture. Which was why I needed his help now. "I need your help. Where are you these days?"

"You need my help? Interesting." I could practically hear his smile growing.

"This was a terrible idea," I grumbled.

"Actually, the best idea you've had all year, I'd guess." A shuffle of sheets sounded through the phone, followed by a soft female voice. "Not now, sweetheart. Daddy has a work call."

My brows rose up my forehead in surprise. "You never told me you had a kid."

His sensual chuckle raked against my thin patience. "I don't. Get to the point, Alec. I have other matters to attend to."

"You're a prick, you know that?"

"You knew that when you called."

I took a calming breath to keep from launching my phone across the yard. "How soon can you get to Texas? There's a case, and I could use your expertise."

"You mean my amazing hacking and investigative skills."

"Yes," I gritted out. My hold tightened on the phone. "She was—"

"Ah, there it is," he cut in.

"What?"

"The reason you set aside your obvious annoyance with me to ask for my help. She must be something special. Can't wait to meet her."

"Charlie, I swear—"

"Calm down, Hulk. Don't go ripping your pretty pearl snap shirt. I won't hit on her, Scout's honor." That meant absolutely nothing since I knew for a fact neither of us were ever Scouts. "I can be there in the morning. It's not a long flight from Nashville. But for me to drop everything I have going on here, I'll need something from you."

"Yeah, of course. I'll call your boss and request your help."

"Not that. Well, that, and something else."

I groaned and tilted my face to the night sky. "I don't even want to know."

"I've heard through the water cooler gossip that you have a friend in the BSU. I want an interview."

Pain radiated along my jaw from my clenched teeth. "I can't guarantee you an interview."

"Sure you can, if you want my help to save your girlfriend."

Bastard. "Fine. I'll get it arranged after we solve the case."

"Perfect. See you in the morning," he said, his voice full of victory.

"Wait," I snapped before Charlie could end the call. "You don't know where we are."

An exasperated sigh poured through the phone. "Bronson. It's me. I'll pinpoint your location via your cell after I'm done with this naughty little devil beside me. It'll take me less than five minutes to locate exactly where you're standing at that moment. Tomorrow." The line went dead.

I slipped the phone back into my pocket before I crushed it within my white-knuckled grip. He was right about one thing: Rae *was* something special if I broke down and called him for help. He wasn't a bad guy, just cocky as hell and would hit on any available female in a one-mile radius.

As I walked down the path toward my truck to retrieve my bag, a nagging thought pestered at the back of my mind. Her reaction to something I said seemed off, like she was avoiding or hiding something, but I couldn't for the life of me remember when or what we were talking about.

Whether it pertained to this case or something else, I wasn't sure.

But I sure as hell would find out.

8

RAE

A roar of curses and pain-filled groans snapped me awake the following morning. My heart raced at the sign of someone in my home before the prior day's events caught up with my sleep-addled mind.

Almost arrested.

One phone call.

Alec Bronson.

The much older, muscular brute known as Alec Bronson who was currently in the next room clearly upset about something. There was something wrong with me that his shouts didn't set me on edge but offered relief, meaning he didn't die in the middle of the night.

I was a whack job. But when you'd been surrounded by death as much as I had, I figured I was fairing pretty well. I hadn't gone completely insane—yet.

Slipping out of the cool sheets, I padded to the dresser and retrieved a heavy sweatshirt. It was warm in the house, but I'd rather be hot and braless than cool and have to put a bra on before stepping into the living room. Twisting the knob, I pulled the door open and walked straight into a solid wall of muscle.

"Ouch," I exclaimed, my hand flying up to my nose to rub the soreness away. I retreated a step and glared up at Alec.

Bloodshot, tired eyes stared down from where he towered over me. The deep purple, swollen bags made his gray eyes appear almost black. I winced at the irritation radiating off him.

"Sleep well?" I cringed.

The old wood groaned under his tight grip on either side of the doorframe. "Either I sleep in your bed tonight or we're staying in a damn hotel. I will not sleep on that miniature-ass piece of furniture you call a couch one more night. Do you understand?"

I nodded, unable to speak. The sheer dominance in his tone and the way he stood over me sent a flutter straight to my core.

"Good. I need a shower."

Snaking my arm past his waist, I pointed toward the bathroom. "That's the only one. I put a towel in there for you last night."

He was still on the phone when I'd locked my bedroom door and crawled into bed—after retrieving the box of notes from under the couch and shoving them back into their hiding place under the bed.

His eyes narrowed further as he leaned deeper into my bedroom. His arm muscles flexed at the cuffs of his white undershirt, threatening to rip at the seams as the lower hem rose slightly, displaying a row of taut ab muscles. My fingers twitched at my side, desperate to reach out and feel the ridged surface.

"This house is not big enough for the two of us."

"Then leave," I said with false bravado. I really didn't want him to, nor did I want to go to a hotel. There had to be a compromise. "You're the one who's all 'I can't leave, you're under my control,'" I mocked.

A sharp gasp seized in my throat when he quickly closed the space between us, putting us toe to toe. Each step I retreated, he moved closer until my back hit the tall dresser.

"Make no mistake"—the words vibrated in his chest with his deep, menacing tone—"you are mine, and I protect what's mine. It's you and me, Sunshine, against the world." His voice deepened as his gaze slipped to my parted lips. "You've always been mine."

Before I could register what was happening, his lips slammed against mine and a hand fisted in my sleep-tousled hair. It wasn't even a thought when I kissed him back with the same amount of intensity, pouring out my hurt, fear, and loneliness.

Then he vanished from my room, leaving me panting, wet, and so fucking confused.

It took several minutes before my legs would hold my weight and I could shuffle to the kitchen. I flipped off the closed bathroom door as I passed. What an asshole, playing with my emotions like that. Yet I'd let him. It wasn't like I pushed him off or told him to stop.

"I'm a lost cause," I muttered to myself as I filled the coffee filter with grounds. I tossed an extra scoop in for good measure; the way this morning started out, I would need the extra caffeine to get through the day. I flipped the switch, which turned bright orange as the machine gurgled to life.

The counter edge dug into my lower spine as I watched the dark liquid drip into the glass carafe. Did he really just kiss me? Morning breath and all. And he called me his. Or was that a dream? I pressed two fingertips to my lips. Maybe I'd become that delusional to daydream something and believe it actually happened.

The clang and roar of the shower turning on had my gaze slipping to the kitchen doorway. I hadn't imagined the kiss. Or the possessive gleam in his eyes, or the desperation in his hold in my hair.

Holy fuck, that was hot. Even just thinking about it made my entire body quiver. When we were younger, we never went all the way. Just a few stolen moments toward the end, before he left, where our make-out session went a little too far. I loved the feel of his hands on my skin, and I still remember the first orgasm he pulled from me with a few delicate touches.

The Alec back then treated me like I was made of glass. Too perfect and innocent. Grown Alec, the man now naked in my shower hopefully using my loofah, was demanding, dominant, and I wanted more. So much more.

A shouted curse snapped me out of my lusty haze. My feet

pounded against the worn hardwood as I rushed to the bathroom, where another shout still reverberated against the walls.

It was my house, my lame excuse for why I didn't knock. Steam billowed out of the small room into the short hall, most still clinging to the inside of the bathroom.

"Everything okay?" I asked, taking a step into the bathroom just as he tore the shower curtain back.

I opened my mouth to say something, only to shut it again when no intelligent words formed in my stunned brain. All I could do was stare. Ripped abs, chiseled heaving chest, thick corded forearms, and strong biceps were all too much to take in at once. Then my gaze slipped lower and my heart stopped. Holy hell, he was huge and hard. His dick twitched under my full focus.

"Rae." My name was like a whip, the word sharp. I tore my gaze upward to meet his hooded lids. "Eyes up here."

I hummed in agreement, still not trusting my voice.

"Did you forget to tell me you have all of seven minutes of hot water?"

"Water, yeah."

Droplets flicked off the ends of his drenched hair with the shake of his head. "Never mind. You should go."

"Why?" Not sure if that was the right response, but it just slipped out.

"Go, Rae. Now." That commanding tone sent me back a step. "And shut the door."

Damnit.

Ducking my head, embarrassment finally catching up now that my brain registered what I'd done, I closed the door and turned to the living room.

Screw coffee, I need a cold shower now too.

Several minutes later, he finally emerged from the bathroom—fully dressed, to my disappointment. Sitting on the couch, I sipped my coffee, watching as he stormed around the room, shoving his dirty clothes into a duffel bag.

"Shit night sleep, hot water vanishing before I...." He cast me a

Chapter 8

wary look. "And Charlie flying in at some point. It's shaping up to be an interesting day already."

And that kiss, I wanted to add. Was that part of the shit day or a bright spot he obviously wanted to forget and not mention? Instead, I hooked my thumb toward the kitchen. "At least there's coffee."

"Thanks," he said over his shoulder, already entering the kitchen.

"Who's coming today? Charlie?" I shouted so he could hear me. This was a safe conversation, not approaching the fact that I stared at his dick for a solid minute earlier. Did all guys get hard in the shower? That seemed odd unless he was....

Oh. Ohhh.

Now I understood why he was so grumpy.

I smirked behind my coffee cup as he reentered the room, a steaming cup in his hand.

"I need some help with the details of the case. He's with the FBI, and I've worked with him on other cases before. He can help me retrieve everything the police have on each of those unsolved cases. We can review them one by one and see if anything was missed or maybe look into other suspects they had."

"Great," I replied, not knowing what else to say with the tension mounting between us. As the quiet seconds ticked by, it grew stifling. "I'm going to get ready for work. Be ready to leave in thirty?"

"Great," he grumbled, attention stuck to his phone.

I had to agree with him on one thing: today was shaping up to be an interesting day.

Okay, what is his deal? I glared over the stack of books that needed inventorying to the man I couldn't decide if I wanted to strangle or wanted him strangling me.

I needed professional help.

Across the library, he sat at one of the three open tables, leaning forward with his elbows digging into his thighs, studying his phone. We didn't talk about what happened earlier, my stare-off with his dick or the kiss. In fact, we didn't talk at all. We had to do something or this awkwardness would eat me alive from the inside out. But how did you bring something like that up to someone clearly set on avoidance as the best option?

Maybe I should pass him a note.

The thought made me chuckle. We used to pass a dozen notes a day back in school. I didn't hold on to all of them, just the ones that had some kind of deep-rooted meaning to us as a couple. It was pathetic that I still had them, but for someone who had very little hope in her life, holding on to those words of his somehow kept me strong through it all.

Did he ever think about me the way I'd thought about him? Wondering what would've become of us if he hadn't disappeared from my life? I still didn't know where he went, and I was too afraid of the impact of his answer to ask.

A dark shadow crept over my desk before a man stepped into my line of sight, blocking my view of Alec. The overpowering body spray sent me reeling back a few inches to catch a clean breath. Long stringy hair hung to his narrow, scruffy jawline. Cold lifeless eyes stared down at me, but he didn't say a word.

I wasn't surprised by his somewhat disheveled look.

"Need to use the computers to build a résumé and look for jobs?" I questioned but already knew the answer. When I stood, the man took a shaky step back. "It's okay. I'll show you to the computers and help you get started. Sound good?"

He gave a weary nod in answer.

"Follow me." My flats padded against the thin multicolored carpet. A deep line indented between Alec's brows, his eyes tracking the man's every movement as we walked past. "How long have you been out?"

"One week."

I nodded.

"Congratulations on your release. We'll get you back on your feet in no time." The chair slid easily away from the desk as I motioned for him to sit down. He slumped into the curved plastic, shoulders rounded. "Hey, it's okay. It's easier than you think. I'll get a résumé template started for you."

Once he was all set, I left him to fill out the information on his own.

"Who's that?" Alec asked, his intense focus still zeroed in on the only other person in the library.

"No one you need to worry your pretty little head over," I said lightly. "We get visitors like him all the time. We're the only library on this side of town, so their probation officers send them here to use the computers to look for work."

"Probation officer," he nearly growled. The hand wrapped around his phone tightened. "This happens when you're here—alone. I don't like it."

I shrugged. "Fortunately, you don't get an opinion. Most I've met were sentenced for petty theft, minor drug charges, things like that. Nothing violent. If someone with a dangerous record stops by, their probation officer usually calls and gives us a heads-up, but I've never felt threatened. Most come in here hoping to turn their lives around, and I enjoy helping."

Alec groaned and eased back into the chair. "Same old Rae. You always were the type who thought everyone deserved a friend."

I wanted to remind him not to bring stuff like that up, but today it felt different. It felt good and comforting that he remembered specific things about me.

"What's for lunch?" he asked. "I'm starving."

I forced a smile into a blank stare. "We just ate breakfast."

"It was cereal, not breakfast. And that was two hours ago. I need a snack. You don't look like this without constant calorie intake." For emphasis, he patted his flat stomach.

"Wish snacking did that to me."

"You're perfect from my point of view." He visually traced over every curve, every dip of my body.

I snapped, the tension from this morning and now this making me hit my breaking point.

"No," I said and jammed a finger into his chest, hurting me more than him. "You do not get to say shit like that. You do not get to kiss me and walk away. I'm tired of your mood swings." I chanced a glance at the man at the computers, his rapt attention on us. Shit. I was yelling in a library. I lowered my voice and hissed, "You do not get to act like any of this is okay. Not when you're the one who left. Not when everything we were clearly meant nothing to you."

"Who said it didn't?" he rasped. "You don't know what you're talking about, Sunshine."

"Stop making me feel something you clearly don't," I whisper-yelled. I held my ground under his challenging stare. "You either want me or don't. Stop playing with me."

"I'm not doing this here," he said through gritted teeth. "Actually, we're not doing this at all. This is strictly business, nothing more."

"Then what about that kiss?"

"A slip in judgment."

I reeled back, his words a slap to the face and knife to my heart. Tears welled, but I wouldn't give him the satisfaction of letting them fall.

"Am I interrupting something?" said an unfamiliar voice filled with amusement.

Who the hell is that?

9

RAE

"Want me to come back later or grab some popcorn? I'm down for either," he added.

I blinked, slowly taking in the striking man.

Dressed in an all-black suit, he stood just inside the front door, smiling like a Cheshire cat. His bright blue eyes held my considering stare, giving me a moment to come to my senses. Tattoos decorated the hands clutched around two bag handles. Everything about him screamed asshole, but he wore it well.

Very well.

"Good of you to join us," Alec said, stepping around me to block my view of the newcomer. Turning, he fixed his narrowed eyes on me. "That conversation is *not* over."

"Yes it is." Side-stepping around Alec, I strode toward the man, hand outstretched. "Rae Chapin. You must be the agent Alec mentioned. Thank you so much for coming to help."

His head tilted, those blue eyes staring straight through me. When they slipped over my shoulder, he nodded toward me. "I like her. She has better manners than you, Hulk," he said while taking my hand.

"Hulk?" I questioned. Turning, I had to step back to keep from eating Alec's chest. "Fitting nickname."

"I thought so too. Agent Charlie Bekham, at your service." While keeping his gaze locked behind me, Agent Bekham drew my hand up to his lips and pressed them against the back.

"Knock it off, Bekham." With a gentle swat, Alec broke Charlie's grip and once again stepped between me and the agent. I frowned at his muscular back. "Thanks for coming. What do you need to get started?"

"Can I set up here?" He hitched his chin toward the empty table Alec had previously occupied before our fight. "All I need is an outlet and Wi-Fi."

"Yeah, we have both. Set up what, exactly?"

I followed the agent, trying to forget about the asshole following too close. At the desk, he carefully laid one bag on the table and dropped the other haphazardly to the floor. While he began pulling out various objects from his bag, I leaned to the side to check on the visitor from earlier. His attention was no longer on us, rather solely focused on the computer screen in front of him.

"This." Agent Bekham's word brought my attention back to the table as he opened a fancy laptop. "Now," he said to Alec without looking away from the screen, "what do you need?"

"Every file that lists Rae as a suspect or she's at least mentioned."

The agent's dark brow rose. "Someone's been a naughty girl." He laughed through a wince when Alec smacked a palm against his head. "Got it, files and no hitting on your girl."

"Not his girl," I chipped in.

"This keeps getting more and more interesting. Okay, so files on Miss Chapin here, also known as not Alec's girlfriend. If I have some parameters to narrow down the search, it'll take less time."

"Is this legal?" I asked, studying the two men.

Both shrugged.

"It will be with the waiver Alec here is about to sign giving me access past their firewalls, which I just broke through. Make sure you backdate that form, pal." Charlie smirked.

Chapter 9

I stepped away from the table, hands raised in surrender. "They cannot associate me with this. I'm already in hot water with the police."

"I'll take the fall if there's backlash. There shouldn't be, though. As a Ranger, I have authority over every police department in the state and can bring in other agency liaisons as needed without approval."

"So fancy," Agent Bekham whispered under his breath. I chuckled behind my hand at the frown that tugged at Alec's lips. Apparently the two didn't get along. "What am I looking for?"

"Wait." I swallowed hard. "You're a hacker." The agent nodded, making my stomach drop. I couldn't risk someone like him diving into my personal records and online activity. I hadn't prepared for a hacker. "You're only looking into the cases, right? Nothing else?"

The agent's fingers paused over the keyboard, and he slowly raised his gaze to peer over the top of the laptop. Alec also stopped what he was doing to stare across the table at me.

"What would I find elsewhere, Rae?" the agent asked. All lightness and humor vanished from his tone. "What are you hiding that you're afraid I'll find?"

Shit. Shit. Shit.

I had to think of something. Too many were counting on me to keep them safe. No one, especially not these two, could learn my dark secret. I blurted the only thing that came to my mind.

"Porn." I internally cringed, then made it so much worse. "I like to watch a lot of lesbian porn."

Fucking hell. Cheeks on fire, I turned on my heels and all but sprinted back to my desk to hide behind a stack of books.

"Now *that* I want to see." Agent Bekham's purring voice carried through the entire library. "Together, maybe. Ouch! Stop fucking hitting me."

I laughed behind the books, knowing exactly who'd hit him.

The laughter faded when the realization of what I needed to do next hit me. Now I had to download a ton of lesbian porn to make my story legit. On the library server, no less, because I didn't have internet at home.

I really hated myself sometimes.

Determined to shake it off, I sat up straight in the chair and began the process of cataloging the stack of newly received books. When Alec's presence loomed over me, I ignored him and kept working.

"Lesbian porn?" I refused to look until he tugged the book I was working on off the desk and held it high, forcing my gaze up. "That seems odd, considering."

I knew not to take the bait, but I did.

"Considering what?"

Placing the book on the desk, he pressed both palms to the surface and leaned in close. "Considering how you studied every inch of my cock this morning and looked ready to fall on your knees willing for me to fuck that sassy mouth of yours."

My lungs seized while my heart attempted to thrash out of my chest. I wanted to scream at him and tell him he was wrong, but that would've been a lie. I just hated that he read me so well, saw exactly what I wanted, what I needed from him. I swallowed hard, trying to shove away that mental picture of me worshipping him from my knees.

"Just makes me wonder, Sunshine," he whispered. I sucked in a breath when his exhale brushed over my ear. "What are you hiding?"

"Nothing," I murmured, too distracted by him to worry about anything else. "Girl on girl, yay." *Yeah, that totally sold it.*

"Right." The desk slid an inch when he pushed off. Slipping both hands into the front pockets of his jeans, he studied me. "Don't lie to me, Rae."

"Or what? I mean, I'm not." *Smooth, Rae. Real smooth. Now he not only knows you're hiding something but, bonus, knows you're a kinky ass and like the idea of a punishment for lying.* "Please stop distracting me. I have to get back to work. Lots to do."

He stood there a second longer, watching me attempt to work before turning and striding back to the agent. I relaxed against my chair and let out a long breath. *Holy hell, that was intense.* Fanning my

Chapter 9

fiery face, I scanned the library to make sure no one heard the conversation when I noticed the empty computer area.

Huh. Usually the older ones were here for hours trying to figure out the computer nuances. Grabbing the cleaning spray and rag, I went the long way around the library, zigzagging through the shelves to not pass Alec and the agent. Childish, yep, but I was okay with that.

Spraying down the chair and desk area, I wiped up the cleaning fluid, hitting the mouse. The screen brightened to life, showing the blank résumé template he'd been working on, not a single thing changed.

"What the…?" I muttered under my breath. If the guy didn't want to do the work, then why the hell did he let me walk him through it for fifteen minutes? Jerk.

The mouse slid along the pad as I moved it to click out of the document.

A grainy picture flashed, now visible after the document was gone. I squinted and leaned in closer to the screen. It was dark, but the details of the person in the picture were ones I knew well considering I'd been studying him since yesterday.

Alec.

I covered my open mouth with my fingers as I clicked to the next picture.

Alec, earlier in the day.

Then the next.

Alec and me in the truck.

I tried to call out to the two men, but nothing would come out. Fear seized my throat.

I knew what this meant. This wasn't a warning but a promise.

Someone was watching me, and Alec was the next target.

"I'm not changing my mind," I stated as I slammed my shoulder against my front door, shoving it open. My soles let out a squeak as I whipped around to slam the door shut, but his square-toed boot slid between the door and frame before it could.

"For the hundredth time, Sunshine, that's not happening." His fingers curled around the door. Careful to not push me over, since I was leaning all my body weight against it to keep him and Agent Bekham out, he inched the door open until a gap appeared, wide enough for him to slip through with Agent Bekham hot on his heels. "You're acting like that was only a threat to me. There were pictures of you too. Fuck, Rae." He stopped and turned, running both hands through his hair. "You're in danger, and I'm not leaving until you're safe."

My heart clenched at the word leaving.

"You were the focus of the pictures." I sighed, exhausted from the last twenty-four hours. "I can't ask you guys to stay knowing you're in danger because of me. Please, please leave so I don't have your death on my conscience too."

"This means we have proof someone is following you," Agent Bekham cut in. I raised both brows in question. "Alec filled me in at the library while you were demanding we leave." He dropped his stuff by the couch and fell onto the cushions with a groan. "That helps with clearing your name. Not finding this guy but proof that your story about someone committing the murders because of you is true."

I groaned and covered my face with both hands. "Agent Bekham—"

"Call me Charlie, please."

"Or Charles," Alec chimed in.

"Fuck off, Bronson," Charlie snapped.

"Charlie, Alec is...." Not wanting to face him while saying this out loud, I turned and reengaged all the locks. "Alec is all I have left. I can't let someone take that from me."

The weight of those words hung in the air.

Wine. I needed wine.

But when I turned to the kitchen to pour some, I pulled up short as Alec walked through the doorway, a glass of white wine in his hand.

"Here." I took it from him, too stunned to speak. "Go change. We'll finish this conversation when you're done. I'll order food. What do you feel like?"

I was still staring at the very full glass of wine. "Um, what?"

"Food, Rae. What do you want for dinner?"

"Noodles, Thai maybe. Do you remember where the menus are?"

"I think I can manage. Go change. We'll be out here waiting." When I was halfway to the bedroom, Alec called my name, making me check over my shoulder. "Don't think about running. I will find you if you do, and I won't be happy."

That should not make my stomach clench. That should not make my panties wet.

"You're a conundrum, Alec Bronson," I said and took a sip. The crisp flavors exploded on my tongue, and the chilled liquid soothed my too hot skin.

"I've been called worse." He chuckled, a small smile on his lips.

Is this his way of apologizing for his remark earlier?

"Yeah, by me," Charlie said from the couch. "And just because he's all fun and games with everyone but me. It hurts, Bronson, cuts me deep."

"Oh shut the hell up." Alec laughed. "Get back to work on pulling up those files. I'll order food, and Rae will—"

"Devise a perfect plan to get you guys out of my house, keeping you safe from the curse that's darkened my life and turned my soul to ash?"

"Wow," they both said in unison.

Not holding back, I smiled widely at the two and turned for the bedroom. Once I'd closed the door, sealing me in privacy, I stared into the wineglass like it held all the answers.

He said that kiss was a mistake, a bad judgment call. Then he went and brought me wine and ordered me to change, knowing I liked my routine. He was so damn confusing.

I tried to not take it personally, that maybe it had something to do with my full figure and his perfect Adonis body. But self-doubt continued to creep in, making me question every word, every look he sent my way.

Why in the world would someone like him want someone like me? It was what I'd struggled with daily when we finally moved from friends to a couple. Everyone told me it wouldn't last, that I wasn't worthy of the rich stud football player. Because I was me, Rae Chapin, too short, too fat, too poor, and he was everything I wasn't.

Lips to the glass, I took another gulp and eyed the bed. Kneeling, I groped around the darkness beneath, searching for that damn shoebox. Finally my fingers scraped against the old cardboard and tugged it free. This was a record, going down memory lane twice in a week.

After removing the lid, I flipped through the hundreds of folded square papers, searching for the one I needed the most tonight. The one I only read once but kept as a reminder. When the sharp edge of the note scraped against my fingertip, I withdrew it from the others.

My name in his writing stared back at me. After downing the remaining wine from the glass for liquid courage, I pulled the edge, opening the full sheet of notebook paper. The words on the page hurt as much now as they did then.

> This is for the best.
> Goodbye, Sunshine

The paper trembled in my hand. It wasn't so much the words but the timing. The day before, we'd planned a future together. He'd made promises, and then he left. No explanation, just a fucking note left in my locker that I found when he didn't show up to sit by me at lunch. The bastard didn't even have the guts to say goodbye to my face.

"Food's ordered."

I hastily wiped at the few stray tears, then shoved the note back into the box and returned it under the bed.

I deserved an answer, to know why he left me crushed and inconsolable with heartbreak.

He owed me that.

Maybe I could demand those answers and finally have some closure to the most genuine relationship I ever had.

10

RAE

"You okay?" Alec asked, concern tightening his features.

"Yeah," I said with a forced smile. "What did you order?" Hopefully that would distract him from my clearly puffy and red-rimmed eyes from the few rogue tears.

"Thai like you wanted. I didn't know what you'd like, and I'm starving, so I ordered the entire menu." His shoulders rose and fell in a disinterested shrug. "Whatever we don't end up eating can go into your to-go shrine you have in your fridge."

"Funny." I bypassed the living room and went straight to the fridge to pour more wine. But when I wrapped my hand around the bottle, I paused. If we were going to discuss the case, I needed to have a clear head, and if I poured another glass, there would be several more to follow. Setting the bottle back in the fridge, I grabbed a glass from the cabinet and filled it with tap water instead.

Look at me being responsible.

Back in the living room, the two males huddled around Charlie's computer, whispering between them. I chose the three-legged stool I usually used as a side table and sat without a word.

Alec studied me. "We have the files pulled up on the five cases, the four older ones and the most recent. Ready to clear your name and find the son of bitch stalking you?"

Hope bloomed within me as my hand tightened on the slick glass. "Yes. Hell yes."

His answering smile turned feral. "So are we." Turning back to the screen, he continued. "They're searching for the man from the library today. Thankfully he didn't wear gloves when he inserted the thumb drive he left behind, so we know who he is."

"Jason Pouch," Charlie stated. "Thirty-nine—"

"Thirty-nine." Disbelief shadowed the word. "I would've said late forties at the youngest."

"Meth and a bit of jail time will do that to you. Recently paroled from a three-year stint for possession." Charlie's brows furrowed as he concentrated on the screen. "Looks like it wasn't his first time either. Maybe he's a small-time dealer or runner. If we can narrow down which kingpin he worked for, maybe that'll help us narrow the search for the man after Rae."

"That's a good angle. Or I can find out exactly who the fucker is once they apprehend this guy and I can question him." Alec's fists flexed in his lap.

"As long as I don't have to go back to the station with you," I said with a frown. "I hope I never have to see Detective Asshole and Guard Pencil Dick again."

Alec froze with a predatory stillness. A flash of worry crossed Charlie's face.

"Interesting names. What happened before I got there?" The protective edge to Alec's voice sent a shiver down my spine.

I licked my lips, suddenly nervous from the thrumming tension filling the room. "The detective never told me his name, just accused me of kidnapping someone, then made a comment or two about my weight. Which was dumb because that asshole was twice my size, and he made it seem like I was the size of a damn cow."

"What?" Alec practically growled and leaned forward, shoving the computer aside. "What exactly did he say, Rae?"

"I don't want to repeat it," I whispered and avoided his stare. "It's embarrassing."

"Why?" To my surprise, genuine confusion clouded his voice.

"Because what he said was true."

"The fuck it is," Alec shouted and stood. "What did he say? Exact words."

I couldn't deny his steely command.

"He said I probably killed the guy who's missing because he turned down my advances, which wasn't true. Then he said it wouldn't have surprised him that the new victim would've turned me away because someone like me would smother a guy like him."

When I dared a peek toward the couch, Alec had both hands interlaced behind his head, his chest heaving.

"Calm down, Hulk," Charlie placated, both hands raised in surrender like he would approach a wounded bear. "He might have been using it as a tactic to get her to confess, catching her off guard to make her slip up."

"And the guard?" Alec questioned, ignoring Charlie.

"Careful what you say here, Rae," Charlie whispered out of the corner of his mouth. "He's about to Hulk out on us."

I angled my head in confusion. "Why?"

Sympathy softened his eyes. "You have no clue, do you?"

"No clue about what?"

"Rae," Alec snapped. "The guard. What did he say?"

"He, um," I stammered, searching for the right words to not upset him further. Running trembling fingers through my ponytail, I pulled it over my shoulder and played with the ends. "He basically said the same thing, but what he suggested made me the angriest."

"What did he suggest?" His words came out more of a hiss.

Oh boy. Alec was really worked up. "He said it to the woman in the cell with me." I chanced a glance at Charlie, hoping for help on how to calm Alec down. "If she wanted to get out of holding sooner, then she knew what she had to do. I read between the lines."

Alec's stormy gray eyes shuttered as his hands dropped to his side.

The new wave of calm was more frightening than his vibrating anger. For a second I wondered if he planned to kill both the detective and guard.

"I need to make a call," he said, his tone unnervingly flat.

"Stay inside?" I half questioned, half pleaded. After those pictures, my anxiety around their safety ran rampant.

That stony mask slipped a fraction for him to shoot a small smile my way. "Sure, Sunshine. Can I use your room?"

After my nod of confirmation, he spun around but didn't immediately walk away.

"Do you have any sound-canceling headphones in that bag of yours?" he questioned Charlie, who dipped his chin. "Good. Give them to her, and don't let her take them off until I'm done, understand?"

When he stormed off, I tensed, prepared for the bedroom door to slam and shake the entire house, but it never came.

"Here." A set of huge headphones dangled in front of my face. "Boss's orders. What do you want to listen to?"

"Why can't I hear the call?" I slid the expensive-looking headphones off his finger and turned them this way and that, inspecting them.

"I have a feeling he doesn't want you hearing him. No one wants his girl to hear him at his worst."

I wanted to tell him, again, that I wasn't Alec's girl but moved past it to the more troubling word. "Worst?"

"Yep."

"Care to fill me in?"

"Nope."

"Why not?" I sighed and rested the headphones on my lap.

Charlie studied me for a second, the bright light of the screen highlighting his chiseled features. "Because I value my life and his trust."

"You trust him? I thought you two didn't like each other."

A lopsided smile tugged at his lips, making him appear years younger. "We get under each other's skin, sure, but I trust him with my life. Now"—he nodded to the earphones—"put those on before the yelling starts."

Charlie's words still hung in the air when Alec's shouting voice boomed through the house. In a rush, I slipped the headphones over my ears, the room immediately going silent.

"These things are awesome." I might have shouted, but I couldn't tell. "Have any eighties love songs?"

Charlie's nose scrunched in disgust with a quick shake of his head.

"Beatles?"

That earned me a smile and nod. Seconds later, the soothing sounds of my parents' favorite group filled my ears. Closing my eyes, I lost myself in the music, allowing the memories to flitter through, reminding me of a time long ago when I was truly happy.

I lost track of time listening and flipping through a *Wired* magazine Charlie had dug out of his laptop bag and tossed my way. Alec's movement, as he sat on the couch with a dozen bags covering the coffee table, drew me back to the present.

He motioned for me to remove the headphones. "Food's here." I handed the amazing bit of technology and magazine back to Charlie with a smile of thanks. "Let's eat." The rip of paper bags and delicious aromas filled the small room. My stomach growled with ferocity at the same time as Alec's. "Where are we?"

"While you handled *that,* I pulled up everything they have on Rae's parents' murder." I felt the blood drain from my face. My hand froze over the chicken curry. "The evidence was circumstantial." While Charlie rambled on, Alec pushed the chicken curry container my way with his chopsticks. "Bloody footprints, but more dots than large amounts, unlike the puddles surrounding the bed—"

"Easy, Bekham," Alec cautioned.

I forced a smile and began eating the noodles and chicken, but it tasted bland after hearing that. "It's okay. I need to hear it all."

"There's only one set of soaked footprints, when she ran from the bedroom. Then the obvious rage in the overkill."

I cringed. That was a new detail. "What do you mean, overkill?"

"They both died of stab wounds to the heart, but there were dozens of other lacerations along the torso. Your mother's body had the most." Charlie chewed on the end of a pen that he'd been using to take notes. "They were already dead, so why keep killing them? I'd wager to say this was personal. Which is why they suspected Rae's involvement. From the police notes, the Chapins didn't have any known enemies and really kept to themselves."

"If it was personal, that means the person knew Rae was home."

The noodles near my lips slipped from the chopsticks as I stared wide-eyed at Alec.

"There's more to confirm that." Charlie's fingers flew over the keyboard, that pen now clenched between his white teeth. "But first, look at what they found on the bodies, mixed in the blood, which meant it was shed during the murder or when Rae found her parents. The hair length and color doesn't match her parents, and visually, the color matches Rae's dark brown, so they never sent it off for DNA. They just assumed it was hers."

"Lazy bastards," Alec snapped. "Get that evidence from the station and to the FBI office in Dallas, labeled priority by the Texas Rangers."

"Slow your roll there, Hulk. I plan to, but before I rush over there and demand they shift through cold case files, I wanted to make sure there isn't anything else they've overlooked or maybe we could have reanalyzed with the latest technology."

"Smart. But call me Hulk again and see what happens." He tossed one empty container to the coffee table and searched through the others before picking up one that looked questionable to me. "Damn, this is excellent food."

After finishing my food, I set the empty box on the floor and picked up the container with warm soup.

"Where the hell do you two put all that food?" A bit of wonder laced Charlie's voice. "Have to watch every calorie and work out like a madman to keep this amazing physique." He waved a hand down his lean chest.

"Um, pretty sure you can see exactly where I put mine," I stated dryly before shoving a spoonful of soup past my lips.

"Don't judge yourself or what you offer by the poor judgments of others." I blinked up at Alec. "Those bastards wouldn't know a real woman if she sat her pussy on their faces."

I covered my mouth to not spew out soup with my laugh. Alec grinned and went back to devouring his food like it might run away from him.

"What else, Charles?"

"You're a fuckhead," Charlie grumbled.

"Yeah, Charles?" I added. "What else did you find?"

"Et tu, Brute?" Charlie mocked. "I have half a mind to not tell you about the blood trail they found leading from the parents' bedroom to Rae's, which was how she ended up with those blood dots on her socks."

"What?" Alec said around a mouthful of food.

"Looking at the pictures and diagrams of the crime scene, the trail of drops of blood go from her parents' room to Rae's. The distance between each drop suggests the blood flowed down the killer's hand and dripped off the blade of the knife as he walked the short distance to Rae's room." Pausing, he leaned back and pinched the bridge of his nose. "There was also a significant puddle just inside her room."

"I don't... I don't understand." I absentmindedly set the soup container on the coffee table, my mind whirling with questions.

Alec's features turned grim. "It means whoever killed your parents was in your room that night."

Charlie sighed, drawing my wide-eyed gaze. "And stood there long enough for a small puddle to form inside your room."

I almost died right there and then. The man, the person tormenting me, watched me sleep with my parents' blood on his hands. Breathing turned difficult, my throat closing as my mind raced. Heart thundering, I swayed on the stool.

"Rae, breathe."

Alec's voice continued in the distance, but the buzzing in my ears made the words too muffled to understand. My vision narrowed, tunneling to black as little sips of air slipped into my lungs before everything went dark, oblivion sweeping me away for the time-out my body demanded.

11

ALEC

Rae slumped into my awaiting arms. Tucking her to my chest, I studied her lax face, panic restricting all reasonable thoughts. Only the rise and fall of her chest in a slow and steady rhythm kept me from losing all semblance of control. My thigh muscles tensed and bunched as I stood and adjusted my hold to support her neck.

"Get some water," I ordered Charlie as I strode to her bedroom.

With a gentleness I didn't know I possessed, I laid her on the unmade bed. Two fingertips to her throat, I held a breath until the steady, strong beat of her pulse thumped against them.

"Rae," I whispered. Knees pressed against the hardwood floor, I drew closer to her side. Hand hovering over her face, I brushed loose strands of dark hair from her forehead. Reaching back, I removed the tie containing her thick hair so she could lie flat against the pillow. Unable to stop myself, I dragged my fingers through her silky strands as I studied her beautiful, petite face.

"You look like a creeper." A glass of water dangled over the bed. "She's fine, just overwhelmed. I can't blame her."

I set the full glass on the nightstand. "Finding out you could've died the night your parents did would be a lot to handle for anyone. Why didn't he?"

"Well, that's confusing." I tore my focus off Rae to Charlie. Something silver rolled along his lips.

"Do you have a fucking tongue ring?" I said, completely surprised. Few people could surprise me, but *that* left me shocked.

Charlie grinned down at me and slid his tongue out, showing the silver bar punctured through it. I frowned. How had I not noticed before?

"It's new. Don't beat yourself up about it. We can still be friends."

"Debatable. And I don't feel bad," I said carefully. "I'm just wondering."

"Wondering what?"

"Wondering when we stepped back into the nineties when those things were cool."

Charlie's roaring laugh echoed in the room. "You're funny for a Texan."

"And you're not so bad for a dumbass." Rae stirred along the bed, soft mumbles whispering past her parted lips. I watched her for any signs of discomfort. "What's confusing about the case, not your choice of body piercings."

"First, the ladies love it. Especially when I add ice to the mix and—"

I held up a hand, cutting him off. "I don't need details."

"Obviously you do."

"What's that supposed to mean?" I challenged.

"It means that woman doesn't know you've dropped your life to come save her from this mess. If memory serves me right, and the bit of research I read on the plane, this isn't your territory, which means you had to jump through hoops to get assigned this case."

I frowned and watched Rae for any signs of her waking. "She doesn't need to know, and probably wouldn't care. She called me," I said with a sigh. "Which means she knew how to contact me and only did so when she needed me. Not because she wanted to see me."

"What happened between you two? It's obvious you both want the other, but you're both holding back."

"We were just kids, but what we were, what we had, was real. The only thing like it I've ever had." Damnit, why was I spilling my fucking guts to this asshole? But now that I started, I couldn't stop. "Bottom line, I left and never came back. And to make it worse, I left after I promised her the world. Promised her a future."

"Why?" I shook my head and waved off his question. "You're both hiding something."

"Damnit, Charlie, just answer the question about the case." I fisted the quilt to keep from lashing out and punching the smirk off his face.

"The pool of blood in her room. I figured it could mean one of two things. Theory number one, the killer killed her parents and came to her room to let Rae know they were dead, meaning she was awake, knew the murderer, and helped plan the attack." Sitting on the bed, he leaned back, situating himself too close to Rae for my liking. With a growl, I shoved his shoulder until he rolled off. "Fucker, we're both dressed. Your possessive side needs work."

"Whatever you say, Charles," I mused, loving the glare he shot my way. Who knew why he hated that name, but because he did, I kept using it. Getting under other people's skin was a fun hobby of mine.

"Second theory." He kneeled beside the bed and pressed both elbows onto the mattress. "The person responsible knew Rae and changed his mind about killing her, which doesn't make much sense. Unless he was instructed to only kill her parents, but then why the overkill if it wasn't personal?" He paused. "I'll look into her financials. I can do more digging than the local police could back then. Maybe I can identify some suspects that they couldn't."

"Rae mentioned meth swept into town around that time, but her parents didn't seem like meth heads. They were good, hardworking people when I knew them." A slow grin spread up my cheeks. "Her dad hated me."

Charlie scoffed. "I bet he did. I'll check the blood work in evidence to be sure. If they were on something, that would fit in with the second theory."

A string of softly spoken words drew our attention to the beauty who was slowly coming to.

"Look into her too," I said under my breath. "I agree with you, she's hiding something. Find out what it is." When I didn't get a response, I looked at Charlie. His face pinched like I'd said something wrong. "What?"

"If you go down that road, you can't go back. If she finds out you were looking into her background, that you don't trust her, it'll end badly. You sure about this, Hulk?"

Was I? I didn't want to hurt what little trust Rae had in me, but I still had a job to do. If it turned out Charlie's first theory was true, there would be other clues that would tie her to the murders. I was almost positive she wasn't the suspect we were trying to find, but almost wasn't good enough.

"Do it."

Rae's lids fluttered open. After a few long blinks, her dark eyes frantically searched the room, stopping on me. With a gasp she sat up, both palms sunk into the bed behind her.

"You passed out," I explained. Sliding my fingers through her hair, I urged her back to a prone position. "Don't sit up too fast or it could happen again."

"How did I get in here?" she rasped.

Slick, cool glass of water in hand, I lifted her head off the pillow a few inches and pressed the rim to her lips. Rae downed several sips. "I carried you."

Water spewed from her sputtering lips across the bed and showered my face. Raising a shoulder, I wiped my face with the sleeve of my T-shirt. I shot the cackling Charlie an unamused scowl.

"You did what?" Rae exclaimed.

"I carried you." I kept my words soft and slow, not understanding why she appeared to be freaking out.

"How?" She blinked at me, expecting an answer.

"Um." I curled my arms, mimicking how I carried her bridal style. "Like this."

"Is your back okay? Are you hurt?" Worry knitted her brow as she scanned my shoulders and leaned forward to see my back.

Ah. Now I understood. She actually believed those fucksticks' comments about her figure. If she only saw herself the way I did, she'd know she was perfect. All woman, fully capable of taking everything I could give her. And that ass would look perfect, pink from my hand, as I slammed into her from behind, making her scream my name.

"Alec? Shit, are you okay? I hurt you, didn't I?"

I shook myself out of the erotic daydream and casually reached down to adjust my hardening dick. This had to stop. No losing control around her, not again. It was for the best. At least that was what I told myself for years after I left Sweetcreek, and what I needed to remind myself of now.

"Rae, I think you see yourself much differently than I do."

"I'm no fool, Alec. I can read the double-digit size listed on the back of my clothes. Don't attempt to convince me I'm small."

"You're not big either," I stated, but she snorted and shook her head, dismissing my comment. Pushing off the floor, I stretched my arms high overhead and groaned. "You stay in here and rest, and we'll keep looking into the other cases." Grabbing Charlie by the back of the neck, I practically dragged him to the door.

"Alec." I shoved Charlie out of the room and turned to Rae. "You're sleeping in here tonight, right?"

I wasn't sure which seemed happier at that reminder, my heart or my cock.

Both needed to chill the fuck out.

"Yeah, Sunshine. I'll be quiet though in case you're asleep."

Before the door closed behind me, she called out my name again. "Yes?" I asked, poking my head through the door.

"Why would he watch me sleep?"

A surge of possessive anger flared, and my grip tightened on the doorframe. "Who watched you sleep?"

I'd kill them. Rae was mine to watch.

That internal declaration smacked me in the gut, that immediate urge to inflict harm the reason why I was bad news for someone as sweet as Rae. Why I was always bad news for her.

"The person who killed my parents. Why did he not kill me too?"

Sitting up, she wrapped an arm around her bent knees. Watery eyes found mine. "I wish he would've."

In three long strides, I crossed the small room and scooped her off the bed, placing her on my lap. Her shoulders trembled. Quick breaths brushed across my neck as she sobbed against me. Each soft cry ripped a new shred through my heart for this woman.

Running my fingers through her strands in long soothing strokes, my chin to her crown, I closed my eyes, fighting back the waves of regret and grief her sadness conjured.

If I hadn't confronted Dad that day, we wouldn't have fought, which means I would've stayed in Sweetcreek, none the wiser of the monster I would become.

"Sunshine, don't say things like that. You don't mean it."

"You don't know how hard life was after they died. Foster homes, figuring out how to make it on my own, then more death and accusations and more death. Everything I've loved ripped away from me. I'm so tired of it all. It's not getting better, and now it's happening again."

"Hey." Finger beneath her chin, I tipped her damp face up. For a second I allowed myself to become lost in her dark chocolate eyes. "It is getting better."

"How. How is it getting better? They threatened you today."

I forced a cocky smile. "Well, for starters, I'm here."

Some sadness lifted with her almost laugh. "And?"

"Isn't that enough?" I joked.

"For now. But how will I go back to my normal life when you leave me? Again."

My lips parted to reassure her, but I couldn't think of a damn thing that wasn't a lie. I would leave. Again. We both knew that.

"It's okay," she whispered with a watery smile. "I survived you leaving me once. I can do it again." Fuck, that hurt. The accusation in her harshly spoken words made me blanch. "Go work on the cases." She slid off my lap and stood. "That's why you stuck around this long after all, right?"

I was a chickenshit. I was a motherfucking Texas Ranger, and this little sassy-ass woman's words made me desperate to tuck my tail and retreat. There were many things I could tell her to make her understand why I left and why we couldn't be together now, but instead I stood from the bed and walked out without a second glance.

If she only knew I wouldn't leave because I didn't care. It was the opposite. I cared too much about her. Fuck, I was pretty sure I still loved her, which was why I had to leave.

I swore a long time ago to protect Rae. And now I had to protect her from me. Even if keeping my hands off her tested the limits of my control. I had a sinking feeling I wouldn't be able to hold out much longer.

Especially with us sleeping in the same bed.

That lumpy couch seemed a better option now that I thought about it. Sure, it would be uncomfortable, but so would lying beside the woman I was desperate for and forbidden to touch.

Tonight's gonna be another long night.

12

RAE

Their murmuring and occasional burst of laughter stopped minutes ago. The clock read two in the morning. I'd been in this bed since Alec walked out hours before. Sleep evaded me this entire time, leaving me listening to make out any details they discussed and staring at the closed door, willing it to open and for Alec to charge through saying he was sorry.

He was holding back, that was clear. But why, fuck if I knew.

Rolling over, I released a long breath. It was almost like he didn't trust me with the truth, which hurt, but then again, I hid something from him too. So who was I to cast the first stone?

The fan whirled overhead, helping cool my skin. It was warm in here, but July in Texas meant nighttime temperatures sometimes didn't drop below eighty degrees. And my house was ancient. Any cold air my struggling AC could pump out sucked through the creaky floors, through gaps in the walls, and out the uninsulated attic.

A creak drew my gaze to the opening door. Through the darkness, I tracked Alec's silhouette as he lumbered into the room. Shortly after he paused at the bedside came a rustle of clothes, then the clang of a belt and soft stomp of a boot.

My breathing kicked up to match my heart rate. *Is he getting naked?*

The thin sheet lifted off my body, and the mattress dipped under his weight as he slid onto the bed beside me. He wiggled and shifted, getting comfortable. A few times his thigh or arm brushed against my own.

Every place he touched felt like a brand, my skin burning with the need for more.

"Hey."

He stilled at my word.

"Why are you still awake?"

"Can't sleep."

He hummed in a noncommittal way. "Want to talk about it?"

"Not really." I sighed. "I don't want a reminder of everything we covered tonight or the fact that you have a target on your back because of me."

The bed jostled. "I can take care of myself." His voice was closer, like he hovered an inch from me, lying on his side. "It's you I'm worried about. Charlie and I made some good headway with the other cases tonight. We'll find this guy soon, promise, Sunshine."

I stayed silent for a second before blurting, "I'm still upset and confused about why you left, but thank you for coming now when I need you most, Alec. It's nice having you in my life again, even if it's just for a little while."

"Did you miss me?" he asked, the words rumbling over my heightened sensitive skin.

"Yes. Every day." I licked my lips, eyes fixed on the fan, too chicken to turn and face him.

"Sunshine, everything I did was for you. Please don't hate me for leaving."

"I don't hate you, Alec," I admitted to him and to myself. "I could never hate you."

I sucked in a harsh breath when a ghost touch caressed my shoulder.

Chapter 12

"We're playing a dangerous game, you and I." Fingertips brushed over my exposed collarbone. "But right now, with you in bed beside me panting like you'd die if I didn't touch you, I can't stop myself."

"Please don't," I pleaded. "Don't stop."

"It would help you sleep," he hummed to himself. His palm encircled the column of my neck. My throat worked against his grip.

I nodded. If he didn't finish what he just started, I'd have to do it myself with or without him in the bed with me. Already my underwear and sleep shorts were damp between my thighs.

"Two rules." I listened with rapt attention. "First, this is only tonight. Agreed?"

"Yes," I said, the word a hiss from the pleasure pumping through my system.

"Second." I felt his lips hover over my ear. "You'll have to stay quiet. The bedroom door is open, and Charlie is just outside still working."

I sucked in a shaky breath. Why did that make my entire body shiver?

His deep chuckle vibrated against my skin. "You like that idea, don't you? My sunshine has a dark side." Teeth sank into my lobe, and I bit my lip to keep from moaning. "So do I."

A scorching hot palm slipped from my neck, lower and lower. Dipping below the light lavender cami I wore, he circled one pebbled nipple with a blunt nail and then the other, never touching where I needed.

"Please, Alec," I begged.

Two fingers latched on and pinched. I moaned, my back arching off the bed as pleasure spiked through my veins. *More, more, more* was all I could think. I slid my hand across the sheets and skimmed up his massive thigh, but a hand encircled my wrist, stopping me.

"Three rules," he groaned. "No touching me. If you do, there won't be any way I'll hold back from bending you over and fucking you all night long."

"But—"

"Let me touch you tonight, Sunshine. Give me tonight." Before I could respond, his hand moved to my other nipple, pinching and twisting, while his tongue flicked over the tip of the one he'd just tortured.

Any argument died on my lips as they parted with a throaty moan. The sheets were too rough, too hot; I kicked them off until the covers bunched at my feet. My cami snagged beneath Alec's fingers as he stroked three along my belly and then dipped beneath the elastic band of my matching shorts.

"How wet are you, Sunshine?" Alec purred against my neck. His tormented groan vibrated against my skin when his fingers slipped between my drenched folds. "Holy fuck, baby. You're so damn perfect. I can't wait to taste you."

A thick finger pressed against my opening before pushing inside. I gasped at the intrusion. Knees bent, I pressed them to the mattress, opening myself to whatever he had planned.

Another finger slipped inside, the fullness beyond any pleasure I'd ever felt. My hips moved against his hand.

"That's it. Ride my fingers." Alec's voice was guttural as he curled those fingers against my sensitive walls. "How about this?" With a twist of his wrist, the heel of his hand pressed against my swollen clit.

I cried out, completely forgetting about the open door and the FBI agent in the living room.

Alec's dark chuckle filled the room. In and out he thrust those two talented fingers while rubbing that bundle of nerves. Stars exploded behind my shut lids as an intense, body-shaking orgasm ripped through me, back arched off the bed, fingers fisting the sheets as I let out a silent cry. He continued to push into me, drawing out the orgasm, and sending aftershock ripples shivering down my arms and legs.

I panted, blinking at the rotating ceiling fan as I slowly came down from the high. A soft moan slipped past my lips when he withdrew and pulled that hand from my shorts. Alec's hungry moan had me whip my head along the pillow to face him. He had two fingers plunged deep between his lips.

"Delicious," he said around those fingers I couldn't tear my eyes away from. "Just like I dreamed." *Dreamed? He dreamed of me?* I thought it was just me who had lusty midnight fantasies starring us. "Now go to sleep, Sunshine."

He fixed my top, carefully tucking my exposed breasts beneath the soft cotton, and retrieved the sheet, laying it over us both.

"Sleep?" I huffed. "After that? Are you kidding me?"

The bed shimmied as he shifted to plop on his back. Two fingers latched onto two of my own and squeezed.

"Rae." His voice was gruff, forced almost. "I want—" He cut himself off and sat up straight in the bed.

"Alec?" I questioned, not understanding what happened and why he was now on high alert.

"Shh." Without a sound—which was impressive for a guy his size—he stood from the bed. He picked up something off the floor before creeping toward the open bedroom door.

I felt the blood drain from my face. Something was wrong.

The sheet tangled around my legs when I tried to follow Alec as he disappeared into the living room. Throwing it off, I scooted to the side and rushed on my tiptoes in the same direction.

My bare feet skidded to a halt, but I wasn't fast enough to not slam into Alec's back. A single lamp in the corner shed soft light across the dim room. Charlie, very shirtless and tattooed—*wait, are those nipple piercings?*—stood with his gun drawn, his stance mirroring Alec's. An arm wrapped around me and tugged me to his chest.

"What's going on?" I asked, frantically searching the room to see what set them on edge.

"I heard something," Alec whispered. "He heard it too."

"And it had nothing to do with what you two were doing earlier." Charlie's voice was no longer light and fun as he stared down the length of the gun barrel held between two hands. "Come over here, Rae."

"No, I want—"

"Go, Rae. I need to check the perimeter, but I can't with you unprotected." With a firm squeeze to my side, Alec all but shoved me toward Charlie, who caught me with ease. The room still spun when the distinct click of the deadbolts releasing met my ears. "Stay with her. I'll be right back."

"Don't," I gasped. "Don't go out there."

"I have a gun" was his indifferent response.

"Actually, you have three." I turned and studied Charlie, his normally cocky features now set in a firm line as he surveyed the entire room. "The one in his hands and his arms. It was a joke."

"Oh." It was all I could think of as a response.

"It was funny, just bad timing," Charlie grumbled.

"Knock it off, you two," Alec snapped, ear pressed to the front door.

I held a hand over my chest, pressing hard to keep my heart from pounding out and sputtering to the floor. Dread and anxiety fought for dominance, making my stomach churn and washing away all remaining effects of the mind-shattering orgasm.

Shoulder against the door, Alec leaned close and peered through the peephole. He shot a cautious look my way before stepping back and reaching for the knob. Bile rose up my throat. A loud protesting groan emitted from the door when Alec tugged it open an inch.

"What the—" He stopped as he opened the door all the way. I stared into the darkness outside the door, squinting to see what he saw. "Call the police."

Distracted, I moved out of Charlie's arms and raced to Alec's side.

"Rae, no," he said, voice slightly panicked. Only when I stood right by his side could I see what was there.

I slapped a hand over my mouth to keep from puking all over the dead body just outside the doorway.

"Fuck." With a hard shove that pushed me back into the house, Alec leapt over the body and raced down the stairs. Before his bare feet landed in the grass, Charlie had an arm around my waist, dragging me across the living room.

A wall pressed against each shoulder when Charlie pushed me into the far corner, the one not visible from the front door.

"Do you know how to shoot?" I shook my head. "Do you understand the basics?" After cocking a second black gun, he held it out to me. "Point toward the bad guy and pull the trigger."

"Charlie, I can't—"

"Rae, listen to me. You can and you will. You're stronger than the fear that's trying to take control. Don't let it win, you hear me?" I nodded and took the offered gun. "Repeat it back to me."

"Don't let fear win. Point and pull the trigger." Palming the rough grip, I held it tight between two hands and pointed the barrel to the ground in case I got spooked or trigger-happy. Accidentally shooting an FBI agent wasn't something I wanted to add to my record.

"Exactly." When he turned, I reached out and latched onto his lean, muscular, fully tattooed arm. "I'm not leaving you," he told me firmly, "but if someone comes through that door ready to finish what he started with you, then I need you prepared to defend yourself. We're assuming this guy works alone, but what if he's not? I'm not risking your life because I assumed something."

He uncurled my fingers from around his bicep and stepped to the center of the room, where he could see both me and the front door. Phone pressed to his ear, he described the scene unfolding around me and then hung up.

"Police will be here shortly."

"Who... who is... who is it?" I stammered. "The body." I cringed just saying the word.

"I don't know. Can't see much detail from here, but what I can see...." He stopped and tilted his head. "It's not pretty, Rae. Looks like whoever this unlucky bastard is was on the wrong side of a rage-fueled beating."

"Do you see him? Alec?" I shivered, only now realizing I still wore my skimpy cami and shorts. I tried to cover myself as best I could—not that Charlie was looking at me—but couldn't do much with the gun in my hands.

"I don't, and I don't hear him anymore—" He stopped and held a hand in the air, palm out toward me. I held a breath, trying to hear what he heard. The floorboards creaked and groaned as Charlie crept toward the front door.

I heard it then, a rustling sound, footsteps maybe. Charlie sealed his back to the wall, slipping out of sight from the front door, and held the gun tight to his chest as I watched the door. Pounding steps shook the house, and a familiar annoyed groan and curse overtook the summer bugs' chirps and buzzing.

"Charlie," Alec's voice bellowed through the house. "Lend me a hand with this one. Unconscious, not dead like the other one."

Charlie stepped into the doorway, his eyes wide at whatever he found there. After securing his gun into the back of his gray sweatpants, he held out both arms. He grunted and tilted forward as if Alec deposited a massive weight onto his outstretched arms.

And it was.

Arms underneath a limp man's armpits, Charlie dragged him away from the doorway and laid him flat. Alec stepped through the doorway half a second later. His white undershirt stuck to every curve of his chest, the cotton nearly translucent from sweat. When his searching gaze landed on me, some tension eased from his shoulders, dropping them an inch.

Until he noticed the gun.

"You gave her a gun?" he said dryly, turning, his bare feet squeaking on the hardwoods.

"I didn't know where you ran off to. I wanted her prepared just in case." Charlie nudged the unconscious man with a toe. "Isn't this guy convenient."

"The police on their way?" Charlie ran a hand through his black hair as he nodded to Alec confirming he made the call. "This makes little sense, doesn't it?"

"What are you two talking about?" Moving along the wall, I gently set the gun down and grabbed the blanket I'd set out for Charlie to use tonight. After securing it around my shoulders, I moved toward the men.

"It all seems too easy. This is the guy from the library, and now he shows up to dump a dead body on your porch. It would be easy to assume this was the guy who was stalking you and killed all those people."

Eyes wide, I took in the familiar man. I expected for hate or anger to well inside me, but I felt hollow instead. "But that's too easy. That's what you said."

Alec nodded and turned for the front door. His thighs bunched when he squatted low to get a good look at the dead body. "What if the real bastard doing all this used this guy as patsy so we'd leave?"

"That would make sense. He'd know he couldn't get through both of us to her. When that threat against you came to the library, he didn't know about me being added to the protection detail mix. Then when I showed up, disrupting his plan, he needed to get rid of us to get to Rae."

"Who is that?" I asked, pointing to the body at my front door.

"Guessing by the smell, he's been dead a few hours. In this heat, it doesn't take long for the stench to become unbearable. But the coroner will tell us exactly when and how he died. There's too much damage to his face to get a good ID, but I'd wager this is the guy who went missing three nights ago."

My hand rose to cover my open mouth.

No.

Tears welled and slipped down my hot cheeks. I'd hoped we could save him. Somehow prevent the inevitable that came with knowing me. Guilt slammed into my stomach, shoving the earlier Thai food up my throat.

The blanket slipped from my shoulders as I raced to the bathroom. I made it to the toilet just in time. Every time I thought about that kid's smiling face, the joy in his spirt, and the now dead body at my doorstep, I heaved into the toilet.

Abs sore, throat burning, I turned and sat on the cool tile when the nausea finally subsided. I squeezed my eyes shut.

This was my fault. If I hadn't engaged, if I hadn't gone out, that man would be alive.

But now he was dead. Violently dead.

That was on me.

I thought about the two men arguing in the living room.

If they wouldn't leave, then I would. There wouldn't be any more death because of me. I would leave this town full of painful memories and never come back.

13

ALEC

"Now what?" Charlie questioned as he secured zip ties around the man's wrist and feet. It would be terrible if I had to knock him out again if he woke up and tried to run.

That was a lie. I kind of enjoyed it the first time.

Something wasn't adding up. I looked between the body and the man from the library.

"If this guy here isn't the one we're after, then he knows who is." I turned at the sound of the bathroom door opening. Rae stormed out, marched to her bedroom, and slammed the door shut. "She's not taking this very well."

Charlie laughed as he stood from the floor. "You're a moron if you thought she would. There's a dead body on her porch and an unconscious man on her living room floor. What did you expect from her?"

I pursed my lips. The urge to run in there and wrap her in my arms, to protect her from any harm, was overwhelming.

"This place isn't safe."

"Was it ever?" Charlie scoffed. "You need to get her out of here. Out of town for a few days until we get this worked out."

"What about him?" I nudged the now groaning man with my heel. "We need to question him."

"I'll stay here, interrogate our little friend, and keep working on the case. At some point, I need to get that evidence out of the cold case files and search for more shit they missed. Don't worry about me. I'll stay in a hotel or something."

The slam of drawers and other sounds coming from Rae's room drew my attention. I stared at the closed door. The idea of getting her out of here, this town, me included, sounded fantastic. My home had security and was actively monitored, a great place to hide out until we had better leads and knew more about what we were dealing with.

"I'll go talk to her." I ran a hand along my scruff-covered jaw. "She won't like it, but it's for the best. Can you dig up the number for her boss at the library? I'll call her and let her know she won't be coming in until we solve this."

Charlie grinned. "Oh, this will be fun to watch."

I slammed my shoulder into his on my way to the bedroom.

The knob turned freely. A good sign, I hoped. But that hope vanished when I took in the state of her room. An open, half-full suitcase lay on the bed. Rae knelt in front of the dresser, tossing clothing over her shoulder from the lower drawer onto her bed.

"What are you doing?" Maybe she heard us and was excited to get out of town.

"I'm leaving," she said, not looking up from the clothing.

"Yeah, Charlie and I were just discussing that. You and I are—"

"No." The dresser rocked with the force used to close the drawer. Wild brown eyes glared at me from her spot on the floor. "I'm going alone. I'm leaving this town and never coming back." Her bottom lip quivered. "I won't be responsible for any more death."

I cringed. Thank goodness the police weren't here yet or they'd take her statement the wrong way. I knew what she meant, but others... not so much.

"You're not going anywhere alone," I stated and crossed both arms over my chest. It was hard to feel commanding when standing in only boxers and an undershirt.

"Yes. I. Am." Rising, she pulled a sweatshirt over her head, whipping her loose hair from inside the neck to sway along her back. "I'm leaving you. Charlie. Everyone who has ever spoken to me. No one is safe around me. I can do this on my own."

I sighed. Tugging on my jeans, I left the front hanging open. "Rae, you don't have a choice in this. You're coming with me. It's not safe."

Her laugh sounded hysterical, maybe even bordering on crazy. "Oh yeah? I'd love to see you try to stop me."

Slamming the top of the suitcase closed, she zipped up the sides. I shrugged and dug through my duffel. Her back was still to me when I pulled out the steel handcuffs.

"What the—" She gasped, eyes wide, as I gripped her wrist and pulled her to the bed. Her back bounced on the mattress. "Alec, what are you—" She stopped when I slipped one cuff onto her left wrist. She followed the movement as I pulled her arm out wide, securing the other end of the handcuffs to the metal headboard.

I dug through my bag, searching for my spare set, all while she screamed to release her and tugged on the cuffs, the clang of metal thundering through the room.

"This is for your own good." She moved her hand this way and that to keep me from securing the other wrist. "You're the one who threw down the challenge, Sunshine, so don't get pissed that I accepted."

"You're crazy," she said through gritted teeth. If her glare could kill, I would've died three times by that point.

Finally I snatched her free hand and cuffed it to the bed. Standing back, I smiled at my work.

The way her chest heaved, from exhaustion or something else, told me she wasn't hating the idea of being tied up. To test my theory, I circled her bare ankle with a single finger, monitoring her reaction.

"I'm liking this scenario," I admitted, trailing that finger higher to stroke over her calf. "You've been a bad girl, Sunshine, challenging me and expecting me to back down. What should I do with you?" Goose bumps pebbled her skin as I made my way up her inner thigh, but unknown voices entering the living room made me pause. "I have to go deal with the police and coroner. I'll come check on you in a bit to see if you need anything."

"I need to leave," she hissed. She kicked at my chest, but I dodged it with ease.

"Not going to happen. So get comfortable." That earned me a string of curses. "I'll come get you when it's time to leave."

"I'm not going anywhere with you."

At the door, I turned with a vicious grin. "Yes, you are. You're not safe here. We now know for certain the person after you knows where you live. Charlie and I can't secure every inch of this house at all times. We're leaving. Now get some sleep."

I slammed a hand over the light switch, dousing the room in darkness. Her anger-fueled screams filtered through the now closed door as I stomped away.

Didn't she know I was only doing it for her safety? She was my responsibility until we figured this out. And even if she wasn't, like I'd let her run off to some strange town with nothing but a suitcase. The bastard tormenting her would probably follow her and start this all over again when she set up a new life away from Sweetcreek.

I fisted both hands at the thought.

Charlie's brows were nearly at his hairline as he glanced from me to the bedroom. "What did you do to her?"

"Handcuffed her to the bed. She wanted to leave on her own."

"Kinky."

I smacked the back of his head. Three officers stood outside, one taping off the crime scene, the other two helping the coroner. A man in a suit stood writing in a small notebook just a few feet away.

"That the new detective covering the case?"

Charlie nodded, his shit-eating grin wide. "Did you have the other guy fired or reassigned?"

"Reassigned," I grumbled. "They said there wasn't enough documentation to fire him outright. Fucking red tape. Let's get this over with so I can get Rae out of here."

He tilted his head toward the detective. "Think they'll be okay with you taking their only suspect out of town?"

"I don't give a fuck if they are. We're leaving in two hours whether they, or Rae, like it or not."

"You're a cocky son of a bitch, you know that?" I nodded as we moved toward the detective. "But that's what makes you good at what you do. Don't worry about things here while you're gone. I'll keep working and keep you updated. You just keep her safe."

I tightened my lips and looked toward the bedroom. The calls for help and thrashing had subsided. Why couldn't Rae see all I wanted to do was protect her, keep her safe? Hopefully she'd have realized that by the time we needed to leave. The last thing I wanted to do was keep her restrained. Well, outside the bedroom. But I'd do whatever it took to get her out of town.

Earlier she said she could never hate me. With any luck, that would stay true after today.

RAE GLARED out the passenger window, her anger and frustration palpable. The barren West Texas landscape was all around us for as far as we could see, glinting in the red and orange sunrise. Only two more hours until we arrived home.

Home. I leaned against the door and gave a side-eye glance toward the passenger seat. *How nice would it be for her to call that place home too?*

I rolled my eyes at the thought. I was a fool if I thought that could ever happen.

I was evil, broken. Dangerous. I needed to be alone in this world to keep my anger and rage controlled. I saw what could happen to those people like me claimed they loved. It ended in broken bones, bruises, and lashes.

I refused to be that to anyone, but especially Rae. She deserved so much better than me, than what I could offer her. Her future would be as bleak as my mother's if I gave in to the urge to claim Rae the way I wanted—the way my body demanded.

"I won't jump out of the car," she said, her exasperation clear. "Can you unlock me now?" For emphasis, she rattled the handcuffs that were looped through the handle above her head and secured to her wrists. "Can't believe you didn't even let us have coffee."

It looked slightly uncomfortable.

"I didn't want to stop every thirty minutes for you to pee. I'm exhausted too." Neither of us had slept in nearly twenty-four hours at this point. "Plus, I asked you if you wanted the easy way or the hard way." She huffed and shifted in the seat. "You're the one who tried to outrun me, Sunshine. So no, I think you'll stay secured, because I'm not sure you won't jump out of a moving truck. Your self-preservation skills are lacking, by the way."

"Screw you, Alec."

"You sure wanted to last night." Her roar of rage proved that was the absolute wrong thing to say. Frustration brewed at the entire situation. My grip tightened on the steering wheel. "Sorry, I just…. I need to keep you safe, and you're making it difficult pushing me away. The last thing I want to do is hurt you, Rae."

"I know." She blew out a hard breath, sending a few stray hairs floating away from her face. "I'm just so mad."

"Understandable."

"I've lived with this for so long, and for a while there last night, I thought… I don't know, that maybe all this would be over soon. That we would find the information to not only clear me but enough to find the actual person behind all this. And then the dead body and the guy from the library…." Leaning forward, she pressed her forehead to her bicep. "It seems like this will never end, and I'm not okay with that, but I'm also not okay with kidnapping."

I chuckled against the fist pressed to my lips. "I didn't kidnap you."

She rattled the cuffs. "Really?"

"Okay, fine, maybe I did, but I promise you'll like where we're going." She turned, angling her back to me. "Come on, Sunshine, don't be like that. I have a pool." I drew out the word to make it sound enticing. It worked, her body shifting an inch away from the door. "And a…." *Huh, how would I describe Sherry?* "A housekeeper who's a mean cook and says food is her love language."

Chapter 13

Rae turned to face the windshield. "Housekeeper? Not girlfriend?"

I cringed. "No."

"Have you ever been married?"

That made me adjust in my seat, suddenly feeling like I sat on the receiving end of an interrogation. "No."

"Engaged?" she prodded.

"Nope, and before you ask, I've never even dated someone long enough to consider that." *Except you.* But I left that out. The clang of the cuffs drew my focus from the road. "Listen, if you promise not to jump out of the truck, I'll uncuff you. Do you promise?"

"Cross my heart." She mimicked the sign as best she could while restrained.

I flicked the blinker and pulled over to the side of the two-lane highway. Key in hand, I stretched over the center console, reaching for the cuffs. Her dark brown eyes tracked my every move as I crowded her space.

"Alec?" she whispered and licked her lips.

I turned, putting us face-to-face. All it would take for me to close the short distance between our lips was a simple shift forward.

"Yeah, Sunshine?"

"I like these." Blush brightened along her cheekbones, but she didn't look away. "A lot. Are you sure about last night being a onetime thing?" No. I wanted to say, "Fuck no," and seal my lips to hers, to devour her from the inside out. But I wouldn't. "Why does it matter? Why can't we have fun until we solve this and you leave?"

A slight begging lifted her voice. Add that with her restrained and obvious desire rolling off her, and I grew hard in my now tight jeans.

I clenched my teeth to leash my desire and maintain control. "You don't want to know the answer to that, Rae."

"I do. Fucking hell, I do. This is torture, Alec. Having you, yet not. I don't care why you left me after making all those plans and promises. I don't care that you left me with a shattered heart for years. I want you, even if it's only for right now. Is it because of me?" The vulnerability in her tone cut like a knife to the heart.

I dove my fingers into her hair and tugged, arching her neck back. "Never, for one damn second, think any of my mess is because of you. You're perfect. Too perfect and good. I would destroy you, Rae. Don't you see that?"

"No, I don't, Alec. Why do you think you would do anything to hurt me? Don't you see what I see?"

I let go of her hair and made quick work of releasing her hands. I massaged the ring of red skin around each wrist, avoiding her stare.

"I've always cared too much when it comes to you. You're my weakness and my strength in one flawless package. I don't trust myself with you. And I'm afraid...." I stopped myself before I could reveal my dark truth. "We can't happen, Rae. Just accept it and move on."

"I don't think I ever mattered to you at all." My shoulders bunched at her words, my muscles tense. "Or you would've come back for me. Hell, you wouldn't have ever left me the way you did." She scoffed and yanked her wrists out of my grasp. "A fucking note."

"I did what I had to do." I settled into my seat and slammed the truck back into Drive. The back end fishtailed on the blacktop as I sped down the highway.

A deafening shrill blared through the cab, causing us both to wince at the intrusion into our tense conversation.

"Bronson," I snapped after hitting the button to answer the call.

"Should answer 'Dumbass'," Rae grumbled.

"Ranger Bronson?" the voice on the other end of the line asked tentatively.

"You've got him." I shot Rae a warning when her lips parted, ready to say something derogatory, no doubt. She sealed them shut and rolled her pretty brown eyes. I fought the urge to pull the truck over and spank her fine ass. I tightened the grip on the wheel. "Who is this?" I demanded.

"Maxwell Chisom. The man with the missing wife."

Rae's eyes went wide, staring at the display screen.

"Mr. Chisom, right. What can I do for you?"

"My wife is still missing, and I want her back."

Chapter 13

I frowned at the windshield. The undercurrent of anger, something I was familiar with, and the possessive verbiage made me pause. From the way Rae's eyes narrowed, I assumed she'd picked up on the same thing.

"I have someone looking into it now, as your wife wasn't the only one who's gone missing in the past few years."

"I don't give a fuck about those women," the man bellowed so loud, his voice rattled the windows. "I want Shannon back home where she belongs."

Another red flag waved in my mind.

"Either way, we're looking into all the cases. When I have additional information, the Sweetcreek police will reach out to you. Until then, there's nothing I can do."

A click, and silence filled the cab.

"What an asshole," Rae muttered.

I couldn't have agreed more.

14

RAE

I chewed on the end of my ponytail, thinking over the call that just ended. It seemed Alec felt the same way I did about the jackass. Anyone who would talk about their wife like that with so much anger was not someone I ever wanted to know. If Alec ever found out about—

"Miss me already?" Charlie's cocky voice spilled through the speakers, severing the downward spiral my thoughts had taken. "Can Rae hear me?"

"Yes," I responded, unsure why I was smiling. Charlie made things easier between Alec and me, buffered the ever-growing tension between us. What would we do without him these next few days?

"Your couch might be the worst couch in the history of couches. My shoulders and lower back are solid knots."

"It's a great couch," I defended, even though I knew he was right. Alec said just as much the first night he stayed with me. "Next time you can take the bed with me and Alec."

"The fuck he can," Alec snapped.

"Why do you care, Mr. I Did What I Had To Do?" I mocked.

"Don't start with me, Rae," Alec said, shooting me a serious look. "I'm doing what's best for you."

"Don't you dare suggest you know what's best for me, Alec Bronson," I hissed and pointed an accusing finger across the center of the truck.

"Um, guys? Not sure what happened in the last hour since you left, but I really don't want to be the third wheel in your lovers' quarrel."

"We are not lovers," Alec and I said at the same time.

"Not how it sounded last night." Charlie's resounding chuckle had my downturned lips ticking upward. "Was there a reason for this call, or you just wanted to check in on me?"

Alec shifted in his seat to sit up straighter. "That other case I asked you to look into last night before I went to bed, the missing women."

"I remember. Several women missing over a few years. You wanted me to look into their online history and see if I could track them down that way."

I stilled. My breathing picked up as my anxiety grew.

"The most recent woman who went missing, Shannon Chisom, look into her background and the husband's. Specifically hospital records or ER visits."

"Got it. Anything specific I should look for? Oh, and by the way, the coroner just left. Said he assumed the COD was blunt force trauma to the head, but because of all the blood, he couldn't be sure until the autopsy. The beating seemed like overkill to me, same as the others, but this time the bastard used his fists instead of a knife or gun. He's all over the board with how he kills these people. The only signature is the rage behind them and the connection to Rae."

I pressed a hand to my stomach, hoping to calm the queasiness.

"Let me know what he says after the autopsy. And for the other case, I want to know if they visited the ER or hospital for broken bones, bruises, sprains, things like that. Anything common with domestic violence."

A long pause weighed heavily in the truck before Charlie spoke again. "You think there was a reason for the women to go missing."

"It's a hunch. Shannon Chisom's husband called, and it rubbed me the wrong way. Maybe domestic abuse connects them all. If we find the connection, then we can uncover who's taken them."

Closing my eyes, I leaned a warm cheek against the window, trying to drown out their conversation. I couldn't think about those women and what they lived through. I hated my lonely life, but at least I didn't live in fear of going home because of my spouse and what he might do. I shivered at the thought of always walking on eggshells around the person who should be your partner in life, not the villain.

"On it," Charlie said. "Oh, Alec?"

"Yep."

"Stop being a dumbass." With those parting words, he ended the call.

I smiled with my eyes still closed. "I like Charlie."

"I'm not a dumbass," Alec grumbled like a pouting toddler. "You don't understand, don't know the full story."

My lids flew open, and I swiveled in the seat. "Then tell me, Alec. I'm all ears. You know the worst about me, about my shit of a life since you left. How can what you have hidden in your closet be worse than mine?"

"Drop it, Rae," he warned.

"You're scared," I said, finally getting it. "It was a woman, wasn't it? Some woman broke your heart and made you scared to get close to anyone again. So now you won't open up, too afraid I'll hurt you too."

The muscle along his jaw twitched, his posture now tense, as if prepared to pounce. "No."

"A friend maybe, someone who you thought you could trust but stabbed you in the back." I was grasping at straws, but I had to know. Had to understand what was holding him back from telling me why we were such a terrible idea.

"You need to drop it. Now."

I held my ground even though that commanding voice sent a

shiver of fear through me. Maybe I should've stopped, heeded his warning. But I didn't, because with Alec, I wanted it all. All of him.

"Or maybe it was your mom who—"

My seat belt snapped against my chest, and a scream tore up my throat as the truck skidded to a stop. Dust and smoke floated past the truck, which was still in the middle of the highway. Chest heaving, I turned my shocked face to Alec.

Both hands gripped the wheel, his full attention out the windshield. The quick rise and fall of his chest plus the flex of those biceps and forearms spoke to the taut tension pulsing off him in waves.

"You have one thing right, Rae Chapin." *Oh hell. I got the full name.* I swallowed hard. "I am scared. Fucking terrified that if I let you in, allow your kind, sweet spirit to break past my walls, you'll see the monster lurking inside and run. I can't take that chance." He slammed a tight fist to his chest, just over his heart. "I am who I am, but I sure as hell can stop the cycle from repeating, even if that means depriving myself of the only thing I've ever truly wanted. You."

I flinched back at the passion in his words. "Alec," I breathed. "Who said you were a monster? I've known you, I know you, and you're—"

"My father."

I sucked in a breath, my nostrils flaring as a swirl of emotions flooded. His father was a notorious asshole in the community. The richest man in town could be, I guess. But how could anyone say that about their son, especially Alec? Sure, he got into fights when we were kids, but that was just him protecting or sticking up for me or other weaklings.

"What?" It was all I could manage. Too many other words lodged in my throat.

"My father. The last time I saw him."

I shook my head in disbelief. "Why would you believe him enough to make you alter your life around this lie?" Anger began festering in my chest, not for me but for Alec. If he truly believed that about himself all this time, I hated his father for doing that to him.

Chapter 14

After pulling the truck to the side of the highway, he put it in Park and leaned his head back, closing his eyes. Those dark lashes fanned across his naturally tan skin.

"Because he was right. He said I would grow up to be just like him. A mean bastard to the ones he claimed to love. Too high expectations, too much anger and harsh punishments. A wife beater and child abuser. A fucking monster hiding beneath a businessman's mask. It runs through my veins, that constant simmering anger. I know I'm destined to be just like him, Rae. Now you understand why I push you away, why I left. I would rather cut out my heart with a dull blade than ever hurt you."

I stayed gaping toward the driver seat as he thrust the truck back into Drive and slowly eased back onto the highway. All I could do was stare at him, fighting back the pity and anger that warred inside me. I wondered if he'd ever spoken those words out loud, ever told anyone what damage his father had done.

Child abuser and wife beater.

Those two hideous labels clanged in my head. How did I not see that in school?

"How did I not know?" I whispered, choking back the tears that were building and burning my throat. Was that why he never let me touch him back in high school? Why he seemed determined to only focus on my pleasure?

"He was good at hiding who he truly was and hiding the evidence on Mom and me. Now you understand, you see why this"—he motioned a finger between us—"or any relationship can never happen. I refuse to be my father."

I pressed my lips into a thin line as I stared at him.

If he didn't see how amazing he was, then it was up to me. He seemed to see only the beauty in me; it was my turn to make him see the good in himself.

"You're a fool, Alec Bronson." His head whipped my way, eyes darting from the empty road. "If you won't fight for you—the real you, not the monster you think you're destined to become—then I fucking will."

I held a breath. Maybe that was a little too much? But he had to know it wasn't true. The lie he'd believed for too long was just that, a big fat fucking lie.

"What did you say to me?" he said, the words hissing through his clenched teeth.

How did he not see it? Not see what I saw. What anyone who ever met him saw. Hell, even the reporters made him out to be a saint, and those people didn't like anyone.

"You heard me. Pull over here," I demanded, finger pressed to the window in the direction of the rest stop we were about to blow past. "I'm not having this conversation while you're driving."

Nothing. Not a twist of the wheel or motion toward the blinker.

Hell no. He thought he could drag me around, restraining me and kidnapping me, but he couldn't pull over at my request?

I lunged across the truck and yanked the steering wheel, careening the front of the truck down the off-ramp.

"What the hell?" Alec yelled as he fought for control of the wheel. "You're going to get us killed, Rae. Let go."

Once we were halfway down the ramp, I released my tight grip, giving him control once again. "Pull into a parking spot. We're going to talk about this. Now." With a harrumph, he whipped the truck into an angled space and slammed on the brakes. For the second time in less than twenty minutes, the seat belt snapped against my chest, knocking the air from my lungs. I shot him a glare. "Real mature."

Just over the hood, several concrete picnic tables and rusted grills secured to the ground dotted the rest area, all vacant. The rumble of the truck silenced.

"There's nothing to discuss. I made my decision a long time ago, and I'm not changing my mind." He crossed both arms over his broad chest. "Sorry, Rae. It's just not in the cards."

"Well, here's the thing, Alec." I inhaled a deep breath and released it slowly. "Even if I wasn't insanely attracted to you, or still hopelessly in love with you after all these years, I'd still fight for you. Because, Alec Bronson, you're my friend. You've been my friend since elementary school, became more in middle school, and stole my heart in high school. And I'm not the type of friend who will let their friend believe lies. Just like you wouldn't allow me in middle school. When all those girls called me fat, shouted nicknames like 'porker' or 'fat trash', you never let me believe them. You fought for me to know the truth, and I'm doing the same thing now for you.

"And as your friend, I'm here to tell you I know firsthand you're not the monster you think you are or will become. I've seen you, know you inside and out. Even as kids you were the good guy, defending those who couldn't defend themselves. That's not the heart of a monster, that's the soul of a hero."

He scoffed. "Tell that to the guys whose asses I kicked. It was happening then. I couldn't stop myself. I needed that outlet." His gray eyes turned cold. "What will happen if I need that outlet and you're the only one around? Do you think you'd stand a chance against me, Sunshine? If I explode, I'd destroy you."

"First, you never hit a girl or woman. All those guys back then, sure, maybe you picked some of those fights, but it never made you a bad person. It doesn't mean you would grow up and be a man who couldn't learn to channel that anger toward something else. And you know what? Even if you get that urge or are so pissed you want to take it out on someone and I'm the only one around, I know in my heart you would never hurt me. Because I know you, Alec. I know your heart. I'm not scared of you," I whispered and stretched across the cup holders to grab his fisted hand.

Eyes distant, he shook his head as though deflecting my words from seeping deep. He didn't believe me or chose not to hear my heart-filled argument. Maybe he needed a demonstration. To see I wasn't scared of him, that even if he was pissed to the point of explosion, I knew he wouldn't hurt me.

I racked my brain. A slow smile grew on my face as I formed a plan.

Good thing I knew his one major trigger. One that sent him boiling over within moments.

Me.

"It's because I'm fat, isn't it?"

"Rae," he seethed. "Don't do that."

"Do what? Tell it how it is? That you're this Greek god lookalike, actually better because you're real life, and I'm me." The truth in my words left me breathless, my insecurities leaking into this brief therapy session I concocted for him. "I'm nothing special."

His entire body vibrated with restrained anger. He needed another push to send him over the edge.

"Well, I guess if you're going to deny this between us, then I'll just ask Charlie—"

Just like that, he was in his seat and then not. I gasped as he crowded me against the door. A hot palm slid around the back of my neck and tightened, arching my neck and angling my face to his.

My breaths were shallow and quick. Desire twisted and trembled low in my belly. The soft cotton of the sleep cami I still wore beneath the sweatshirt scraped against my sensitive pebbled nipples. His heavy breaths fanned across my face.

"I'm still not scared of you," I whispered.

He scoffed. "You sure about that?" His grip tightened. My lids drooped in response, my focus going from his intense gaze to his lips.

"Alec." I glanced up and pleaded with him through our locked gaze. "You're not your father."

With a frustrated growl, he closed the small distance between us, crashing his lips to mine. When he pulled away, no doubt struggling internally with this turn of events—doubting himself, his control—I gripped the front of his T-shirt and tugged him close. Parting my lips, I slid the tip of my tongue along the seam of his mouth, begging him to open for me.

"You're a stubborn woman, Sunshine." His lips moved against mine, brushing and teasing. A sharp bite of pain along my lower lip snapped my eyes open. Those gray eyes danced with mischief as he nipped at my lip again. "Are you sure you want this? Want me knowing—"

I cut him off with a kiss. "Yes. I want it all, everything you're willing to give me. I know it won't be easy, that you've believed some-

Chapter 14

thing for so long that isn't true, but I'll be here for you. We'll walk through it together. I want you, the good and the bad."

"I'm not gentle, Rae. I have particular... tastes and triggers." His free hand slipped between my pressed thighs and cupped my mound. "I take what I want."

"Oh hell," I moaned and relaxed into the hold he still had around my neck. "Please."

"You think you can handle me?" Alec shoved his fingers down the front of the gym shorts he dressed me in before dragging me out of the house earlier. A low hum of approval filled the truck when his fingers slid against my wet slit. "You like this, don't you? Just like the handcuffs."

"Yes," I breathed. The back of my sweaty thighs slid along the leather seat as I widened my legs, offering him more room.

"You want me to fingerfuck you right here in the truck, don't you?"

I nodded, unable to speak with his finger circling my clit.

Every nerve ending was on fire. My head swam with desire as he teased me with his fingers and lips. The bastard knew what he was doing, and I loved every second.

"You're so damn beautiful," he whispered into my ear. "If I ever hear you degrade yourself again, Rae, hear you mention one negative thing about your perfect body, I'll punish you for it. I'll spank that fine ass of yours red and fucking love every second of it."

One breath he was hovering over me, the next he was gone.

His fingers, his lips, his touch all gone.

"What?" I pouted. "Where did you go? Don't stop. I thought we got past that?" My voice was low with frustration. "You're good. I'm good. All good."

A wide smile split his face, that dimple gone with his bunched cheeks. "I told you before that I like control, and I say not now, not here."

"Why?" I whined.

He raised a hand and pointed out the passenger window. "Because a family just parked two spots down."

I sucked in a breath as embarrassment flooded through me. I hastily sat up straight in the seat and made sure all clothing was situated before turning to see where he pointed.

Sure enough, a family of five were making their way toward a picnic table, the older male dragging a heavy ice chest behind him.

"Right." I unbuckled my seat belt and reached for the door handle. Alec's hand wrapped around my wrist, soft enough to not hurt but strong enough to keep me inside the truck. I gave him a small smile. "I'm not running, just going to pee. It's been like an hour."

Outside, the sweltering July heat smacked me in the face, making the sweatshirt heavy and constricting. Hopping onto the sidewalk, I turned and squinted to see inside the truck. Alec stared back, a disbelieving smile on his face.

I gave him a gigantic wave and turned for the bathrooms.

Had my life just veered because of him? Was the course I was now on toward happiness and love instead of death and loneliness?

I sure as hell hoped so, and that somehow it involved Alec.

15

RAE

"Home sweet home." Alec shoved the tall wooden door open. With a wide palm pressed to the center, he held it open and gestured for me to enter. "Ladies first."

I bit back a smile and stepped into the... home? No, this place wasn't a home.

"This is an estate, not a home, Alec. The driveway was the longest part of the trip." Slight exaggeration, but it was the longest gravel driveway ever.

He softly shut the door behind us and dropped both our bags on the polished dark hardwood. "I like my privacy. Which reminds me, I have security cameras placed all around the property's perimeter and in the house. Plus security alarms, glass-break sensors, and motion alarms. We're safe here."

"Fort Knox," I muttered under my breath. But it was a relief. This place, the faraway location, was a relief. I inhaled deep, feeling like a free woman. "It's beautiful, Alec." I continued to inspect every inch of the entryway and the two adjoining rooms. To our right was a large living room full of leather furniture and a stone fireplace, to my left a personal library.

I held in my squeak of excitement at the stuffed shelves. My fingers twitched at my side to brush along the spines.

"You were right," I said, turning to him. "I needed this. I already feel better, like the weight of the world has lifted from my shoulders. I know I fought you at first"—I shot him an annoyed look at his smirk—"but I'm glad you kidnapped me."

A shy grin, one I'd never seen before, made his features soften, giving him a younger, less authoritative appearance.

"Come on." He grabbed my hand and interlaced our fingers. "I'll give you a quick tour, and then I need a nap." He covered a yawn with his free hand. "I haven't slept in twenty-four hours."

A yawn of my own had my mouth opening. "Yeah, I'm exhausted." Which I was, and I had a feeling being here, with him and the security, I'd sleep harder than I had in a long time. I chased that deep sleep with wine all the time but could never fully allow myself to be that vulnerable. But not here, not with him.

We passed a gym and a bedroom before the hallway gave way to a massive open space. The kitchen, a cozier living room, and the dining room all flowed together with a wall of windows on the other side. I removed my hand from his and moved to that bright wall to get a better look outside. To the left was a pool with a cabana, seating area, outdoor kitchen, and pergola. Opposite that was nothing but beautiful Texas landscape.

To the non-Texan, all they'd see was rocks, dirt, and piles of dust. But not to me, and apparently not to Alec, if he made these windows to stare out all day.

"Wow." I glanced over my shoulder, smiling. "It's beautiful."

He nodded, his face unreadable as he watched me. "Come to the kitchen." He held a hand out for me. "We skipped breakfast, and it's almost lunchtime. I need food."

I placed my hand in his. "Tired and hungry. That can't be a good combo. I'm starving too."

"A woman who likes to eat. I like her already."

I turned toward the feminine voice. An older woman with the

sweetest smile strode across the room, wiping her hands on the front of the pressed blue floral apron that hung from her waist.

I shook my hand out of Alec's and swiped the sweat from my palm onto the sweatshirt before jutting it out between me and the woman. "Hi, I'm—" My grunt cut off the next words when she bypassed my hand and wrapped her arms around my shoulders in a tight bear hug. I stood stiff, not knowing how to respond, but the longer she held me the more relaxed I became in her arms.

How long had it been since another woman, a friend or motherly figure, had wrapped me in a loving hug? Tears threatened at the sadness and joy that swirled from this simple kind gesture.

"You must be Rae." She finally released me but still held on to my shoulders at arm's length. "I'm Sherry." We both turned at the sound of the fridge opening. "You two must be exhausted from the trip and"—she fluttered a hand in front of her face—"everything you've been through. I'll make you both a heavy snack and bring it to your rooms. I'm sure you'll want to shower before crawling into bed."

"You're a gem, Sher Sher," Alec drawled and shut the fridge. "If I could sleep-eat right now, I would. Damn, I'm exhausted."

I nodded in agreement. Him mentioning it was like a trigger to my exhaustion. I could barely keep my eyes open.

"I'll get Rae settled into one of the guest rooms." Alec's lips pursed unhappily about that revelation. Quite frankly, so was I. "Then I'll bring you something to eat in your bedroom. It'll be there before you're out of the shower."

Before I could agree or disagree, Sherry herded me toward another long hall. Before we slipped out of sight, I checked over my shoulder for Alec. He stood with his hip pressed against the counter, smiling as if everything was right in his world. I smiled back, loving that for the first time since he found me in the jail cell, he appeared genuinely happy.

THE SUN WAS high in the sky, its bright rays burning through the large window, when I awoke hours later. Groggy from sleep, I sat up and rubbed my eyes. I surveyed the room I was too tired to appreciate before sliding into the softest sheets and instantly falling asleep.

Soft blues and yellows sprinkled around the room on pillows, the fluffy duvet, and accented with a few pictures perfectly hung on the wall. It was cute, quaint. There was no way Alec decorated this. The front living room that was 100 percent masculine, yes, but not this room. This spoke to a female's touch. Sherry's maybe?

The urge to use the restroom forced me out of the comfortable bed before I was ready. Padding to the door, I pulled it open and checked up and down the hall before hurrying to the bathroom across from my room.

I winced at my reflection and did my best to tame my wild mane. I knew better than to go to sleep with it wet. Thankfully I found a stack of unused hair ties in the drawer, saving me from looking like a hot mess.

Minutes later, I stepped out of the bathroom refreshed and feeling more like myself, only to draw up short when I found Sherry going through my drawers. No, not going through them—filling them. The suitcase I had hastily packed earlier sat open on the bench at the end of the bed, half empty.

"Hi," I said shyly.

Sherry whipped around with a smile. "Hope you don't mind. I just wanted you to feel settled. Alec mentioned you two would stick around for a few days."

My ears perked at the mention of him. "Is he up too?"

She nodded. "Out by the pool, waiting for you when you're ready."

I turned my attention to the suitcase and frowned. I hadn't packed a bathing suit, mostly because I didn't own one.

"You can borrow one of my suits. We're about the same size, and I have a brand-new one I haven't used."

My frown deepened as I studied her frame. "Um, I don't think—"

"Nonsense. Of course you can use it. I'd be delighted. I'll go get it and be right back so you can change."

Chapter 15

I held up a hand to stop her, but she was gone. With a reluctant sigh, I sat on the edge of the bed. Only a minute passed of me staring at my hands before she returned, a beautiful black one piece in her hand.

The material was smooth as I rubbed it between two fingers. Trepidation built in my chest as I turned it to look at the size. My brows furrowed at the double-digit number. I glanced up at Sherry through my lashes.

"I don't understand. How did you know my size?"

"I didn't." Sherry shook her head, confusion clear in her fluctuating tone. "I bought that for me."

"But you're, well, to be blunt smaller than me."

Understanding brightened her eyes. "I think you're mistaken. Try it on. I'll grab you a cover-up and be right back."

I stared at the swimsuit, only knowing she left the room when the door clicked closed.

Ten minutes later, I was dressed in a matching sheer black cover-up, flip-flops, and wide brim straw hat. None of it my own, yet it all fit perfectly. That still made little sense. I thought it over as I made my way down the slate walkway, the borrowed flip-flops smacking against my heels with each step.

The sun blazed overhead, instantly making sweat bead along my spine and forehead, but thankfully the hat kept the harmful rays from hitting the fair skin of my face. The rest of my body was just as fair, but hopefully since it was late afternoon, I wouldn't burn without sunscreen.

I rounded the full outdoor kitchen, and the pool came into view. Oversized with a diving board on one end, its clear water sparkled and glinted. A dark form speared through the water, bubbles and waves emerging in its wake. Alec's dark hair breached the surface first as he came up for air. Water cascaded along his tan skin, sprinkles raining from his strands when he shook his head and rubbed at his eyes.

A wide smile broke across his face when he found me staring

from beneath the shade of the pergola. Treading water, he hitched his chin.

"The water feels great."

"Looks great," I muttered beneath my breath. Clutching the cover-up tighter, I shook my head. "Sherry said she'd bring out some snacks." And wine. The wine was what I needed the most for liquid courage. Anyone like me half naked around this Adonis would need it too.

His arms cut through the water as he swam toward the ladder. Hands gripping the rails, he hauled himself out. Water slicked down his taut pecs and weaved through his ripped ab muscles.

I licked my lips and all but fell into a chair, my knees literally giving out at the sexiest sight I'd ever seen.

"I was beginning to think you'd sleep forever," he joked, shooting a wink my way. A tall wire shelf stood just off the pool, adorned with stacks and stacks of thick white towels. He grabbed one and pressed it against one eye, then the other.

"You been up long?" He shook his head, sending water to sprinkle my bare legs. He smiled at the sight and did it again. I shifted with a squeal. "Such a kid." While he dried off, I took in the expansive pool area. "This place is amazing. From the house to this, I'm a little intimidated, to be honest."

He cocked his head to the side. "Why?" The genuine confusion in his tone made me chuckle. He had no idea how all this could make a commoner, someone like me, feel. Add his sexy self to it all and I felt way out of my league.

"Because you're you." I waved a hand up and down his chiseled body. "With all this." I gestured toward the house and pool. "And I'm me, with a one-bedroom cottage that's falling apart." I avoided him, choosing to watch the pool water lazily lap against the tiled edge.

"Rae, look at me." Reluctantly I leaned back in the chair so I could look up. "None of that matters. Don't allow this stuff to intimidate you."

"How can I not? You have a live-in housekeeper, Alec. That's not normal."

He shrugged off my comment. "What is normal?" Metal screeched against the stained concrete as he tugged his own chair away from the matching metal table and plopped down. "My mom's family was wealthy, so when she... died...." He struggled around that word, making me wonder what really happened. "Her trust was split between me and my sister."

"I barely remember your sister," I mused. She was older than us and never really did much around school. A sinking feeling turned my stomach sour. "Did your father treat her the way he treated you?" I didn't want to use the word abused in case it sent him into defensive mode. Talking through all this was fresh for him; it would make sense if he had triggers that would shut him down.

I would know, had seen it many times before in the haunted eyes and reluctant tendencies of abused women. I wrapped my hand around my charm bracelet tightly.

Alec pitched forward and pressed both elbows to the tops of his thighs, clasped hands dangling between them.

"I took the brunt of it." Water dripped from his hair onto the concrete he suddenly found riveting. "She never needed as much discipline as my mom and me. I was the one who needed to toughen up, to be a man." The knuckles on both hands went white as he tightened his hold. "She left to study at Oxford and never came back. We still keep in contact, talk once or twice a year. We never talk about what happened during our childhood."

"Sounds healthy," I joked, the lightness in my voice forced, trying to ease the growing tension from his raised shoulders.

"You're the only person who knows what went down that last day, what he said." Slowly, he lifted his face, those gray eyes locked with mine. "I told no one what he said. Sherry knows the basics." He grimaced like he hated that minor fact. "She's been the one to slap sense into me when I lose myself to the memories."

"And you never hurt her." It was a statement—I knew he would never—but he needed to see that. My faith in him couldn't carry him through the healing he desperately needed. He had to believe in himself too.

"Of course I never hurt her," he huffed.

"So if she saw you at your worst and survived without a bump or bruise, then why do you think it would be different with me? Why are you determined to push me away when the evidence of your control over your actions and emotions lives here with you? And I can tell she cares about you, deeply."

He glanced away, dismissing me.

"Why can't you see yourself the way we do? The truth?"

His gaze slowly traveled back to me. With a brow arched, he leaned back in the chair and rested an arm on each armrest. "I could ask you the same thing."

I paused, not expecting that response. "That's different," I breathed. "Totally different."

"No, it's not. You keep believing some false narrative about your body, about what you offer, refusing to believe others find you beautiful." Rolling his lower lip between his teeth, he tilted his head. "Do you think Sherry is too heavy to be beautiful?"

"Well no, but that's not—"

"It is the same. You're wearing her bathing suit right now, are you not?"

I narrowed my eyes at him. *How the hell does he know that?* I sealed my lips, refusing to answer. This conversation was over.

"The same bathing suit that looks damn good on you."

Okay, maybe it wasn't. The gurgle of the pool and buzz of the overhead fan inched up my anticipation wondering what he would say next. "We've both believed certain lies about ourselves for over three decades. None of that, how we view ourselves, will change in a day."

I mulled that over and nodded. "Agreed."

"I will add this to the conversation, because it would be wrong of me to not bring it up." I swallowed and inched to the edge of the metal chair, my full attention on Alec and his next revelation. "As attracted as I am to you physically, it's who you are that entrapped me from the start. You were always so damn happy." A wistful look washed over his features. "Did you know I was jealous of you, of your life?"

"Mine?" I huffed.

"You had it all. You were—" He smirked as though he found his next words funny. "—sunshine personified. Kind to everyone, even those bitches at school. You believed everyone deserved a friend, a smile, and I was hell on wheels. Everything in my life revolved around rules and punishments and pain." Vulnerability flashed in his eyes, making me itch to go to him, but I stayed rooted in my seat. "You were the only good in my life. I looked forward to seeing you at school, for that beautiful distraction you offered with your smiles and laughs. I wanted what we planned together that night," he admitted hoarsely. "And I'm sorry I promised you the world and then walked away."

"Wow," I said in a long breath.

The shuffle of footsteps stopped me for asking for more, digging into his reason for leaving and finding out where he went, where he'd been all those years. A round plastic platter hovered in front of my face before settling down onto the table. A bucket filled with ice and a bottle of white wine rested beside it.

Without me asking, she poured half a plastic stemless glass.

"Thanks, Sher Sher," he said with a lopsided grin. He licked his lips as he stared at the platter stuffed with cheeses, meats, fruit, and crackers. "I'm starving."

I'd barely gotten out my own thank-you before she left, saying something about getting things started for dinner. Without bothering with the serving utensil, Alec began picking meats off the platter and shoving them into his mouth. He caught my amused smirk.

"What?"

"Where in the hell do you put all that?" I said around a laugh. Leaning forward, I plucked a strawberry off the platter. The juices slipped past my lips and rolled down my chin as I sank my teeth into the perfectly ripe fruit.

"I work out a lot," he said absentmindedly, watching the juice slide down my chin before I could wipe it away. "I picked up boxing in the military."

"How did you end up in the military?" I grabbed a cracker and nibbled on the edge. "I read where you spent time in the army before going to the Dallas police force, then became a state trooper, but I never read how it all happened. Figured you would've gone into business like your dad, but now I know why you didn't."

That damn teasing smirk popped his adorable dimple. "You read my Ranger bio?"

Well, shit.

"Maybe?" I shoved the rest of the cracker into my mouth and gave him a tight-lipped smile. "I just wanted to know what happened to you, where you'd gone. I always wondered."

Alec finished chewing a few grapes and swallowed. "I never forgot about you either. Wondered how you were, what you were doing. Who you were with." A flash of anger hardened his features.

"Really? I figured you forgot about me the day you left. Since you never came back, I just assumed I didn't matter." Inhaling deep, I studied the half-eaten platter of food. "I used to dream you would come back for me, would save me from what my life had turned into. Honestly, I'm not sure how much of what I held on to was young love or desperation to cling to the last time I remembered being happy. But you never came for me, and I guess year after year, each time something bad happened, then my self-inflicted isolation, you became the only dream I had left. That sounds so pathetic, but I could imagine, could dream of what could've been, a fantasy of a better life with you." I peeked up through my lashes. "And seeing you like this"—I flicked a hand toward his hard bare chest—"does not help with the minor obsession I developed over the years."

"Obsession?" His tone indicated he liked the sound of that.

"That's what you heard?" I tossed a green grape at his head. "Whatever. Enough about me being a freak and hopelessly infatuated with a man I once knew. You were saying something about boxing and the military."

He nodded. "It helps get my aggression out. Some days are harder than others to forget and move on. Punching the shit out of something helps on the bad days." His lips parted, ready to say something else when his phone vibrated along the table. He flipped it over and checked the screen. "Charlie," he said to me.

My stomach sank.

What now?

16

ALEC

"What do you have for us?" I asked, brows narrowed in concentration at the phone.

"I'm headed to the police station to pick up that evidence from the first murders and send it to the Dallas FBI office. Rae, would you mind me taking a sample of your hair from the house for comparison reasons? This way we can either prove it's yours from when you tried to wake up your parents or rule you out completely. If you're ruled out, we can run it through the national DNA database and maybe identify a new suspect."

"Um, sure."

The rustle of clothes filled the phone. "I'm getting dressed now. I also want to meet up with the coroner to go over the autopsy results. I want to know cause of death and see if this body has the same anomaly as the others."

"Anomaly?" Rae and I said at the same time.

"I found something that might connect the victims. Even though they were killed in different ways, there was something similar among all of them besides the overkill. A red, raw abrasion emerged around each of their throats, like they were strangled either before, during, or after death."

"Interesting," I mused. "Why didn't they see this before?"

"They probably never lined up the autopsy photos side by side. That's how I noticed. Whatever he used was the same with each victim. The abrasion had a fabric-like pattern. I want to see if this new victim has the same."

"His signature. Excellent work. Let me know what you find and if you need me to push through any red tape. Did you get anywhere on the background of the missing women?"

Annoyance filled Charlie's huff. "Kind of been busy proving your girl's innocence and finding the actual killer. Speaking of which, Rae, I have a question for you."

I swept my gaze to where she now sat ramrod straight in the chair.

Interesting.

"What's up?" Her lips parted as her chest rose and fell with her quick breaths.

"A package arrived for you before I left for the hotel." I watched her every move. "It didn't have a return address on it, so I opened it in case it was another taunt from the unsub. Do you want to know what was in it?"

Her fingers gripped the armrests. The way she avoided my questioning stare spoke to the fact that she was hiding something. But what?

"Oh, the charm I ordered, I bet?"

The silence from the other end of the line was deafening. It seemed Charlie suspected she was hiding something too.

"Yes, it was a charm, yet it didn't have a sales slip, return label, anything inside except for the small silver charm." I waited, anticipation mounting with each detail Charlie gave. "And how did you buy it? You don't have a cell phone, no Wi-Fi at the house, and your internet history is basic from the library—much to my disappointment."

"You checked my search history?" she asked breathlessly.

"What can I say? Girl-on-girl porn piqued my interest." I could've hugged Charlie for not mentioning I asked him to look into her more deeply. "And to my surprise, I didn't find lesbian porn like you promised."

Fingers in her hair, she loosened the messy knot she had it tied in and nervously raked her fingers through the long tangled strands.

"Guess I'm good at covering my tracks."

Something wasn't adding up, but it was clear she wouldn't tell us with this line of questioning.

"Let me know what you find out from the coroner," I cut in. "You questioning that bastard I caught after?"

"Yep. I'll let you know what he has to say. Later."

I stared at the beauty sitting across from me while she did everything she could to avoid my gaze. The chair rocked back when she sprang to her feet and pulled the sheer material up and over her head, giving me an unobstructed view to the lush curves beneath.

I called out her name in question as she raced toward the pool, but instead of stopping, she dove into the water. There was no doubt she was trying to distract me from asking about that charm and oddly avoiding behavior.

But it worked. That flash of fair skin, the look of her in that swimsuit, and I forgot about it all. Leaving the towel in the chair, I strode to the pool and dove in after her. I wrapped my arms around her waist and pushed off the bottom, rocketing us to the surface.

Her back to my chest, I moved her hair to one side and kissed along her neck, the taste of her and a hint of salt water washing over my tongue. Treading my feet through the deep water, I kept us afloat.

"Now that you can't escape my questioning..." I said against her skin. She squealed when I rotated her, putting us chest to chest, her palms pressing against my pecs. I tightened my hold, pressing her lower body tighter against my own. "What's with the charm bracelet?"

"It's nothing," she breathed, pushing with all her strength to break my hold. "Just let it go, Alec. Please."

"Why?" Keeping one arm around her waist, I grasped the wrist with the curious bracelet and held it up between us. "What are you hiding?"

"It has nothing to do with the case," she said. That felt like a truth. But what *did* it have to do with, and why wouldn't she tell me?

I sucked in a breath, ready to ask more questions, but forgot anything and everything when her lips sealed to mine. The taste of the salt water from the pool mixed between our moving lips as I deepened the kiss.

Pulling back, I gave her a devilish grin. "I know what you're doing." Her features dropped. "But I don't mind."

This time it was me who pounced, holding her tighter, grinding my now rock-hard cock between her legs as I kissed her. I flicked my tongue against her, swirling with the preview of what I could do—no, *would* do—between her thighs. Fuck, I couldn't wait to eat her, to taste her orgasm on my lips as she screamed my name.

I shuddered at the thought. We had to get out of this pool now.

I moved an arm through the water, directing us toward the shallow end. Every thought, every action revolved around getting her naked and making her mine. Right here, right now.

I stood once I had my footing along the pool bottom. She slipped in my hold, but she reached up and wrapped her arms around my neck to stay secured.

Panic bolted through me, devouring any hint of lust or pleasure.

My heart raced as the memories of being restrained and the following pain flooded my mind, overtaking every sense. I released my hold on Rae and shoved her away, sending her floating backward with a look of shock on her petite face.

Ignoring the blooming guilt, I gripped the ledge and hauled myself out of the pool with ease. Snatching a towel off the rack as I left, I snapped it to the side and wrapped it around my waist, not once looking back as I headed inside the house.

Glass condiment bottles and other containers lining the shelf rattled as I yanked open the fridge and grabbed a beer. I twisted the cap off with my bare hand and tossed it to the counter.

I was weak. So damn weak. Even after all these years, something as insignificant as Rae wrapping her arms around my neck sent me into a frozen panic. That hurt and confused look on her face was like a knife to my heart, but I still walked away. Because I couldn't explain to her what happened. For years I'd worked on minimizing any overreaction when held or restrained, yet what just happened made it so clear that I was still fucked in the head.

That was why I should've told her to stop. I should've backed the fuck off and never touched her. She was too much. She was always too much, infiltrating every inch of me, making me feel and be too much. I had no clue how she did it, how she made me feel so fast.

The bottle slipped in my tight grip as I raised it to my lips.

"I know that look." I ignored Sherry and kept guzzling the cold beer. "Alec Bronson, you look at me when I'm talking to you." The laundry basket she'd been holding smacked to the floor at her feet. "What happened?"

"Nothing." I again avoided her stern look and picked at the label on the brown glass. "It's complicated."

"Then uncomplicate it, Alec." She sighed. "I'm going to let you in on a little secret." Elbow on the counter, I rested my head in an open palm and motioned for her to continue. "Women forgive the men they love easily, but they have to understand to forgive. I don't know what happened out there, but if you're in here sulking, you did something wrong, which you need to go apologize for and explain why you did or said what you did."

"Do you know how many times my mom forgave my dad?" I asked through gritted teeth. "I refuse to repeat that cycle."

"You're a damn fool," she snapped, and yanked the beer from my hand.

"I'm a realist." I reached across the counter to retrieve the bottle, but she was too fast. Seconds later, the remaining half of the beer was down the drain. "I've seen the worst firsthand, and I refuse to do that to her. Plus, I'm a fucking mess, Sherry. No one should be tied to that. I won't ask her to be tied to me."

"Don't you dare take the choice between you or leaving away from her. That is her choice. You lay it all out on the table and let her decide." Marching to the wine fridge, she withdrew a bottle of white wine. "Now you stay in here and think about what you did." *Did I just get put in time-out by my housekeeper?* She turned and glared at me. "I'm going out to make sure she's okay and enjoy a glass or two of wine. When I come back, then you can go out there and beg for her forgiveness."

17

RAE

I spun my arms in the water to keep me afloat as I gaped in the direction Alec stormed off. *What the hell just happened?* Lost in desire, loving the feel of him as he ground against me, and then he freaked out.

Like a switch flipped, he went from hot to frigid with zero explanation. He just left me confused, again. This was proving to be an unpleasant habit of his, one I was clearly enabling by constantly going back to him.

I lay on my back, enjoying the water as I thought back to high school and the utter heartbreak that left scars and holes in my soul. All I needed was an explanation, something that told me it wasn't something I did. Because that was how it felt then and now.

A shadow casting over me had me splashing to stand.

"Sorry to startle you, but I saw Alec storm off." Sherry's lips pursed as she glared back at the house. "I thought I'd join you." She held up an empty glass and another bottle of white wine.

I opened my mouth to say, "No, thanks," that I wanted some alone time, but stopped. I was tired of being lonely and not having anyone to talk to. Standing, I waded through the shallow end for the steps.

"You know what? That sounds great. I haven't had someone to drink with in a long time."

After grabbing a towel, I wrapped it around my chest and sat in the chair I'd vacated what seemed like forever ago. When all I wanted was to avoid his questioning. I took a tentative sip of the wine I had yet to touch and grimaced when I found it slightly warm. I might have been okay with cheap wine but warm white wine? Yuck.

Digging through the ice bucket, I pulled out a few cubes and plopped them into the yellow-tinted liquid. The ice swirled as I moved the plastic glass to disperse the ice's cold temperature evenly.

"What happened?" Sherry asked after pouring herself a glass from the opened bottle chilling in the bucket. "He seemed... destroyed."

"That's how I feel, but more confused." I took a drink and savored the cool crispness on my tongue before swallowing. "He's good at that. Leaving without warning and leaving me confused and hurt. I should really stop allowing him to do it, but it's Alec, and I...."

"Love him?" She reached across the table and gave my hand a comforting squeeze. I lifted my wet eyes to meet hers. "I've worked with that man for years, so maybe I can help you understand him, his reactions. I can see he loves you too and didn't mean to leave you hurting. He's just confused and a male, which means he's terrible at communicating his feelings."

I laughed and took another drink. I stared at the wine as it swirled along the sides. "My mom told me he would break my heart, and I didn't believe her. I never thought he'd just up and leave me, not when we were... everything." Emotions clogged in my throat. "For weeks after he left, I sat by our home phone waiting for his call, but it never came. He never bothered explaining why he just left me like I meant nothing to him and never came back. Just like now." My voice broke. "I thought I meant something to him, that we were working toward something together, and then he just walked away. I'm a damn fool falling for him all over again, aren't I?"

"No, honey, you're not a fool. We can't control who our hearts latch on to. Alec Bronson is just as confused as you are, I have no doubt. Did he tell you about his dad?" I nodded while filling my empty glass. "I won't go into detail on what all I know—that's his story to share—but please be patient with him. He's a good man, and his heart is as big as this state, but he struggles with knowing how to communicate what he's feeling and why, which is what probably happened out here. Alec's love language is action, doing things for the person he cares about, not by saying the words out loud."

"What do you mean?"

The corners of her lips tugged upward.

"He might not say the words explaining how he feels about you, but I know he cares deeply. He brought you here, after all, introduced you to me. Then there's him dropping everything, pushing out some time off he needed, to race to your side when you called. I was outside the door when you called. He could barely contain his panic when you said you were in trouble. I saw it in his eyes, in his body language. He wouldn't drop everything for anyone, not when he had to butter up the Ranger over that territory to come help you."

Wait. Sweetcreek isn't his territory? And he did all that so he could help me? That bit of knowledge did something funny to my heart.

"You mean something to him. How far that will go is up to you two, but don't give up on him because he's a fool." She shot me a wink over the wineglass pressed to her lips. "Give him time to figure out what happened. He probably doesn't even know himself just yet. His daddy broke a little boy with his fists and belt." I winced at the thought. "And if you ask me, that little boy is still in there, keeping everyone at arm's length to never allow someone to hurt him again."

We sat in silence for a while, each sipping and watching the water. My mind, every thought, was on Alec and thinking through everything Sherry said. My self-doubt wanted to tell me he stormed off because of something I did or how I looked, but Sherry's words said something completely different. Alec hinted that he had left because of him, to protect me all those years ago. What if it was the same now?

Sherry stood with a groan and switched out the empty wine

bottle in the tub for the fresh one. I downed the remaining wine in my glass and stood to follow her inside.

"Oh no, honey, you stay out here. Drink this bottle and enjoy the pool." My smile of thanks was easy, the pain from Alec's rejection nearly gone. "Just sit out here and wait for a bit."

I crinkled my nose in confusion. "Wait for what?"

Her face turned stormy. "For a damn apology."

I knew I liked her.

18

ALEC

I stayed inside, pounding my fists against the punching bag as I waited for Sherry to give me the go-ahead. That was where she found me about an hour later and forced me out of the house to go grovel.

I was not looking forward to that. Not that Rae didn't deserve it, but it just meant I'd have to lay it all out there. Tell her why I panicked, the stories I really wanted to forget.

On my way toward the pool, the slate stone hot beneath my bare feet, my cell phone rang. I raced toward the table where I left it earlier and answered it.

"What did you find?" I asked, scanning the pool area for Rae, but came up empty. I strode to the pool and checked the water. Nothing. I spun on my heels toward the cabana and released the breath I was holding. She appeared to be sleeping on the mattress, hat covering her face.

"You and Rae fighting again?" Charlie asked.

To keep from bothering her, I moved to the far corner of the concrete. "It's complicated."

"It always is when it's important. Listen, I just left the coroner's office. The new victim had the same strange ligature mark. We've found his signature, and do you want to guess what the coroner thinks he's using as the ligature?"

"No, I don't want to guess. I don't have time for that." I sighed and glanced back to Rae to make sure she was still sleeping. "Apparently I have some groveling to do. Just tell me what the bastard used."

A loud high-pitched whistle belted through the phone. "Damn, man. From what I've witnessed, you're terrible with women. Need pointers?"

"I'm a little out of practice," I muttered. "Rae is different from some random hookup."

"That she is. Hey, if you fuck this up and I—"

"Don't even say it if you value your life," I threatened.

"Right, which I do, so moving on. It was a shoe string. That's what this guy is using to strangle his victims. The coroner also said half the beating happened antemortem. Then he was strangled and beaten some more."

Lips pressed in a thin line, I processed his words. "That's odd. Oddly specific."

"Very. And difficult to trace. I asked the ME to swab the wound to see if we could get anything from it. Maybe we'll be lucky and he's used the same shoestring in all the murders."

"That would be a huge connection clearing Rae's name for sure."

He hummed in agreement. "There's so much more."

"I've missed out on all the fun, it seems."

"Work, you mean. You've missed out on all the work I've been tasked to do single-handedly." I chuckled. He was right. "We questioned that guy, and you'll never believe what he told us. He couldn't give us a name, said the man who put him up to this didn't have a name. And, Alec, this guy literally pissed himself in the interrogation room when talking about the other guy. He's some enforcer, takes out anyone who steals from the dealers or doesn't pay up. So on a hunch, I did a little searching through other cold cases."

"Hacking. You did a little hacking."

"Touché. I found fifteen other murders that might be our guy's. I have a program pulling the autopsy photos now, and I'll check for strangulation marks."

"Fifteen?" I cursed. I stared at Rae, suddenly hating the distance between us. If the guy who'd done this also killed fifteen other people, she'd been in more danger than she realized over the years. "Are you saying a serial killer is stalking Rae?"

"Perhaps, but there's nothing in the cold case victims that tie them to Rae, nor did the other murders have the same level of overkill. I don't know how Rae ended up on this guy's radar, but...."

"This is bad." I could almost hear his answering nod. "We need to find the connection between Rae and this fucker. That's the key to unraveling it all. Did you at least get a description of the killer?"

"White, shaved head, dead eyes."

"Fuck." My stomach tightened with dread.

"I'm digging into her background, financials, and records later today. I sent that evidence to Dallas via courier earlier, along with a sample I took from her house. It won't take long for them to compare the two samples and possibly give us a lead."

I tightened my grip on the phone. "We're staying here, where it's safe, until we know more."

"Yep. I'll call you when I have anything else."

"Charlie," I said before he could hang up. "Thank you for everything you're doing. I appreciate it." I clicked the phone off and tapped it against my chin. This was worse than I initially assumed. A serial killer was stalking *my* Rae.

I'd kill him if he came after her and enjoy every second. One thing was for certain, she wasn't leaving my sight until we caught this guy.

The phone clattered to the metal table. Stealing a few grapes, I popped them all into my mouth and set across the pool deck, ready to explain and grovel to the woman who owned me body and soul, then detoured, jumping into the clear water instead.

I sank to the bottom, allowing the cold water to soothe my aching muscles and calm my racing thoughts. Only when my lungs burned with a desperate need for air did I press the balls of both feet to the rough bottom and push to the surface. Half my face submerged, I glided along the top of the water, my eyes on Rae, who was awake and watching me in return. Apprehension pulsed through my veins as I climbed out of the pool, water cascading down my shoulders and back, which she tracked with a guarded gaze.

"Hey," I said. Grabbing a fresh towel, I wiped the streaming water from my face. Taking one end, I wrapped it around my neck and grasped the other end. "Listen, I...." *Fuck, how am I going to explain this without displaying how much of a shit show I am on the inside?* "I want to explain."

"Alec." She sighed. Sitting all the way up, she stretched those long muscular legs out and crossed one ankle over the other. My fingers twitched to caress down them. "I don't want an excuse. If you're not ready to—" She looked to the sky like the right word was there. "—work at this, then we can leave it. We can focus on the case and nothing more. Because I can't... no, I deserve better than you walking away from me every time you doubt yourself or it gets difficult."

I nodded as I twisted the towel's ends around my hands.

"You do deserve better. You deserve the best of everything, Sunshine, and that's not me. I'm...." I groaned and shut my eyes. "I'm not good at this. I don't open up. I sure as hell don't have any relationship that lasts longer than a night or two."

"Thanks for the visual," Rae grumbled as she picked at the terry cloth towel beside her.

"What I'm trying to say is be patient with me. I don't deserve you, or you giving me a chance to make this right, but I promise to try and be the man who can earn the privilege of being with you." Her gaze softened. "I've always had issues with being restrained. I have little control over who I hurt or how I react when that panic takes over. I thought I'd conquered that defect—"

"It's not a defect," Rae snapped like I'd somehow offended her instead of degrading myself.

"Fine, that *issue*, but today proved me wrong. It's never happened when I was with a woman, mostly because I maintain control the entire time. I never let them have the upper hand. That's probably why I like restraints so much," I mused. "It allows me full control even if the woman gets a little overzealous while we're together."

I couldn't help my grin at Rae's hiss.

"Why are you telling me all this, Alec?"

"Because you deserve an explanation, not an excuse. Earlier in the pool, when you wrapped your arms around my neck, that panic slammed into me, and I wasn't prepared for it. All I could think about was getting out of your hold."

She frowned. "I wasn't trying to restrain you, though."

I shook my head and sat on the edge of the mattress. "You're thinking about it logically. Did I...?" I took one of her arms and inspected the slightly pink smooth skin, searching for bruising or red marks. "Did I hurt you?"

"Not the way you're thinking."

I shook my head in disgust at myself. I wasn't a man; I was a fucking coward who hurt the woman he loved because he was weak.

"I still hurt you. Physically or emotionally, it's all the same to me. I don't want to be that man you're guarded around all the time. And that's all I'll ever be. I'm broken without a way to be fixed, Sunshine. It's why I left all those years ago and why I should walk away now. All I'll ever do is cause you pain."

Her teeth sank into her lower lip in an attempt to conceal her grin. "Pretty sure what you made me feel last night and today in the pool, before you pushed me away, wasn't hurt. I'm feeling a little tortured sexually after being that turned on and left hanging." Releasing her teeth, she let that full smile bunch her cheeks. "You're being too hard on yourself. I'm not great at this either, but I'm willing to try. For you."

"This is serious, Sunshine. I'm trying to give you an out before you get hurt."

"Listen." She pushed off the bed and rested on her knees. "I've had a long time to daydream about us together, and now you're here, with me. I don't want an out, I want you. Broken bits and all."

I sighed and slumped my shoulders in defeat. She wouldn't let me go no matter how many times I warned her away, so where did that leave me?

"I want you, Alec, even if it's just for a little while."

"You're too good for a hookup. You deserve a forever with a man who—"

"Oh for fuck's sake," she exclaimed and tossed her hands into the air. They slapped against her thighs as she turned angry eyes on me. "Please stop telling me what I do or don't deserve and leave that up to me. Right now, I'm just a girl who's really horny after being left hanging and needs you to follow through on what you started."

I blinked, turning to face her squarely. An empty bottle of wine along the bed caught my eye. "How drunk are you?"

She laughed. "Tipsy enough to not have a filter. Your wine is fantastic, by the way. But I'm not drunk enough to not know what I'm doing or what I want."

My cock stirred to life at her suggestion. "You don't know what you're asking for."

"Try me," she stated and crossed her arms. My gaze dipped to her cleavage.

"I have rules. No restraining me. I'm in control at all times. And whatever I say goes. Do you have a safe word?" My chest rose and fell with my rapid breaths. I was already rock hard, and I hadn't even touched her.

"Bananas. I hate bananas."

I smirked. "Bananas it is." Kneeling to the concrete, I wrapped both hands behind her thighs. "Use it if you need to. I'm not gentle," I mused. "But I assume it's been a while for you so I'll go easy – for now."

"A while since sex?" I nodded. "With a real-life penis, yes. Fake, almost every night."

My caressing hands stilled. "Toys. You masturbate with toys. Now *that* I have to see."

"The last time I had sex with a person, it wasn't that great. Terrible, actually. Not that the toys have been that fulfilling lately anyway."

Well, this conversation took an interesting turn. I leaned forward and placed a kiss on the top of her slightly sunburned thigh. "Oh?"

"Yeah," she breathed, those brown soulful eyes finding mine. "It does the job, but it's just not as fulfilling. Like when you get a piece of cake that looks delicious only to bite into it and find out it's gluten-free with sugar-free icing. I mean, you eat the cake because it's cake, but it's not nearly as satisfying as you'd hoped."

"And the gross cake is your toys?" I wasn't sure if I was tracking.

"Yes. And a real cake is a penis attached to a living man."

"Can we please stop saying the word penis?" I grumbled and adjusted myself in my suit.

"And not just any dick, but a connection with the dick. Or the person attached to the dick. Toys don't form a connection, so it's so impersonal. Unless you're drunk and they're anyone you want them to be—"

I pressed three fingers to her lips. "So to summarize, it's been a while since you've been with anyone." My voice rumbled with even the suggestion of another man touching her. Hands beneath her armpits, I stood and tossed her back to the bed. Dark hair fanned around her smiling face. "And your safe word is bananas."

Wrapping a hand around each of her ankles, I pulled her to the edge of the bed, legs spread around me. With a single finger beneath each of the tiny suit straps, I pulled them over her shoulders and down her arms.

She sent a panicked look toward the house. "What if Sherry—"

"She won't. Don't worry, Sunshine, I won't let anyone see you but me." I worked the top of the swimsuit down, exposing her rosy nipples. I groaned and cupped myself, giving my impatient dick a hard squeeze. I wasn't a small guy, so she needed some warming up before my cock could have some fun.

Her lids fluttered closed, back arching when I palmed both breasts, pinching the peaked nipples until she cried out. A dark chuckle rumbled in my chest. I made quick work of removing the swimsuit, tossing it aside as I stared at her weeping center.

Last night was torture, touching her without seeing every inch of her beautiful body. Today, seeing all of her displayed for me, spread around my thighs, was so fucking erotic. I shivered at the sight as I palmed her hips. Her thighs tightened around mine, a look of unease flittered across her face.

"What if you...? Can we go somewhere dark?"

Ah. That's what she was worried about. I dragged a finger through her core and pushed inside. "No. I want to see all of you." Her lips parted. Adding another finger, I pushed both into her and pressed a thumb to her swollen clit. "I said no. We're staying out here. Now relax."

Knees to the pool deck, I yanked her closer and dipped my nose between her thighs. Our matching moans echoed through the pool area, disappearing into the Texas landscape.

Gentle.

Gentle.

Gentle.

I repeated the mantra to keep my control locked in place. Rae wasn't a virgin, but she might as well have been. I would need to soften my rough tendencies for now.

"Tell me, Sunshine," I said while parting her lips with both thumbs. I gave her sweet center a long lick. "Has anyone ever eaten your sweet pussy?"

"Oh fuck," she cried out.

"Answer me," I demanded and pinched her nub for emphasis.

She screamed a "No".

"Well, I think we should change that, don't you?"

19

RAE

Every worry about being naked outdoors, the sun highlighting every imperfection, vanished when he sealed his face between my legs. He licked up my wetness, sucking my clit with every pass. I writhed on the bed's soft mattress, the pleasure too much and not enough at the same time.

I dug my nails into the thin mattress to keep from reaching for his head.

"You're delicious, Sunshine. I could eat you forever and never have my fill."

"Okay," I said breathlessly.

His chuckle tickled. I sucked in a breath when he added another finger, the fullness almost too much. I tried to push away, but a hand wrapped around my waist and held me in place.

"If you want to take me, all of me, I need to make sure you're ready." He thrust those fingers in and sucked on my clit. A rush of pleasure washed away any hint of pain. "That's it, relax. I'll take care of you," he purred.

Back arched off the bed, I squeezed my eyes shut as bolts of desire and pleasure surged through my veins. Sweat slicked my hot skin. Too soon an orgasm ripped through me, tearing me apart in the best way possible. I floated above the bed, breaths coming in rapid succession as I hovered in the bliss only a full, earth-shattering orgasm could offer.

When I managed both eyes open a slit, I found his stormy gray ones on me as he planted soft kisses and nips to my inner thigh.

Pushing up, I reached for his swim trunks but paused, my fingertips brushing the elastic. Peering up through my lashes, I silently asked for permission. With a cocky smile, he hooked both his thumbs into the low-slung shorts and tugged.

My mouth gaped open when his full, hard erection bobbed only inches from my face. A whimper escaped at the thought of him in my mouth. I licked my lips and leaned closer, but a fist in my hair stopped me short.

"If we want this to last longer than a few minutes, then I can't have your mouth on me." He flexed forward, brushing the head of his dick against my lips. "Later." Bending forward, he kissed me hard, forcing my mouth open with his tongue. We lay back on the bed, his massive body covering mine.

Elbow to the mattress, he hovered, careful to not place his full weight on me. We both moaned into the other's mouth when he slid between my folds. Back and forth he flexed his hips, coating his cock in my wetness.

"Alec, I'm not... I mean, there hasn't been a reason for me to be on birth control." I cringed internally, hating that this might have to stop.

He simply kissed and nipped at my lips. "I had a vasectomy at eighteen, determined to not create more monsters like me. And I'm clean."

I groaned in relief.

With a shift, he used his hips to widen my legs and push against my entrance. Lungs full, I held a breath as he pushed forward. Inch by inch he watched me, searching for any sign of pain. Fully seated, our lower halves sealed together. His lids fluttered closed, and a soft groan passed his parted lips.

His heavy breaths fanned across my face.

"Fuck, this feels better than I imagined." Slowly, his eyelids opened. "Every inch of you was meant for me." He thrust, making me gasp. "Inside and out. You're squeezing the life out of my dick," he panted. "I've never felt anything better."

A hiss whistled through his clenched teeth as he pulled out to the tip. I whimpered, missing the fullness, which turned into a groan when he slammed back in and ground against my clit.

In and out he thrust, each harder than the last. The entire cabana bed moved as he picked up the pace, our pants mingling. Sweat dripped from his brow to the sheets beneath me. Still sunk deep inside me, he kneeled on the bed, lifting my hips to rest on his thighs.

A wicked smile spread across his face as he dipped a hand between us and flicked my clit. Another orgasm ripped through me, a silent scream releasing as I shattered. Still, he continued to pound into me. That hand snaked up my stomach, tweaking one nipple and then the other, eliciting a pitiful whimper from me.

That rising hand wrapped around my throat and constricted. A thumb pressed beneath my chin, arching my neck and directing my gaze from where he pounded into me to his strained face.

Another rush of wetness slicked between us at the utter helplessness I had under his control. And I fucking loved it. This was pure trust. The hand cupping my ass, holding me to him, squeezed tightly, shooting a burst of pain.

With a barked curse, he slammed into me and stayed seated as his own release rocketed through him. His muscles tensed and twitched as his hips slowly flexed, wringing out every second of pleasure.

Panting, I tried to shake my head when he released my backside and slipped forward and rubbed against my overly sensitive clit. That hand around my throat tightened a fraction, a warning. Within seconds, another wave of pleasure had me whimpering and squeezing around him.

Lines of sweat streaked down the sides of his face as he panted, smiling. Reaching over, he grabbed the towel I'd discarded earlier and wiped his face, then down his defined chest and rippled abs.

When I tried to wiggle off him, he shook his head and gripped both hips, holding me in place.

"You're not going anywhere, Sunshine. Not now, not ever. Just give me a second to be ready for round two."

Round two?

Hell yes.

THE MOST GLORIOUS hot bath relaxed every single sore muscle and chased away the memory of why I was staying at this glorious estate. Standing in front of a mirror in the expansive master bathroom, I studied my reflection. My grip tightened on the towel secured around my chest before releasing, allowing it to flutter to the floor and puddle at my feet.

My gaze stayed locked on my own in the mirror, too afraid to slip lower. With an inhale for courage, I squared my shoulders and looked down. Alec's praises and compliments of my body, the one I'd been critical of my entire life, sank deep and inspired this. I looked over my reflection, taking in every curve and dimple. If he found me beautiful, imperfections and all—just as I did him, though his were internal— why couldn't I? Why could I only see the bad just like him?

I shivered at the memory of him kissing every inch of my skin, of the pleasure-filled sounds he made while he licked me clean. Palms to my waist, I brought them straight out for a rough gauge to how wide I was there.

Huh. My reflection's head tilted as I inspected the rough measurement. That couldn't be right. It looked smaller, thinner than I remembered.

Doing the same with my hips, I laughed to myself. Yep, those were still wide, yet when Alec's huge hands held me, they felt tiny.

Maybe, just maybe, he was right. I'd allowed society's negative words and harsh looks to alter the way I saw myself. I'd allowed people who didn't know me from Eve, whose opinions did not matter, to make me feel bad about my body.

How fucked-up was that?

I had great legs, a pretty little face, thick naturally shiny dark hair with a soft wave some women spent hours mastering. Sure, there were some areas that weren't perfect, but who was? This was me. I should be proud of that, not embarrassed.

My hands tightened into fists at my side.

How long had I believed I was unattractive because of the double digit on the back of my pants or the small cup size listed on my bras? How long had I failed to see the beauty in myself because I was too focused on the rest?

Shaking my head in disappointment at myself, I tugged on a pair of panties and one of Alec's old army T-shirts. I had plenty of my cute matching outfits in the other room, but this felt better—right, considering I was sleeping in his bed tonight. Collar pressed to my nose, I inhaled, securing his unique masculine scent into my memories. He thought it was odd that I wanted a slightly used shirt of his, but I told him to add it to my list of quirks.

Like the online stalking I'd done the day before he reentered my life.

The tile was cool beneath the balls of my feet as I tiptoed across the bathroom. The cold air-conditioning whooshed over my hot skin when I pushed the door open to the bedroom. Alec lay sprawled across the California king bed, one arm tucked behind his head while he read something on his phone.

Those gray eyes slid to me as I hurried to the bed. "I like you in my clothes."

"Yeah?" I questioned without expecting an answer. Climbing onto the bed, I scooted to the area he patted in request next to him. When I relaxed back, I groaned. "This bed is heaven."

An arm snaked beneath my shoulders and curled, tucking me against his side. I kept my arms close to my chest to keep from wrapping them around his naked waist.

"There, that's better." Keeping me secured next to him, he went back to studying his phone. I smiled at nothing and shifted to find a comfortable spot. Cheek to his chest, I nuzzled his pec like a cat. Several minutes of comfortable silence passed, but the urge to hold him became too much.

"Alec." His skin pebbled where my breath brushed.

"Yeah?"

"Will you tell me why?"

Not tearing his gaze from the phone, he smirked, that adorable dimple popping out to say hello. "I need you to narrow that down for me."

"The restraining. Why?"

I immediately wanted to eat my words when his entire body tensed, my comfortable muscle pillow now stone. I shifted to stare up at his face, but he kept his gaze straight ahead. His Adam's apple bobbed with a hard swallow.

"Did you notice my back earlier, in the pool?" I nodded, too afraid to speak. All those scars. I shivered and nestled closer to his body heat. "When he was feeling incredibly cruel, maybe from a bad day at work or wanting to get back at Mom for whatever thing she did wrong in his eyes, he'd secure my hands and tie me down to anything heavy or immovable." Alec's voice hardened, fury tightening his face. "Then he'd beat the shit out of me with his belt." There was no warmth in the smile that crept up his lips, forming more of a sneer. "He enjoyed using the end with the buckle."

"How did I not know?" I placed a soft sorrow-filled kiss to his skin. "How did no one know?"

"He hid it well and paid off anyone who came around asking questions. My mom couldn't leave, couldn't even trust the police department. My dad had everyone in that town in his pocket."

"Is that why you didn't come back?" I whispered.

Eyes closed, he leaned his head back against the wooden headboard. "That day, the day I finally grew some balls and fought back, was because we'd just made plans. Life plans, and I knew if I wanted any of those to come true with you, I had to stand up to him. So I did. That night I didn't bow down when he came after me. Instead I fought back. We fought, and I won." My head moved with each of his harsh breaths. "And I kept hitting him. Face smeared with blood, eyes almost swollen shut, and I just kept pounding my fists into his smiling face. And I liked it. That's when he laughed and said I'd finally become the man he'd trained me to be, that he was proud of me. That stopped me from killing him. And just like that, fear wrapped around me when his words sank deep. When I stumbled off him, he just kept laughing, saying I couldn't change who I was, what I was.

"And I knew he was right. I could feel it, the rage rolling through me, desperate to finish him. To take my hate out on him." Slowly, those tormented eyes slid to me. "He'd wanted me to attend this military academy for years, but I kept saying no because I wanted to be with you. After that night, I realized I'd only ever cause pain, so I told him I'd go. I dropped off that note in your locker on our way out of town. And I never came back because I knew, I knew if I saw you, I'd risk it all, and that wasn't fair to you. Even after he murdered my mother—"

I gasped and covered my mouth. Pushing to sit up, I stared wide-eyed at his tense face. "He murdered your mother and is still out there living in that damn compound outside town?"

Alec nodded. Twirling a damp strand of hair around his finger, he held his focus there. "The official ruling was suicide, but to me, he killed her. She wouldn't have OD'd on pills if he hadn't beaten the joy out of her life for years and controlled her every movement. She was trapped. Me and my sister got out, but she was stuck there."

"How brave of your mom to wait until she knew you two were safe." I lay back down and snuggled against his side, hoping to offer some comfort even though I couldn't hold him. "I can't imagine living in that kind of hell."

We stayed silent, both of us lost in thought.

"It's why I wanted to become a Ranger," he said after a few moments.

"To protect others." That made sense. If he only knew we both had that same purpose, his way was just legal and mine wasn't.

"Yes, but to be above the law when needed. To be the one person someone could turn to if there was corruption or dishonesty in their town's police force. I can't be everywhere at once, but I offer justice where I can."

Pride pulsed through me at the gorgeous, honest man beside me. "And here I thought you couldn't get any sexier."

He laughed, a bit of that tension leaving his tight face. "Does my badge turn you on, Sunshine?" His gaze flicked to me, those eyes sparkling with heat. The same type of heat that simmered beneath my skin and pooled low in my gut.

"Very much so. But who you are is the best part."

The front of his mesh shorts shifted, ever so slowly tenting, giving me insight to exactly where his thoughts had wandered.

Same as mine.

"Alec," I said, licking my lips. "Can I touch you?"

"Touch all you want, just don't get any ideas of climbing on top." His breath fanned over the crown of my head.

That was fine. My plans had me on my knees anyway.

20

RAE

Trembling fingers danced along his stomach, his ab muscles flexing and tensing in response. At the edge of his shorts, I traced along the fabric, too timid to dip beneath. What we did earlier was him touching me; this, me daring to touch him, was intimidating since I'd never done anything like this before.

"I don't know what to do, just that I want to," I admitted. Heat filled my cheeks. I'd only touched one dick in my life, and it resulted in him crying out in pain. Apparently, jerking wasn't to be taken literally.

"Want some help?" His voice had deepened, a low rumble that sent my heart racing.

My hair shifted along his skin with my nod.

"I love how innocent you are," he hummed in approval. "I like playing teacher."

Wetness seeped into my panties. Apparently my body liked that idea too. I squeezed my thighs together to ease the building throb.

"First, you have to grab me." Taking my hand in his, he dipped both beneath the elastic band. Heat infused my skin. *Okay, so cocks are heaters. Good to know.*

Using our hands as one, he trailed my index finger up and down his length. His grip flexed around me as a heavy breath pushed over the top of my head.

"Just like that," he encouraged. "I like a little teasing." I could hear the smile in his voice. Angling my face up, I smiled in return. His lids were heavy as he watched our hands move beneath his shorts. Daring another few fingers, I gently wrapped around him and tightened. "Fucking hell," he groaned.

Dropping my hand, he tugged at his shorts until they rested just below my fingers.

"That's better." Lust-filled eyes met mine. He licked his lips and bit the lower one. "Only I've done this in my bed, and I'd much prefer your hand wrapped around me than my own."

Pride spread in my chest. Embodied by the knowledge that I was doing okay, I slowly moved my hand up and down, keeping my grip snug.

Alec groaned and closed his eyes. "Tighter." I obeyed. "Faster," he breathed.

A small bead of precum slipped from the thick head. My gaze zeroed in, my tongue tingling for a taste. But that would put me leaning over him, possibly making him feel trapped.

"Alec." My voice cracked from the dryness in my throat. "I want...." I couldn't get the words out. They felt filthy and uncomfortable.

"What do you want, Sunshine?" His voice deep with command.

"To taste." I shook my head. That sounded like I wanted a bite. "I want to feel you in my mouth."

He cursed and flexed his hips, thrusting into my hand. "Thought you'd never ask. Slide off the bed and kneel."

I moved as if the sheets were on fire. Careful to not crawl over him, I moved down the bed and slipped off the end. A cowhide rug tickled my knees and shins as I kneeled and waited.

Legs spread, Alec sat at the edge of the bed, his shorts gone. Gloriously naked. I tilted my head and took in his face. Reaching out, he gripped my chin and smiled.

Hands fisted at my side, I waited for direction. That grip moved from my chin into my hair and fisted at the base. A gleam winked in his gaze as he pulled me closer to his twitching cock until my lips hovered over the tip.

"Is this what you wanted, Sunshine?" With another harsh tug, my lips were pushed apart by the soft head. He groaned and dropped his head back. "My cock looks good between your perfect little lips." Without warning, he flexed, pushing himself farther into my willing mouth, hitting the back of my throat.

I gagged and tried to back up, but that hold in my hair stopped me.

"Breathe through your nose." He pulled back before thrusting in again just as deep. This time I prepared myself for the intrusion and stopped myself from gagging around his thick dick. "That's it. Fuck, Rae, do you know how many times I jacked off to this image of you on your knees, my cock deep in your throat?"

Tears slipped down my cheeks, and saliva dripped out of my open mouth, dribbling down my chin, but I didn't care. All that mattered was that look of pure desire on his handsome, striking face—because of me.

"Hold on, baby. I'm going to fuck your mouth, then flip you over on this bed and fuck your pussy until you scream for me."

I shivered in anticipation, the building pulse between my thighs painful.

Gripping my head with both hands, he shifted for a better angle and plunged in and out, fucking my mouth like he promised. His stomach tapped the end of my nose with each forceful thrust. Remembering a trick I read in a book once, I swallowed, constricting my throat around the head of his cock.

"Fuck," he roared and pulled back, popping his slick and swollen cock from between my lips.

Before I could protest, he hauled me upright and tossed me onto the bed. My stomach and chest bounced on the mattress. A sting bit into my skin when he literally ripped my underwear off my hips. Twisting, I rested a burning cheek on the comforter and closed my eyes, focusing on every place his callused hands caressed.

Skimming up my inner thighs, he pushed my legs wide and stepped between them. My labored breaths pushed against the bed and fanned back onto my face.

Rough hands gripped my hips and angled my ass so it stuck in the air. He squeezed each cheek, his hold tight enough to mingle pleasure and pain. I sucked in a tight breath when he spread my cheeks apart. I wiggled, embarrassed.

"Tell me, have you ever played with your ass?" His voice was a soothing rumble, yet the words ignited dark and dirty thoughts. I didn't answer, not wanting him to know the truth. What did that make me if I said yes?

After dipping a finger through my wet center, he circled around that tight hole. "Ever shove a plug up there, felt the tightness as you fucked yourself with another toy?"

I shuddered so hard my entire body shook. He had to stop or I'd orgasm before he even got inside me.

"I think you have, my dirty little sunshine." His laugh was dark, humorless, making my insides tremble. "Not tonight, but back at your place with your collection of naughty toys." He slipped that finger inside to the knuckle. A groan rumbled through the room. "I think I'd like that a lot."

A pitiful whimper rattled in my chest when his finger disappeared. Fuck, I was a dirty girl.

His dirty girl. I wouldn't want this with anyone else, wouldn't feel comfortable being this exposed. But this was Alec—*my* Alec. And he could do whatever the hell he wanted with my body, and I'd beg for more.

A firm grip on my hip was the only warning before he slammed into me from behind, pushing all the way until his hips hit my ass cheeks. I turned my face to the comforter and bit the cotton fabric to keep from screaming.

"I can't hear you." A crack rang out before the sting of pain radiated along my right ass cheek. Mouth open, I turned, lifting as much as I could to gape at him. "I told you I wanted to hear you scream."

The bastard spanked me.

Chapter 20

And I liked it.

Fuck, there was no coming back from him.

Forever beautifully and thoroughly tainted by his hands, words, and passion.

I couldn't bring myself to care.

THE LOUD RING of a phone roused me from a deep sleep.

"What?" Alec's voice sounded as gruff and out of it as I felt.

I turned and placed the other cheek on the soft sheets to face where he now sat up, phone pressed to his ear. The dark sheet pooled around his body when he leaned to the edge of the bed. I squeezed my eyes shut when he flipped on the side lamp, brightening the room and nearly blinding me. When I could see without dark spots, I blinked and found Alec sitting on the edge of the bed, his back to me.

"You're kidding me. Please tell me this is a sick joke, Charlie."

My stomach dropped. *Charlie? Shit. Shit. Shit.* Something bad happened, I just knew it, but who was there that I cared about who could've been harmed?

"Yeah, okay." A pause as he listened. A balled fist slammed into the mattress and twisted in the comforter. "Yeah, when we get there. We'll leave at first light."

I leaned back to check the clock's red numbers.

Four o'clock in the morning. First light was only in an hour and a half. I fell back onto the pillow and rubbed at my temples as Alec finished the call.

Only when his massive torso fell beside mine did I turn his way. Hands tucked beneath my cheeks, I lay on my side and blinked up at him, waiting.

"There's been another murder."

"Okay," I whispered.

He shot me a quick look before turning his focus back to the phone between his hands.

"Who was it?" I cleared my throat. "I don't have anyone left who I care about. Maybe it wasn't related to me—"

"Your boss. The new victim is your boss." Everything stilled. Even my lungs forgot how to function. "Rae, breathe." I stared wild-eyed at Alec, not understanding a single word. "Sunshine, you're okay. You're safe. Breathe for me." Fingertips caressed along my jaw and down my neck in soothing strokes, easing some suffocating panic. Just enough for a sliver of air to slip inside.

"My boss?" I searched his face. "That doesn't make sense. I don't really like her. She's just a boss, not a friend. Why would this person hurt her?" My words were quick, my breaths more like wheezes.

Alec blanched. Running a hand through his bedhead hair, he tossed the illuminated phone to the bed. "Do you really want to know Charlie's assumption?"

"Yes." Zero hesitation in my response. "I need to know why. Why her? Fuck, why me!"

"I don't know that last part yet. But I will. I promise you, Rae, I'll find this bastard and make him pay for clouding your life, for forcing you into hiding to keep others safe." Pushing off the mattress, he slid off the bed and stretched his arms overhead. "There's no way I'll get back to sleep after that."

"Why, Alec?" I demanded. Sitting up, I allowed the sheet to slip around my waist. "Why does Charlie think he went after her?"

"Rae," he groaned. "Just drop it."

"No, tell me, damnit. I deserve to know."

"He tortured her." I stilled, only able to blink as he continued. "Charlie thinks he went after her because you didn't show up for work."

"I didn't show up for work, so he killed her?" I said dumbfounded.

"To find you, Rae, except she didn't know where you went. Only Charlie, Sherry, and I knew where I was taking you."

I let out the held breath that burned my lungs. "To find me."

"It's the only theory why the torture make sense. Which brings up another concern."

Like a child, I covered my ears with both palms. "I don't want to hear any more."

Gentle hands grasped my wrists and pulled them to my lap. "You need to hear this, Rae. Look at me." Unable to fight the command in his tone, I turned my wet eyes upward. "It means he's looking for you. He's done tormenting you by killing those you love. Now he's coming for you."

Releasing me, he paced the room. Naked. Paced naked. If things weren't so dire, I'd appreciate the way his thighs flexed and shifted with each powerful step. The way his ass bunched and his dick slapped—

"You're staying here. I'll go." I shook my head to clear the zoned-out trance. "I don't want you anywhere near that town until we find this bastard."

"No."

He shot me a hard look without pausing. "You're safe here."

"And you're not there. So no. If you go, I go." His lips parted, but I held up a hand. "If you leave me here, then I'll just hitchhike or call a car or something like that to get back to Sweetcreek. If you go, I go. That simple."

21

RAE

A brooding, sleep-deprived Alec was not a fun road trip companion. Another annoyed grumble from the driver seat had me rolling my eyes, just as annoyed. The sun's first rays made the sky glow a golden yellow as we headed west. Waves of heat rose from the black asphalt.

Maybe when all this was over, I'd leave this suffocating heat, go somewhere cooler in the summers.

I watched Alec out of the corner of my eye. His job was here, so he wouldn't go anywhere—couldn't. What had bloomed between us, the growth we'd both had in just a few short days, was amazing, but was it enough to keep us together forever?

I swallowed hard to push down the rising emotions the thought of him leaving and not coming back dragged to the surface. This was a fling, right? He hadn't promised me anything other than finding the man after me. So why did the thought of never seeing him again hurt like a punch to the gut?

I toyed with one of the silver charms while staring out the window, trying to process everything that had happened over the last several days.

"What's with the bracelet?" I dropped my hand and tucked it

beneath my thigh. Turning in the seat, I gave him a wide smile that I hoped said "I'm not hiding anything".

"I just like them." My shrug was stiff, awkward. "What's the plan when we get to Sweetcreek?"

Alec shot me a knowing look.

The thing was, if he knew the truth, he'd understand, yet he was an officer of the law. An officer of the law in Texas, and what I did, even though it was with the best of intentions, was illegal. I wouldn't tell him the details and make him choose between me and the law. "I think you brought enough guns and ammo to take down a small militia." I hooked a thumb to the back seat, which was literally packed to the brim with most of the firepower from his storage.

"You're the one who insisted to come along, so yeah, I need the guns to protect you. I still don't think you're taking this seriously. This bastard has killed nearly two dozen people—"

"What the fuck did you say?" I blurted and slapped a hand to the dash. "Two *dozen* people, Alec? What the hell are you talking about? I don't know that many people. Why would this person kill so many—" I sucked down gulps of air. The small breakfast Sherry made us eat before we left rolled in my stomach, turning the homemade pastries to lead.

"We're not sure why, but Charlie found a connection between the murders surrounding your life and cold cases. They were all strangled with the same ligature—his signature." He shifted in his seat and gave me an apologetic look. "Sorry, I should've told you. It's why I wanted you to stay at my house. I'll turn around and—"

I shook my head, sending my loose hair to sweep along my upper back. "No, this is my fight too. You just stepped into this, while I've been living it for over twenty years. I want this done so I can move on. Maybe go to college, become the nurse I always wanted to be like Mom. Move to a state that isn't so damn hot fifteen months out of the year."

Alec's smile turned icy. "Is that what you really want? The nursing thing and the moving away?" His words were tight.

"I don't know. I've dreamed of being free but never thought it would happen. All I know right now is I'm ready for this to end."

The tires hummed along the highway, lulling me into an almost sleep.

"I don't want you to leave," Alec mumbled so low I wondered if I was meant to hear him at all.

I dozed off and on the remaining hours of the trip, my dreams filled with Alec, death, and freedom. Grogginess hazed my thoughts, making me sluggish when we pulled along the curb in front of my house. I frowned at the little dilapidated cottage. It looked worse after being at Alec's pristine estate for almost twenty-four hours.

And bonus, yellow crime scene tape wrapped around the porch, blocking the entrance. Had it really only been a day since a dead body was hand delivered to my house?

The door swung open, startling me, but a familiar lean frame stood in the open doorway, tattooed arms crossed, a firm expression on his chiseled features. Dressed in black tactical pants and matching T-shirt, Charlie looked ready for battle.

Apprehension swirled within me as I pushed open the truck door and stepped onto the sidewalk. That wariness grew the closer I drew to the house, Charlie's hard gaze tracking my every move like he thought I might bolt.

"What?" I asked as I dipped under the crime scene tape and paused in front of him, unable to get inside until he moved. "Don't tell me you're mad at me too for coming."

"Oh no, Rae Chapin, I'm very glad you're here. We have some things to discuss."

My stomach dropped at the anger in his hard tone.

Shit. Shit. Shit.

"Let me just go to the bathroom. I really—"

"What's this about, Charlie?" Alec asked at my back.

Sweat built along my forehead as Charlie stared me down with suspicion in his stare.

"Seems your girlfriend here has some explaining to do."

I cleared my throat and took a step back. Charlie gripped my wrist and hauled me inside. I stumbled, my feet made of lead, nearly crashing to my knees.

I wrenched my wrist free and whirled around to face the two men.

Charlie was most definitely pissed, Alec just looked confused.

Shit.

I searched the living room that seemed ransacked. The only order was....

I swallowed down my fear. Five familiar burner phones lay in a line along the top of the coffee table.

"You went through my stuff?" I said accusingly. "How could you?" Hurt weakened my words. "Why would you do that?"

"Charlie," Alec rumbled, his voice full of warning. "What the hell is going on?"

Charlie hooked a thumb to the coffee table, alerting Alec to what I'd already seen. "Want to tell me why you have five prepaid burner phones hidden beneath your bed?" I sealed my lips. "Or why I found razor blades and plastic coating things one would need to make fake IDs?" Alec's arms fell limp at his sides as he blinked disbelievingly at me. "Or these?" Digging in his pocket, Charlie withdrew a baggie filled with small, round white pills. "Tell me if I'm wrong, Rae, but I think these are roofies."

I opened my mouth only to snap it shut.

Fuck.

I am royally fucked.

"Is that how you met him?"

I shook my head, not understanding. I never met the men. "Met who?"

"The local enforcer for several of the dealers in the area. Did you meet the man responsible for all those murders when you needed these drugs and came up with a plan to kill anyone who found out about your habit? Did you roofie people before killing them?"

What? He really thinks I'm in cahoots with this psychopath who's killed almost two dozen people? I shook my head, fighting off the hurt

Chapter 21

his words caused. I retreated a step toward the bedroom. The two men followed.

"Rae," Alec demanded. "What's going on?"

"Nothing. It's nothing," I stammered. "It's not what you think."

"What about the missing money?" My eyes snapped from Alec to Charlie. I could almost feel the anger blazing off him. He thought I'd played him a fool. "Yeah, I checked your accounts. Each month you withdraw a large sum of cash, all in small denominations, leaving you barely enough to cover your bills."

I rubbed at my sternum to ease the building pressure. I couldn't look at either of them. "It's not what you think," I begged. My voice shook with anger and fear. *How dare they investigate me? Me!*

A thought snapped to the forefront of my mind, making me look at Alec. "You knew." He blanched, confirming my fears. "You knew he was looking into my personal finances and history." My voice was now void of emotion.

Charlie had the audacity to look at me with pity in his eyes. Why would he feel bad? That made little sense unless....

Then it all came together.

I balled my hands into fists and pressed them to my hips. "You told him to," I accused. My finger shook as I pointed at the man who I thought trusted me, who I thought I loved. "You told him to look into me because you didn't trust me." I sucked in a shaky breath. "You said you believed me."

An emotionless mask slid over his face, erasing any trace of familiarity to the man I'd allowed myself to fall in love with a second time.

"I am the law. I provide justice. I told you I'd help you find out who was behind this." His thick fingers that caressed my body so gently only hours ago curled into tight fists. "I offer unbiased justice. It's my fucking job to make sure no stone is unturned. Now answer the agent's questions. What is the meaning of all this?" he yelled.

"The agent," I whispered. No longer Charlie or Charles. No joking. This was all business, because they both assumed after seeing what I hid that I was capable of evil. Every ounce of emotion poured through my gaze when I looked into Alec's stony stare. "Do you think

I had anything to do with the murders, that I could kill my own parents? I called you. I'm the one affected by the deaths. Do you think I'm capable of hurting someone else?"

He sucked in a breath and held it, his chest ballooned out as he searched my face. I knew his answer before he said a word.

"Get out." I pointed to the door. "You're just like the rest of them, only seeing what you want to see. Get the fuck out of my house. Now!" I screamed, my voice breaking at the end as tears spilled down my cheeks. The rattle of metal drew my attention to a pair of handcuffs dangling from Alec's right hand. I swallowed back the sorrow and looked to the floor. "Let me go to the bathroom first and change." I peeked up at him. "You know I didn't do this."

"Then explain all this," he roared, waving a hand at the so-called evidence.

"I can't," I stated. "Please, Alec."

"You've played me this entire time, haven't you?" I gasped and covered my gaping mouth. His features pinched like he was in physical pain. "You played on my feelings from when we were kids, knowing I'd do anything to keep you safe like I always did. And you almost got away with it." He hitched his chin toward the bedroom. "Go change. Then we're going down to the station."

Streams of hot tears slipped down my cheeks. A devastated sob bubbled in my chest. Inside my room, I went to shut the door behind me, not daring a look back. But the door didn't close. My vision swam when I glanced over my shoulder.

"Was any of it real?" Alec asked, his face between the door's edge and the frame. "Or just a ploy to keep me distracted from discovering your secret?"

I turned to face the bed, not able to handle his accusing stare a second longer.

"You've always had my heart, Alec. I don't think that will ever change."

The door slammed shut, causing me to jump an inch in surprise.

Crumbling where I stood, I pressed a hand over my mouth to stifle my sobbing. I didn't realize it would hurt so much to see the distrust written across his face. But it did. Holy hell, it felt like... actually, there was nothing to compare the pain to.

I gave myself three minutes to wallow. Three minutes to mourn the relationship I would never have. When those three minutes were over, I wiped at the still streaming tears with the edge of the quilt and stood.

No way in hell would I allow them to take me down to the station and explain myself. I couldn't do that to all those who trusted me to keep their secrets—to keep them safe. I worked too hard to let those two jackasses ruin everything.

Which left me only one option.

I needed to run.

22

ALEC

I stomped from one end of the living room to the other in four long strides, my focus on the row of disposable prepaid phones. The worn rug twisted under my boots as I swiveled, ready to make another lap. The door to her bedroom remained closed, yet her soft pain-filled sobs were loud and clear. Each whimper laced with emotional pain, pain I caused, was an ice pick to my shredded heart.

The evidence before me spoke to her taking part in something illegal. Hell, just the roofies Charlie confiscated could land her in jail for several years. But she didn't trust me enough to explain why she had all the supplies needed to be a criminal mastermind.

I didn't mean to accuse her of conspiring with the unsub, but the hurt and betrayal made me fumble with my words. Now I had to figure out a way to get her out of this shit. To follow the law like I swore to uphold, yet discover a loophole to keep her out of prison. I might have been mad as fuck at her right now for playing me, but I still loved her.

Holy fuck.

I love her.

That realization had my steps stumbling. When did that happen?

When did it go from having to stay away from her to loving her with every square inch of my mess of a heart?

"What in the ever-loving hell was that?" Charlie whisper-shouted, jamming a finger toward Rae's bedroom. He glowered at me from his spot on the couch. "You were supposed to play the good cop, be on her side to get her to open up."

I gaped at the agent, who was now on the verge of being murdered in his own right—by my hand. "How in the hell was I supposed to figure that out while you were throwing accusation after accusation mixed with evidence solidifying her guilt?" I snapped back.

"Because you know her. You trust her. You fucking love her." I hesitated at the fury in his voice. "I expected you to stand by her side, defend her, give her a safe space to explain all this shit." His voice raised with each word.

"I... I..." I stammered, not knowing what to say to that. Dropping my chin, I squeezed my lids shut. "Hell, what have I done? But she's into something, and I can't let that slide, even if I do care for her. She's lying to me."

"I told you, Bronson. I fucking told you this would come back to bite you in the ass. Some people's secrets are secrets for a reason."

"Yeah, I remember." I cursed under my breath and looked at him, feeling helpless for the first time in years. "What can I do now? How do I even begin to apologize and explain I know she's not conspiring with the killer?"

"Yeah, that was bad, man. I'm not sure even I could get out of that one." I snarled and went back to pacing. "Listen, this is what we do. We wait out here for her to gather herself, get changed, and come out of her room. Then you'll explain, maybe while on your knees, that you know she's not a killer or partners with a psychopath. You'll tell her you believe she's innocent." He looked at the evidence and cringed. "Well, innocent-ish. I'm intrigued now. What is she up to?"

"There isn't an -ish with criminal behavior." I shoved both hands into my front pockets and tilted my face to the ceiling. "Roofies. What the actual fuck is that about?"

Chapter 22

"That," Charlie drawled, "I don't know. And what about the missing money? Where is that going?"

"She's not a druggie."

"Agreed."

"So that's out. She goes through a shit ton of wine as her vice." I smirked at the thought, only for it to fade. "She'll forgive me eventually, right?"

"That I don't know. She looked really hurt, Alec." I sighed and nodded in agreement. "So what do we have so far? A multi-dealer enforcer who only rage kills those who are connected to Rae somehow. He's stalked her for years, killing her parents first, but left her alive. Rae has a secret of her own, but my gut says it has nothing to do with this case."

I glanced at the closed bedroom door, the sound of shuffling leaking through the small gap beneath.

"Did she explain the charm bracelet?" Charlie asked. He leaned his head along the back of the couch and closed his eyes. He looked exhausted. "I feel like that's a clue to figuring all this out."

"No," I stated dryly. "She deflected like before."

"She's good at that." A smile tugged at a corner of his lips. "Whatever she's gotten herself into, we'll help her out of it."

"Yes, I will." I removed him from the equation, not liking the idea of him and Rae spending more time together. He was good with women, unlike me.

A groan of annoyance grumbled from him as he shifted to dig a cell phone out of the front of his pants. Earpiece pressed to his ear, he gave a clipped greeting.

Giving him privacy, I made my way to the kitchen. Head in the fridge, I peeled back various container lids, trying to find something edible.

An ominous presence had me turning from the opened brown box to where Charlie stood in the doorway. Phone pressed to his temple, leaning against the doorframe, he stared, gaze unfocused.

"This case keeps getting stranger with every new piece of evidence."

Forgetting about my hunger, I tossed the food back into the fridge and slammed the door shut. "Tell me. What did you find?"

"That hair. The one they found in the blood in her parents' room." The long dramatic pause grated on my nerves, but I kept quiet. "It's a match."

I let out a long breath. That was fine. She already admitted to being in contact with the bodies when she discovered them. That wasn't evidence they could use against her.

"To a sibling," Charlie added.

Every thought vanished as I stared completely dumbfounded at him.

"She... I...." I couldn't even form a full sentence. Hell, I couldn't get out more than a single word.

"I'm assuming you didn't know." I shook my head, eyes wide as I mentally replayed our childhood and everything I knew about Rae's family. "This case"—Charlie grinned like a cat playing with a mouse—"is fucking awesome."

I growled in response to his enjoyment. He jumped out of my way as I barreled through to exit the house. This place was too small for everything I was feeling; I'd end up shattering the entire place. I ripped through the crime scene tape and kept moving toward the large oak tree. Palm against the bark, I rested my head and breathed deep to help clear my thoughts.

"Rae doesn't have any siblings."

"Not according to the comparison of the hair sample I took from her house." Charlie leaned back against the tree and wiped at the sweat already beading along his forehead. "This is curious. You say she never talked about a sibling, and there isn't any mention of a sibling in any of the reports." The little silver ball of his tongue ring rolled along his lower lip, flashing in the sunlight. "I need to do more digging. I'll also run that hair DNA against the database. If we're lucky, the person it belongs to was incarcerated before."

Something Rae had said several times popped in my mind at the mention of incarceration.

"Ten years." The blades of withered grass held my full attention as I pieced it all together. "That's how long Rae claimed it had been since the last murder. If the guy was incarcerated, then the long break would make sense. Probably a drug charge or trafficking at that stint, and you said he was a known enforcer. He couldn't stalk her, couldn't kill anyone because he was behind bars."

"I'll have them run it now." A sharp ding from his phone had us both hovering over the device to see what fresh evidence would throw us for a loop. "Well, there you go," he mused as we both read the report. "You were right."

"Of course I was."

Every single woman who was reported missing also had a string of ER visits in her past. I scratched at the back of my head, hoping to ease the nagging feeling building there. I was missing something, something big. But what? It was on the tip of my tongue, a thought that vanished before it could fully form.

The deafening shriek of sirens had us both standing tall. We glanced at each other as the sound grew closer. Seconds later, two squad cars rounded the corner, their lights flashing as both raced down the street.

"Huh," Charlie mused. "That's odd."

His tone made my gut twist, only to turn sour completely when the tires screeched to a halt alongside my truck. With a shared confused glance, we strode toward the Sweetwater police who stepped out, guns raised.

What the fuck?

"Get on your knees," an officer shouted, his gun trembling.

"Kid, you have the wrong guys. Look at the badge on my belt." Hands still raised, I nodded to my Ranger badge. "Texas Ranger Alec Bronson and Special Agent Charlie Bekham with the FBI. He'll show you his papers if you promise not to shoot him."

"Don't move," another officer shouted.

"Oh for fuck's sake," I snapped. "Lower your fucking guns, or the second we get this squared away, I'll have all your badges stripped." That got their attention. One by one, their gun barrels lowered to point to the dried grass instead of our heads. "What's going on?"

"We received a 911 call stating two men held a woman against her will at this address."

Hands on my hips, I started to say they had the wrong address only to stop when it all came together. "Fucking hell, Rae," I said under my breath as I raced toward the house.

I stormed through the door; the walls rattled beneath my pounding steps. Not checking to see if it was locked, I slammed a palm into the center of the bedroom door. It cracked and split, and the hinges gave way, sending the entire thing flying into the room.

"Rae," I bellowed. The overwhelming anger and confusion shook my loud voice.

Empty.

Panic sank into my chest. In one long stride, I ripped open the closet, shoving aside the hanging clothes and boxes, searching for my missing girl.

Turning, I scanned the room again, looking for any signs of where she could've gone.

I saw it then. The opened window. Only partially shut, like it was haphazardly closed in a hurry.

I groaned, knowing what that meant.

Rae was gone.

23

RAE

What the hell was I thinking?

In a way I felt like a badass escaping those two, yet guilty for the swarm of police about to descend on my house and the two unsuspecting men.

My hair whipped across my face when I dared a glance over my shoulder for the tenth time since I scaled the short chain-link fence surrounding my backyard.

No one.

Disappointment and relief mixed within me at finding no one behind me. I was lying to myself if I said I didn't want Alec to chase after me. I wanted it desperately. Running was a mistake, but any thought of backing out of my spur-of-the-moment plan was dashed when I shimmied open that window and jumped out.

Slowing to a quick walk, I rubbed at the center of my chest to ease the building pain my grief caused. It became worse the farther away I weaved from the house. No, not the farther away I moved from the house but from *him*. I swallowed back the lump of unshed tears clogging my throat.

He didn't believe me. The man I'd dreamed of saving me for so long didn't believe in me. That hurt. No, it was worse than hurt. It crushed me.

That might have been a tad overdramatic.

Whatever. I was committed now, and I had a plan. A plan-ish.

The canvas strap of my hobo bag dug into my palm under my tight grip. It was all I had left and would have to hold me over until... well, my plan didn't really go that far into the future. All I knew was I had to get out of that house and away from them.

Step one complete. Now I had to get out of town without them finding me.

The bus station. I had enough cash on hand to get a ticket out of Texas; then I'd figure it out from there. Maybe Colorado, find a small place to rent and hide out until they stopped searching for me.

Again, that suffocating ache squeezed in my chest.

Would Alec search for me out of duty or more, because of us?

At the corner of two intersecting roads, a siren blare sent me ducking behind a tree. Two police cars roared past, their lights frantically blinking with the sirens wailing.

My tense muscles relaxed a fraction as they screamed off down the road heading for my house. Hopefully those police officers would get there before Charlie and Alec realized I ran away. I called them from a burner phone the moment they stepped out of the house, knowing I would need extra time to put distance between me and them.

If they didn't know I ran before now, they would very soon.

The sudden sense of urgency sent my pulse racing. Turning, I jogged down the street in the opposite way the squad cars vanished. My bag beat against my hip with every step of my tennis shoes as they slammed against the crumbling asphalt. A right and then a left, I weaved through alleys to stay off the major roads, knowing Alec would snatch me right off the sidewalk if I did.

Alec.

Crouching behind some trash cans, I leaned against a faded wooden fence for a quick breather. I wasn't out of breath from the running—okay, maybe a little—but from the enormity of what transpired in the last fifteen minutes that sat heavily on my chest.

I was on the run.

A wanted criminal.

"Fuck," I whispered to myself. Gathering my hair, I twisted it up into a makeshift bun and secured it with the tie I slipped over my wrist at the last second before sneaking out the window. I balanced on the balls of my feet. The running shorts, T-shirt, and sports bra I'd changed into were a smart last-minute decision too.

I bounced and shifted my weight as I thought about my next steps. All I had to do was make it downtown to the bus station. Of course, it would be easier if men like Alec and Charlie weren't hunting for me.

Lips dry from the heat and lack of water, I ran my tongue over the bottom one and pressed them together. Alec would be furious that I ran. Instead of that thought inciting fear, a tingle of excitement ignited in my core. I squeezed my thighs and eyes shut. Sticking around to discover what punishments he had planned for my careless and erratic behavior might be worth the jail time.

Reaching inside the hobo bag, I pulled out the one burner phone Charlie didn't confiscate in his search. The small black device sat heavy in my hand as I debated the pros and cons of calling Alec. I wanted to tell him I was sorry for running, and also a part of me hoped he would apologize. Take back everything he said and tell me he believed me despite the evidence.

Yes, I purchased and hid illegal drugs, but for a good reason. The boards rattled against loose nails when my head thumped on the loose plank. But he wouldn't see it the way I did, even with his history. He made it clear he became a Ranger to uphold the law without prejudice.

I wouldn't call him. Not yet anyway.

Shoving the phone into my shorts pocket, I stood and dusted off my backside with both hands. After checking down the alley both ways, I headed south. Well, I hoped south. I never had to make my way downtown using only the back roads and alleyways.

I'd find out soon enough.

Half an hour later, I was lost, fucking hot, and really had to pee. The heat was my biggest complaint. Sweat slicked every inch of skin, making my shorts and shirt cling to my back and thighs. I lifted my face to curse this damn state and its hell-like temperatures when the wind shifted, suddenly blowing from the opposite direction in forceful gusts.

I smacked the heel of my hand against my forehead. Of course a storm was brewing somewhere close. If I were lucky, it would miss Sweetcreek, but seeing as today was a terrible day, I would bet the storm would tear through the heart of town. Hell, I would raise whoever was betting a tornado or two.

At least the uptick in wind helped cool the sweat dripping down my temples and damp hairline. There was no hope for the small creek that ran between my breasts and collected in my sports bra, though. Still grumbling and cursing under my breath, I paused at a T-intersection, glancing both ways before taking a right.

The cell phone, heavy in my pocket, nagged at me with every step. *I should call him.*

No. The second I do, Charlie will track it somehow. He was a dick for being easy on the eyes, tattooed, and damn brilliant with computers. Actually, he was a dick more for going through my things than his other attributes, even if it was at Alec's bidding.

I paused. A gust of wind sent any rogue strands of hair flying against my face. I palmed the cell phone. At some point, my desperation to hear his voice, to tell him I was okay, turned into an almost physical pain.

The long cracks along the concrete sidewalk held my full attention as I debated my next move. I loved him. I always had and probably always would.

The crunch of gravel beneath tires met my ears. An older-model Chrysler crept along the curb, pausing close to where I stood. My pulse skyrocketed. Slowly turning toward the car, I held a hallow breath. The driver leaned across the seat and manually rolled down the passenger window.

Chapter 23

"Get in." I retreated a step at his demand. "There's a storm coming."

I stared at him warily and shook my head.

"Thank you, but I'm almost home."

It was a lie, and if I wasn't mistaken, the smile that spread along his thin cracked lips suggested he knew it.

I swallowed and turned to walk away. I was never this rude or dismissive, but there was something off about that man, and every instinct told me to run.

Fast.

Blood thundered in my ears, my breaths like shards of ice slicing up my dry throat. Not breaking my sprinting strides, I dug out the phone. Behind me, the man called out. A second later, the sound of a car door slamming shut echoed through the air.

I bit back a frustrated cry. Another alley opening came into view to my right. My tennis shoes skidded in the loose gravel when I took the corner tight at full speed. The phone bounced in front of my face as I dialed the only number I knew by heart.

Please pick up, I internally pleaded as it rang and rang in my ear. Pounding footsteps drew nearer. I fought the urge to check over my shoulder to see how close the man was.

A click sounded on the other end of the line, cutting off the ringing. Hope soared in my veins. But I needed more time. Reaching out, I wrapped a sweaty palm around the handle of a blue plastic trash can and yanked. It crashed to the ground, barely covering a gruff curse that was close—too close.

I had seconds before—

"Alec," I cried into the phone. "Please tell me it's you."

"Rae. Where are you?"

I wanted to collapse at the worry and anger in his tight voice.

That worry told me he'd find me. No matter what happened in the next few seconds, he would find me. Dead or alive. But I couldn't think about that, not when I was literally running for my life.

"I'm sorry," I wheezed. "He found—"

Something thick wrapped around my neck, cutting off my next

words and sealing off my air supply with a hard tug. The phone tumbled from my hand, crashing to the pavement. I scratched and clawed at my neck to loosen whatever was wrapped around it.

Black spots dotted along my vision. Stumbling back to release the pressure, I slammed into a wall. The stench of death wafted off him, a smell locked in my memories, one I would never forget. I tried to scream for help, but nothing came out when I opened my mouth.

"Time's up, sister."

Sister?

That was the last thought I could muster before my limbs fell limp at my sides and everything went dark.

24

ALEC

The drywall crumbled to dust beneath my fist. The echo of my rage-packed roar still vibrated around the room. I could feel eyes on me, but I didn't care. Rearing back, I slammed bloody knuckles into the wall again. And again.

Skin split, blood splattered along the faint yellow paint, I continued to release all the pain and undeniable fear building inside me through my fists and into the wall.

A hand gripped my shoulder. Without thinking, I whirled around, slamming the person who dared touch me against the crumbling drywall. My sweat-slick forearm pressed against Charlie's throat.

The fucker glowered at me.

I could end his life right here, and the bastard dared to look at me like *I* was the dumbass.

"Not. Helping," he rasped.

I slammed a palm to the wall inches from his face. Charlie didn't even flinch. Like he knew I would never hurt him. Just like Rae.

Rae.

All the fight drained from my body, leaving a large gaping hole in my chest.

"Stop. Hulking. Find. Her." His face had reddened; a vein pulsed along his forehead.

I stepped back until I hit the opposite wall and sank to the floor, resting my head in both hands.

"Hulk." I didn't acknowledge him. "Alec." The muscles of my neck strained as I raised my head. "I need your help finding her. I can't do this alone." I nodded. "The clock is ticking."

I sucked in a ragged breath. Pressure built between my pecs. I pressed the heel of my hand to the area, hoping to ease the hurt. A tattooed hand dangled in front of my face, a peace offering, or maybe a call to arms. I followed up the colorful artwork to his calm face.

"Let's find your girl."

My palm smacked into his. With a grunt and groan, he hauled me up to my feet.

"Damn, you're a heavy fucker." He shot me a wink, trying to ease the palpable tension in the air. "I'm running a trace on the call now. I should have the location shortly, but it'll take longer than normal because the call was short."

"Good." Clearing my throat, I squared my shoulders. "Also request a comparison of the unknown sibling DNA to what we have on file for her parents. Whoever this person is, that has to be the connection for why he's obsessed with her."

He answered with a curt nod, motioning for me to follow him. We marched out of the tiny home to the front yard. Snagging his gear from his Suburban, Charlie set up a mobile command center on my truck's tailgate. He continued to insert cords and wires while I verbally walked through a plan.

"Table anything we were working on with the missing women case. Finding Rae and this bastard is priority number one. Even if we do get a location on the phone, we have to assume it was discarded at the abduction scene or somewhere else. How do we find where Rae is right now or where he's taking her?"

Interlacing my fingers behind my head, I let out a slow breath to calm my racing thoughts.

Chapter 24

"The lead from the man I knocked out, about our killer being an enforcer of some kind. I'll run with that."

Nodding, I pressed the cell phone to my ear. Charlie paused what he was doing to shoot me a questioning glance.

"I'm calling in reinforcements." Ted's gruff voice grumbled on the other end of the line. "It's Bronson. That case, it's escalated. I need SWAT on standby, access to the DEA's information on local dealers and those in their top ranks, and maybe a chopper at some point." This was more of a formality considering I was listed as the second lead Ranger on the case.

With zero flair, Ted gave his blessing and ended the call.

"You know, I can hack into the DEA," Charlie mused, his fingers flying over the keyboard, not missing a beat.

"This is faster. We have direct access to all agency files, we just have to request it." Without glancing up from the screen, Charlie raised both brows. "Yeah, we're badass. Maybe you should interview with us instead of the BSU."

His long jet black hair shifted with the shake of his head as he huffed a shocked laugh.

"Once you get access, I want to know the top ten dealers in the area. I want all associates and their arrest records. And current locations, address listed during parole or release. We start from the top down. I'll break down every fucking door in this city to find the dealer who can give us information or a location on this enforcer."

"Sounds like a party." Charlie leaned closer to his screen and smiled. "Got a location. A ten-minute drive from here."

I helped him load everything into the back seat and then climbed into the driver seat. A screech of tires against asphalt and we were off, blazing down the street.

We would get her back.

Unharmed.

Even if I had to set this entire town ablaze to find her.

"You're not helping," Charlie grumbled from where he hunched over his laptop, gaze flicking between the three screens along the desk. "You staring over my shoulder will not make this go any faster. Want to help? Go get me some more of that sludge they claim as coffee." Still furiously typing one-handed, he picked up the empty Styrofoam cup and wiggled it high in the air.

With a grumbled curse, I snatched it from his hand and stormed toward the coffee maker. I lifted the glass carafe. Empty. Of course it was. With more force than necessary, I ripped the damp filter full of used grounds out and chucked it into the nearest trash can.

While I worked on preparing a new pot, I couldn't help my wandering thoughts. *What is Rae going through while I'm making a fucking cup of coffee?*

The metal can bent when I squeezed too tightly as a million different scenarios raced through my mind, each more gruesome than the last. The weight of those images pushed me forward, the coffee can slamming to the table as I gripped the edges and sucked in a harsh breath.

I had to get my shit together. I was no good to her panicking like some overemotional newbie. But that crime scene where we found the discarded phone showed signs of a struggle, and it had done something to me. She'd fought but no doubt was scared, and I wasn't there to protect her. Even if she was the one who ran off, me not being there to keep her safe was my fault. I failed her.

Wrangling my emotions, I finished what I started and clicked the coffee maker on. It bubbled and groaned to life, the sounds of the black liquid beginning to fill the pot growing distant as I made my way through the sea of desks.

We commandeered two desks for Charlie's workstation to handle all his equipment. Trying to respect his space, I stood back and watched him work. It was fascinating, Charlie in his element. And I knew he was working as fast as he could, but I wanted all the answers now. I wanted the list of dealers, associates, the DNA results—

"Results are back," he called over his shoulder. "You were right on your suspicions." Turning in the chair, he pointed to the report

Chapter 24

pulled up on the largest screen. "Rae's parents were not her biological parents."

"What the fuck is going on?" I said in utter disbelief. Running a hand over my tired eyes, I tried to focus on the small font to read the details. "Okay, fuck, where does that leave us?"

Now what? was what I really wanted to say.

Charlie stared past me like he was shifting through files in his brain. "I saw her birth certificate at one point. There was nothing unusual, and I would've noticed if someone else was listed as the mother and father. Which means it was probably forged."

"Forged." The word felt strange to say.

"That's my only guess. Even if she was adopted, it would've had her biological mother listed on the birth certificate."

A thought blinked into existence. "The doctor, the one who signed the certificate, is he still alive?"

The click-clack of keys filled the tense silence as I waited for Charlie's search results to pull through.

"Retired and still lives here in Sweetcreek." Charlie pointed toward one of the screens while typing with his other hand. "And look at that. Rae's mother and this doc both worked at the same clinic for three years." More typing. "And both left the month after Rae was born."

"We need to bring him in. This could be the break we've been looking for." I gritted my teeth to squash the swell of hope. I couldn't let that happen just yet. We needed answers first.

"Already on it. Here." He enlarged a phone number. "I made it extra big for your old eyes."

I smacked him across the back of his head with little force behind it. "Let's call this Dr. Cartwright and tell him his presence is required at the police station, or else I'll send SWAT out to bring him in, wherever he might be."

"He's nervous," I said to Ted as I regarded the sweating older gentleman on the other side of the two-way mirror. I'd reached out to Ted for a third set of trusted hands, and he came eager to help. Charlie was busy working his magic on the documents, sorting through the DEA information, gathering local arrests of known dealers, and working the DNA evidence. Needless to say, I owed him bigtime.

Ted nodded, agreeing with my assessment of the doctor. He was the quiet type, which I appreciated in this situation. No chitchat, straight to the point to bring Rae home.

"You interview, I'll watch and take notes."

With a grunt, Ted left the room. Half a second later, the door to the interrogation room swung open and my colleague stepped through.

Hands on my hips, I scrutinized the doctor's every twitch and blink. The older man paled when Ted sat on the corner of the desk beside him and tipped his white Stetson up with a single finger to the brim.

"Know why you're here, Doc?" Ted's Texas accent drawled each of the words out in a slow cadence.

The doctor shook his head. Using a legit handkerchief, which he pulled from his pocket, he blotted the sweat collecting along the top of his bald head. "No. What can I do for the Texas Rangers?"

"Well, first," Ted mused, rubbing at his gray scruff, "do you remember a previous coworker of yours, a nurse. Stephanie Chapin?"

The man's Adam's apple bobbed with a slow swallow. "Yes, yes I remember Stephanie."

Ted sighed and placed a hand on the doctor's trembling thin shoulders. "Doc, I'll be honest with you. I know you know." The man flinched, but Ted held him in place. "Now, tell me what you know. It'll be better for you in the long run if you do."

I stepped closer to the glass, not wanting to miss a word.

The doctor's chin dipped in agreement. His shoulders slumped, rounding forward.

"I always knew what we did that night would come back somehow." He stared at the mirror, almost like he could see directly through it to me. "Then Stephanie and Chuck died, and no one came asking me why her DNA didn't match the biological parents listed on the birth certificate, the birth certificate I signed off on...." He shook his head disbelievingly. "You have to know we did it to help. It was a victimless crime."

Ted's head tilted to the side as he motioned for the doctor to continue.

"We had just closed up the clinic. It was one of those places in the lower income part of town supported by a church to serve those who needed care but couldn't afford it. It was late, and we were both tired when a woman beat against the front door. Not wanting to turn away anyone in need, Stephanie opened the door and the woman stumbled inside. The first thing I noticed was the blood and fluid that ran down her bare thin legs. Then I saw her pregnant belly. She was in labor. The woman crumbled to the lobby floor, sobbing in pain, and begged us to do something.

"We got her back into one of the already cleaned exam rooms, and the moment we got her on the padded table, she started to push. The first baby was delivered within five minutes of her entering the clinic."

The first?

A rush of air filled the viewing room when the door swung open. I held up a hand as a silent order for Charlie to not say a word.

"While Stephanie got the healthy baby girl cleaned up, the woman began pushing again. Seconds later I held a baby boy in my arms, everyone in the room staring at it with disbelief. The mother didn't know she was pregnant with twins."

"Twins," Charlie said in awe. "There's no way this is real."

"The mother was inconsolable at that point. She said she barely had enough for one baby, that there was no way she could afford two. And the way she looked at the little girl...." The doctor shook his head. "It was fear. She never asked to hold the girl, just the boy, who I wrapped up and placed in her arms. Any time Stephanie brought the little girl closer, the mother would shy away.

"After making sure the mother was stable, I left to call an ambulance. We were in no way equipped to take care of the mother's aftercare and the babies. When I came back into the room, Stephanie was crying, completely infatuated with the little girl in her arms. And the mom was asleep with the baby boy clutched to her bare chest. Apparently when I was gone, the mother begged Stephanie to take the girl, to find her a good home. Stephanie said the way she said 'A good home, where she wouldn't get hurt' spoke to the mother's past abuse and fear for her daughter's future if she were to take her home."

"And you just let her take a baby?" Ted asked.

"Just before the ambulance arrived, the mother woke up and told me and Stephanie she didn't want the girl. She could only handle one, and a boy had a better chance with her. Stephanie and Chuck had tried for years to get pregnant and couldn't afford adoption. It seemed like a win-win for everyone.

"I know it wasn't right what we did. We should've put the baby through the adoption process, but I knew without a doubt that little girl would have two loving parents if she were to go with Stephanie and Chuck. So we made a plan. The mother and the boy went in the ambulance to the county hospital, and Stephanie left with the baby. I later forged the birth certificate when I was at my other job at the hospital." The doctor hung his head. "Before you ask, no, I had never done anything like that before or after."

Ted hummed and stood. "Do you remember the woman's name, the birth mother?" The doctor shook his head as a single tear slipped down his rosy cheeks. "If you covered this up with documents, how did Mrs. Chapin explain a baby to her family, their friends?"

"Stephanie and I cut ties after it was all settled. She quit her job, as did her husband, to move to a different area of town. Neither had surviving family, so that part was easy. Anyone else who questioned it, they said they hired a surrogate but didn't tell anyone because it was a high-risk pregnancy."

"They had it all figured out," I mumbled. I placed a hot palm to the glass and bowed my head. "We need to find the identity of the other baby. Check for boys born in Sweetcreek on the same day as Rae at the county hospital. If we're lucky, Dr. Cartwright signed the live birth certificate of that baby too, making the search easier for you."

In my periphery, Charlie nodded. A paper smacked against my chest. "I'll go run the records now, but I came to tell you we have a list of the known dealers in the area. I've already asked SWAT to await your orders. They're waiting in the bullpen."

"This the list?" I skimmed the lines of information. In the background, Ted continued to ask the doctor question after question, trying to learn new details.

"No. I already had a query running with the parameters of all the missing women and anything they had in common. Credit cards, favorite restaurants, gym memberships, purchase history, delinquent accounts—anything and everything I could track, I compared. That's the list"

My hand fell to my side, the paper dismissed. It wouldn't help me find Rae, so it was useless for now. Folding it in half and half again, I shoved it into the side pocked of my black tactical pants.

That information would have to wait. Right now I had some dealers to interrogate.

My hand paused over the door handle when something the doctor said caught my attention.

"—right. A few years later, I guess. Maybe ten or twelve. They called to say there was a break-in at the clinic. The file room was ransacked and drugs stolen. They called to let me know since some of my employment paperwork had my social security number on it and could potentially be in the wrong hands."

I held a breath.

That had to be how this mystery sibling found Rae and her parents. And if my memory served me correctly, it didn't take him long to find the Chapins and begin his reign of terror on Rae with his first victim.

Her dog.

25

RAE

My head throbbed against my skull, its steady beat a thrum in my ears. My lips parted, but nothing escaped my raw throat and dry mouth as pain radiated through my very existence when I attempted to move. It wasn't just my head, I realized too late. My entire body felt like it'd been tossed around like a sack of potatoes recently.

Even breathing hurt. With each short inhale, musty air coated the inside of my nostrils and coated my lungs with its stench.

What is that smell?

In the dark recesses of my mind, I searched for answers, my eyes sliding behind my closed lids. I ran from Alec and then the man. Fear coiled around me at the memory of his face, the stench of death that oozed off him like black tar.

My neck. Something was around my neck killing me.

Panic surged, making the beat in my head skyrocket and narrowing my senses, hyperaware of every sound, every smell and touch. Something soft yet tight secured my wrists behind my back. I rotated both hands as the material slid, biting into already raw flesh. My muscles screamed at me to stop moving, but I couldn't lie here like a lamb for the slaughter.

My breaths grew shorter, more wheezes than full breaths. I had to fucking calm down or I'd hyperventilate, leaving me more helpless than I was currently. One thing at a time. I had to focus on one thing at a time, catalogue what I knew, and then go from there.

Both feet felt bound too, though that skin wasn't nearly as painful when the binding rubbed against my ankles. Cloth secured my feet instead of plastic or metal.

Metal.

Handcuffs.

Grief slammed into me like a sucker punch to the gut. I curled in on myself, my body protesting. *Oh, Alec.* Tears burned behind my shut lids. He'd never know how I felt, that even without him saying anything or asking, I forgave him for what happened earlier. Hopefully he would feel the same one day. Forgive me for running away when all I had to do was trust him with my secrets. But I didn't, and now here I was.

Alone. Hurt. Restrained. And, based on the wetness around my shorts, pretty sure I peed myself at some point.

A crack of thunder shook whatever structure I was in, sending a tremble along my prone body. *Where the hell am I?* Sweat and tears clung to my lashes, making it difficult to blink without the ability to rub my eyes. Finally, they released. Vision fuzzy, I tried to find anything familiar, but there was only darkness.

Except the far corner.

Blinking in rapid succession, I cleared the thin film clouding my vision and squinted through the darkness to the soft yellow light of a single lamp. It sat on a side table that looked ready to fall over if another boom of thunder shook the place.

Movement snapped my gaze to the recliner. Half doused in shadows, there was no mistaking the lower half of a man that was highlighted by the light. I stared at his moving hands, one in the light, the other hidden in darkness.

Somewhere close, water dripped into a bucket or puddle, making a constant plop. Rain sounded above me, loud, suggesting a metal roof. I focused on breathing deeper to keep the rasps quiet, allowing me to hear if someone approached from behind.

Coarse, stiff fabric scraped beneath my cheek and arm with each movement. With my eyes now adjusted to the dark, I could make out a faint stripe pattern with ribbing—corduroy, maybe? I tore my focus from the man's moving hands to inspect my cage.

The little light glinted off the ceiling, the walls, the floor.

Metal. Metal surrounded me. A container maybe, by the wave of the walls.

A flash of light blinked, blinding me for a second before vanishing.

Leaks and cracks big enough for the flash of lightning to appear through.

An old, rusted container or shed maybe.

I shifted to stare at the man again. Over and over his hands moved in the same repetitive motion, winding something long and white around one hand before moving it to the other.

Another flash of lightning offered a half-second look at his face. I shivered at the hate on his snarling features even that brief light revealed. And like that lightning, his words—really just the one word—flashed to the forefront of my mind.

The bindings at my wrists tightened, biting into my skin deeper with each attempt to wrench myself free.

"Sister," I rasped. The word physically hurt to say, like salt rubbing over an open wound.

His hands stilled. I held a shallow breath, waiting, watching. His predatory stillness struck fear deep inside my soul. Everything inside me screamed to get away, to run from the presence of evil.

Maybe he had the wrong girl, because I was no one's sister. I was an only child to Stephanie and Chuck Chapin. We lived a quiet, happy life together with no other kids around. I think I would've noticed that. That had to be it. He had me confused with someone else. I just had to tell him and he'd let me free.

Right?

I dragged up the courage to speak again, wincing as I opened my mouth, knowing it would hurt.

"Not me," I whispered. My cheek ground against the stiff material. Whatever I lay on was soft in some places, hard or pointy in others. An old couch, maybe. "It's not me. Only child."

That sent his hands back into motion, faster this time.

Around and around that white cord wound around his fists, not missing a beat.

"Please, let me go."

Another rumble of thunder vibrated through the shed, followed by the deafening sound of rain pounding against the metal roof. More water trickled down the walls, fresh streams of water pouring everywhere, including from the ceiling directly above me. The icy rainwater seeped through my shirt, soaking and chilling my stomach. I shivered even though the temperature was sweltering in the small space.

"No." I barely heard his gruff answer over the pounding rain. In one fluid motion, he stood, that damn cord still winding and unwinding between his hands.

"It's not me. I don't know you, I swear," I cried, trying to make my words sound as truthful as they were.

"You're right."

I sucked in a breath. Did I hear him right? Maybe this was all a mistake after all, and he just realized, "Whoops, I kidnapped and restrained the wrong person." I was sure it happened all the time, cases of mistaken identity and such.

"Yet still...." He moved a step closer. I shimmied back along the cushions to put even a centimeter more between us. "I hate you."

Those words, his rigid, evil-laced tone, were like a death toll.

The small sliver of hope I had vanished. I cried and sobbed uncontrollably.

"Not me, not me, not me," I sobbed over and over. "Not me."

"Want to know why?"

I sucked in my lower lip and held it to keep my wailing to a minimum, then nodded. His form blurred in my watery vision as he went back to that chair and sat. I really didn't want to hear his crazy speech, but the longer I kept him talking, the longer I was alive and gave Alec time to find me. Save me. I just had to give them time. I had to do what I could to stay alive until they broke down the doors, wherever they were, and free me.

As the rain continued to drain from the roof onto my clothes, the runoff slipped along my sides and pooled on the couch. An idea formed, only to vanish with his revelation.

"Did you know you have a twin?"

I gaped at him. "No," I drawled. "I'm an only child."

He leapt up from the chair and took a menacing step toward me. "You callin' me a liar?"

I blanched. "No, no, of course not. It's just—" I licked my cracked lips. "—improbable."

His laugh held zero humor. "They never told you that you weren't theirs to begin with. Of course they didn't." That white cord went taut between his hands. "Wouldn't want to ruin the happy family lie."

I wanted to scream that it wasn't a lie but kept my mouth sealed shut. But his words…. I'd always wondered why Mom and Dad were so small and I so big. I didn't match either of them, actually. My features didn't resemble either of them. I shook my head to dislodge the thought. I couldn't let his delusions suck me in too.

But I had to humor him.

"So, if I'm this twin, your twin, why would you hate me? Why, when we've never even met?"

"Because," he said, the word a hissing sound, "you left me."

I blinked. And blinked some more.

"As a baby," I added incredulously. "How would that be my fault?"

"It wasn't mine either."

"What?" I asked.

"Being born." Back and forth his hands wound and unwound the cord, but he seemed lost in thought, no longer interested in telling me why.

For several seconds, maybe minutes, only the sound of the heavy rain outside and the occasional clap of thunder sounded.

"Do you know what happened to me after you left? What was happening to me while you lived your perfect"—he spat the word like a curse—"safe life."

My stomach rolled. No, no, I didn't want to know. For him to be this bitter, depraved, it had to have been horrible, the things of horror movies and nightmares.

"How do you know it's me?" I asked to distract him from giving me the horrible details I knew without a doubt were about to spew from his cruel mouth.

He leaned forward in the chair, his dead eyes moving into the light. My heart stopped.

"Our mom." I wanted to scream, "Not my mom." My mom was dead, and even though he hadn't confirmed my suspicions, I assumed she and my father died at his hands. And almost two dozen other people. "Before she died. OD'd because of him." Thin lips pressed tight, he snapped that cord between clenched fists. "Everything happened because of him."

I really didn't want to know who this *him* was.

"But I took care of him when I could. Too late for her, for me." I almost didn't hear the last two whispered words. "Now," he said with conviction, maybe relief, "it's your turn."

"Why?" I cried and fought against the binds, trying to ignore the searing pain it caused. "It's not me."

"But it is. And now you'll pay just like her."

"Who?" My voice quivered.

"Your fake mom. The one who took you." His chest heaved like he'd just run a full marathon. "Took you from me." Standing, he stormed over to where I lay. I cowered into the crevice of the couch, but still his hand found a way into my hair, gripping hard and tearing out a chunk as he hauled me upright. "Why?"

"Why what?" I sobbed from the pain and fear of my impending death.

"Why not me!" he screamed into my face, sending spittle and the scent of decay over my skin. "What made you so fucking special?" His vacant eyes scanned my face. "You're just like me. A no one, trash used and tossed." He threw me back to the couch with more force than I expected from the thin man, and my head slammed against the armrest. "We were born to be no one together," he raged. "And you left me to live it alone."

I tried not to move an inch, keeping as still as possible to not draw his attention as he paced.

"So I made you feel it. Gave you a glimpse into my pathetic life, but it would never be enough. Until now." He turned on his heels and stared me down. "It ends soon for the both of us."

Tears clogged in my throat, choking and strangling my shallow breaths.

That cord went taut as he stepped toward me, toward my throat. I begged for help, for anyone to save me, for him to listen that he had the wrong person.

"Not me, not me, not me," I repeated over and over between shouts.

Smooth, almost soft thin cloth pressed to my throat.

A sharp ringing sound chirped over my sobbing and the raging storm.

He cursed and stepped back. I sagged in relief and tried to regain control over my breathing to not pass out. Against the wall, he held a flip phone to his face and squinted at the screen. He smacked the phone closed when he finished reading, the sound lost in another roar of thunder.

Exhausted emotionally and physically, I didn't move when he approached and squatted so we were at eye level.

"They released my messenger. I need to kill him before we can finish this." I shuddered at the ease he spoke about killing someone. "Wouldn't want him telling anything more and cutting my time with you short." Out of nowhere, he withdrew a short blade. The hard, sharp steel caressed down my cheek, slicing as it went. I felt my hot blood glide down my cheek and neck. "Because I have plans for you. So many plans."

With a rush of warm wind, he and the knife disappeared. Heavy steps grew distant behind me, followed by a groan of heavy metal screeching in protest. Then a bang rattled, vibrating through the entire room.

The rain steadily hammered the roof, unrelenting as time slowly passed. After a few minutes, I talked myself into believing he truly left, that I was alone. It was time to get myself out of there.

Heart hammering against my chest, I sucked down gulps of air to calm the panic that had frozen me in place. Eyes squeezed shut, I focused on the one thing that could calm me down, that gave me a sense of control and comfort.

Alec.

Over and over I told myself he was out there searching, doing everything he could to find me. I thought about his smirk and dimple, his protective spirit, and stormy eyes. Slowly my breaths deepened, calming some of my anxiety, enough to move at least.

I twisted to stare at the ceiling, at the streams of water pouring from the cracks and holes above. A quick flash of lightning sparked, highlighting the hundreds of tiny openings along the metal roof.

I had to break free and find a way out before he came back. Now was time for courage, not fear. A renewed sense of purpose rejuvenated my depleted energy, calming my panic and drying my eyes.

Yes, Alec would come for me, but who knew how long that would take? Today there would be none of this waiting around for Prince Charming bullshit. I could be my *own* hero for once.

26

ALEC

The sound of Velcro ripping, magazines clipping into automatic rifles, and the low murmur of male voices filled the back of the SWAT van. As we loaded up ten minutes ago, one fucker suggested I watch from the sidelines. A part of me felt bad for his resulting bruised spleen.

The tires bumped along, hitting every damn pothole on the street as the driver steered us to a known dealer's location as fast as he could without tossing us around in the back. It'd been a while since I took part in any type of tactical assault, but if you'd done it once, your muscle memory set in place, allowing your body to move as if you went through training the day before.

My hands flexed and tightened, reopening cuts and abrasions lingering on my knuckles.

"Bronson." Charlie's voice crackled through the radio waves, tickling my ear. "I have a name."

Every man in the van stilled. Eight sets of eyes focused on me as they listened to the same message pouring through the community channel.

"The DNA got a hit. They sentenced Jared Kent Stark to ten years in jail for possession and intent to sell meth. Arrest record shows the arrest happened here in Sweetcreek, and he was released eight months ago." My gut tightened. We were close, so close. "His record is extensive." Attention focused on Charlie, I didn't miss the strain in his voice. "I unsealed his juvie file, and fuck, man, this guy had a rough life."

I checked my watch. Ten minutes until our expected arrival time at the dealer's location. "Tell me everything."

"The birth certificate is genuine. His birth date coincides with the date and time of Rae's. There was nothing on him until age six. Hell, even his vaccines were up to date, and at five, they enrolled him in kindergarten. A year and a half later, someone alerted CPS to his mom's apartment. Looks like a neighbor called about the kid. The statement says she left the boy alone often, and he'd become malnourished and sullen. Huh, looks like his mom started getting in trouble right around that time too. Drug charges, even a few for prostitution. CPS investigated and...." Charlie's angry curse had us all jumping at the sudden loudness in our ears. "They took him to the hospital for evaluation. The report reads of clear physical and sexual abuse, and abrasions covered the length of his neck. Some old, some new, like someone repeatedly wrapped a cord or cloth around his throat. There are pictures, up-close pictures, and those scars look exactly like the ones around our victims' necks."

"Fuck," I said on a whooshed breath.

"My thoughts exactly. Report says Jared didn't speak a single word, but they had enough with the physical evidence."

"What happened to him?" I asked, fully engrossed in the poor kid's horrifying life. "Was he moved into foster care?"

A pause. "Looks like he vanished from the children's home about a week after they processed him into the system. The police searched the mother's apartment but came up empty. After a couple weeks, the trail went cold, and... well, they stopped looking. He didn't appear again until they found his fingerprints in several home invasions around town, and one clinic burglary. A couple years later, at the ripe age of seventeen, Jared Stark broke into Rae's home and murdered her parents."

Chapter 26

I hung my head, nostrils flaring with a deep calming inhale. Could I have ended up the same way if I didn't have Rae, Mom, and my sister to show me love? Maybe that was why Stark focused on her. He held her responsible for not being there for him.

"We can only assume his life after CPS gave up looking for him was worse than before. They hid him from authorities." Nausea rolled my stomach. "Where is he now?"

"I'm looking for anything to tie him to a location." My knee bounced with impatience as I waited for his search results. "The only solid lead I have is the trailer park where they arrested him. I have an address, but it's not much to go off—"

"Send it to the SWAT lead," I ordered. Releasing my tight grip on the AR, I banged a clenched fist on the metal wall separating us from the front. "Change of location. Check your phone." My tactical pants slid along the metal bench as I turned back to face the other men. "What are the odds we'll find Stark there, Charlie?"

"From what I can tell, it's the trailer they raided and arrested him in. There's still consistent electric use, and water and cable bills are in good standing too. It's a rental, but I guess the renter pays in cash because I can't find anything to match the woman's name on the utility bills. I'm running her name through the system now, but I don't know what you're walking into, Alec. Be careful."

The soft static in the background silenced when he cut off his side of the line.

"Twenty minutes," the team lead called from the front seat.

Resting back, I shut my eyes and focused on breathing deep and the soothing beat of rain against the top of the van. A name. We had a name and a location. This was good. One step closer. Yet a deep pit of worry gnawed at my gut, saying this was too easy. Instead of relaxing, my mind played new darker scenarios of Rae under Stark's cruel hands.

With an annoyed snarl, I leaned forward, pressing both elbows into the tops of both thighs, and held my head. I needed to stop thinking the worst or the worry and fear would drive me crazy.

Fumbling for anything to take my mind off the unknowns, I

reached into my side pocket for my phone only to catch on a piece of paper. The side sliced across my fingertip.

"Damnit," I grumbled. Ripping the offending paper free, I snapped it open. Squinting at the small font, I held it closer to read the various lines. Categories grouped everything with each missing woman's name listed beneath who fit that parameter. The grouping with the most women, but not all, was a certain grocery store chain. "Fucking nothing fits all the women." Shadow of additional print on the back had me flipping it over. Fully expecting the same inconclusive results on this side, I briefly scanned the information and started to crumble the useless paper when the very last category caught my attention.

I flattened it out against my thigh and angled it toward a light. I read it twice. My eyes widened further with each pass.

"Holy fuck," I cursed under my breath.

"Charlie," I snapped while pressing the side of the radio.

"Yes, dear?" he responded, tone dripping with sarcasm.

"I looked at the information you gave me earlier on the missing women. Seven used a credit card at the library. It was a minimal amount charged, probably something like an overdue fee or used book purchase, but it's there. All different days." I paused, skimming each line. "The years vary too. I'm willing to bet the ones without a charge have a library card."

"That's the connection. Wait, do you think...?" Charlie trailed off, knowing we were on a public channel.

"Yep. We'll talk about this later." I ended the call and stared at the paper.

Talk to Charlie, yes. Spank that fine ass of Rae's for being reckless, yes. Why didn't she just tell me? Especially after learning about my background. She had to know I would be sensitive to those women's desperation for an escape.

The weight of my own words the night before was like a kick to the balls.

I understood why she ran today instead of opening up about her illegal smuggling of abused women out of Sweetwater. My dumb ass

Chapter 26

told her I became a Ranger to serve justice no matter what. To be the law. No wonder she ran, so I wouldn't have to choose between her and the law.

Rae ran *for* me, not from me.

Anger boiled my blood, my skin itchy with the building heat. I was a damn idiot.

When I found her, I'd tell her I understood. Hell, I found what she bravely did on her own fucking amazing. Now I just had to find her so I could fall to my knees and beg her for forgiveness.

"Approaching the new location. Be ready," said the man beside me.

I nodded in acknowledgment. On autopilot, I palmed the magazine, ensured it was fully loaded, and slammed it back into place. I repeated the motion with my sidearm and spare strapped around my thigh.

Eight men swayed forward as the van came to a hard stop. Piling out of the back, we lined up along the side of the van that faced away from the trailer. I peeked around the bumper. A few feet separated us from the small front yard of the single-wide trailer. Lights glowed from every window, including a single front porch light.

"Someone's in there," I said over my shoulder.

"We'll clear the trailer," said the team lead. I readied to tell him to fuck off, that there was no way in hell I wouldn't storm the trailer with them, but he shot me a firm glare, stopping me. He hitched his chin toward me. "You're too close to this. If we find him inside, you'll put a bullet between his eyes before we locate Rae Chapin."

Valid point.

"I'm not sitting this out," I ground out.

"Take Pensin and check the property. The satellite photo that Fed of yours sent me showed two structures in the back."

I nodded and tapped the man he indicated. "Let's get into position."

My boots sank into the barren yard as we prowled through the chain-link gate. Six SWAT team members stayed straight, headed for the trailer. Pensin and I veered off toward the side yard. The rain had slowed from the earlier monsoon, but thick droplets still assaulted the top of my head and blurred my vision. Thick gray clouds blocked the fading sunlight, making visibility complete shit. Too bright for night vision but too dark to see anything beyond basic shapes.

Not ideal, but time was running out. We couldn't wait for the ideal conditions; who knew what that fucker planned to do... or did?

A dog slammed into the neighbor's chain-link fence with a ferocious bark. It startled me back to the present and the task at hand. Gun raised, I swung it around, looking through the scope, but found only the dog ready to maul my nuts off. Swinging back straight, I jogged forward, knees bent and ready for any signs of Rae or Stark.

We crept along the fence. The shape of a shed or barn materialized through the rain. Fist raised, the man behind me stopped in his tracks.

"I'll take this one, you the other," I said over my shoulder. In my ear, the other SWAT members shouted as they entered the home.

Ignoring the chaos going on in my ear, I stepped on silent feet toward the building I needed to clear. Ears straining, I listened for any sign of Rae or the bastard holding her captive.

I paused at the metal shed door. Rain continued to slick down my face, soaking me to the bone, but that didn't matter. Every nerve, sense, and cell focused on the shed as I reached for the metal bar securing the double doors. Black glove wrapped around the handle, I adjusted my grip and huffed three breaths in quick succession.

A twist and pull and the door flung open, the entire latch ripping from the thin metal with the force and flying into the center of the soggy yard. The double doors squeaked open, revealing only darkness. Not a single hint of light. Throwing the doors wide, I stepped inside, my boots landing on dry plywood. It groaned with each quiet step. The end of the barrel swept through the small area as I checked every nook and cranny for any signs of Rae.

"Clear," I said into the radio. Seconds later, a chorus of the same word poured through the earpiece.

My stomach dropped with disappointment. Not a single mention

Chapter 26

of finding Rae or her brother filtered through the back-and-forth conversations.

Raindrops splattered against my face as I stepped out of the shed and back into the storm. To my right, the other SWAT agent strode across the grass, his head shaking.

"Damnit," I roared, the sound swept up by a hard gust of wind.

"Bronson." My name crackled over the radio. "You need to get in here and see this."

Gun draped across my chest, I jogged toward the trailer. The back door stood open, the SWAT team lead holding it open as he watched me climb the three rotten wooden steps. I gave him a questioning glance as I passed by and stepped into the trailer.

Mud and water soaked onto the floral floor mat. Unable to keep up with the amount of water sliding off me, little rivers ran over the rubber rim and onto the fake wood laminate floor.

"What is it?" I asked the team lead, catching the kitchen towel he tossed my way. The soft scent of fabric softener wafted up my nose as I scrubbed my face. Lowering the towel, I took in the details of the trailer. Clean pictures hung along the walls, dinner on the stove.

This was a home.

I followed his pointed finger down the narrow galley kitchen into the living room. Blinking, I studied the woman sitting on a plaid couch, her thin arms wrapped around two wide-eyed children.

A boy and a girl about the same age. No, *the* same age. They had to be twins.

A girl who had a mane of dark hair and petite features, both similar to another woman I knew all too well.

I swallowed hard and weaved through the crowded trailer toward the small family. The mother tightened her arms, curling the boy and girl tighter to her side. That protective move softened my vibrating tension.

Her tired face tilted up to meet mine with a determined look.

Right, towering over her was probably making this worse.

The coarse fabric of my soaked pants chafed across my clammy skin as I squatted to her eye level, keeping a couple feet between us to help put her at ease.

"I don't know where he is," she said, voice trembling. "I told them that when they broke down my front door." She shot the team lead a hard glare. "I haven't seen him since—" She stopped and pursed her lips. "It's been a while. And no, I haven't seen him since his release."

"How did you know him?" I asked. Removing the gun, I blindly handed it to one of the other SWAT officers.

"Can they go to their room?" I nodded and gestured down the hall I assumed held the bedrooms. She murmured something to the two kids and gave their shoulders a squeeze. Only once they disappeared down the hall did she turn her focus back to me. "They know about my past, but that doesn't mean I enjoy talking about it in front of them. Jared was my dealer, but he never wanted money." Her voice was so soft, I leaned closer to not miss a word. "He liked kinky shit, and only a few of us would agree to it. I never told them about him, about who he is and what he's done. Didn't want them to know their daddy is one scary guy who I screwed for drugs, you know."

Her frail fingers wrung together.

"I swear I haven't seen him. After I found out I was pregnant, I stopped doing that stuff. I changed, I swear." Her eyes pleaded with me. "I'm doing all I can to take care of those two on my own. I wouldn't mess it up by turning back into who I was."

Her words and tone spoke true. I believed her, but that didn't leave me much. Good for her turning her life around. But I needed to find Stark.

"Were you here during his arrest?"

She nodded. "Sometimes he dealt out of here and I was too high to care. They went easy on me, only eight months in jail, then probation. I found out I was pregnant in jail, and he was inside too, so...." She shrugged like that said it all.

But it didn't. I needed more.

"Has he reached out to you, stopped by?" I fought to stay calm, keep my voice even, but I needed more. Needed to know where this fucker was keeping my girl.

Thin bleached hair swayed with the shake of her head.

I needed a fresh line of questions; these would get me nowhere.

"Does he owe you child support?"

Her face paled. "He doesn't know about them. Please don't tell him. He's... not a good person, and I don't want him around my kids."

I held up both palms to calm her clear worry that I might tell the psychopath he'd fathered twins.

Twins.

"Did he ever mention a sister?" I asked.

She nodded. "I never met her, though. One time when he was high, he mentioned her. But nothing specific."

Another dead end.

My knees popped as I stood to full height. With a smile of thanks, I strode from the trailer out into the evening air. I popped the earpiece out and pressed the smooth cell phone screen against my cheek.

"Did you find her?" Charlie asked, desperation in his tight voice.

"No." I worked my jaw back and forth. "We need another angle. I was calling to ask about the woman it lists on the utility bills. Find out everything you can on her and her two kids. Nothing urgent, but I need a full report later."

"On it. Think she's hiding something?"

"No. Call me if you find anything else we can use to locate Stark. The clock's ticking, Charlie. We have to find her soon."

I ended the call and slipped the phone back into my pocket. Dogs barked and howled all around me; the sound of thunder rolled in the distance. Dark gray clouds covered the stars and moon, making it darker than normal for eight.

Almost twelve hours we'd searched for Rae and still nothing.

A name was all we had to show for our efforts.

We needed to find her soon. Every hour that passed without us locating her lowered the probability of us finding her alive.

Worry clenched my gut.

What if we were already too late?

27

RAE

I am a badass, a fighter who doesn't give up.

I continued the internal pep talk as I gathered the courage to roll off the couch. With my legs and feet secured, there was nothing to ease the impact of the brief fall to the ground. That pain wasn't something I looked forward to. This escape attempt could cause a broken nose or smashed teeth, neither of which I wanted to add to my current list of injuries.

But I couldn't just lie around and wait for my death. I had to do something before that psychopath came back.

My brother. Yeah, right. He was a messed-up freak who zeroed in on me because he thought I was someone else. There was no way.

If—and that was a strong if—he'd told me the truth, then that meant I'd lived a lie my entire life. My parents looked me in the eye and lied to me every day. That wasn't possible. No, they couldn't have done that. And there was no way in hell that man and I were related.

"Who does that?" I said, talking to myself to keep the suffocating silence at bay. "Goes around claiming someone is their sibling, then says they have to die? Crazy-ass people, that's who. And I need to get away from said crazy-ass person who looks dead inside." I shivered at the memory of those haunted, soulless eyes. "Okay, Rae, you got this.

On the count of three, rip off the Band-Aid and roll off the couch. One." I sealed my eyes shut and inched to the side. "Two." Humid air filled my lungs as I sucked in a deep breath. "Three."

Nothing happened.

The air whooshed through my blubbering lips in disappointment.

This was ridiculous. The pain that monster planned was no doubt worse than what the abrupt fall could inflict.

Shimmying back to the edge, I didn't give myself a second to chicken out and just tipped myself over. In the short free fall, realization hit too late that I could've eased my feet off the couch to help cushion the landing, or slipped off backward to help save my face.

Well, fuck. Apparently I didn't perform well under pressure.

My cheek slammed to the ground. Something sharp bit into the skin, tearing it open. One shoulder and both knees followed, the floor shaking with the impact. A groan slipped out as I rolled onto my back and blinked up at the ceiling. The taste of copper slid across my tongue and down the back of my throat.

Now what? Still bound, just at a different elevation. Really, really should've thought this through better than I did. I could blame it on the soul-trembling panic, or even dehydration for causing my thoughts to lag. The way my mouth felt filled with cotton balls, my throat so dry it might crack, the dehydration excuse seemed the most valid.

I tried to swallow, but only thick blood coated the back of my tongue.

When was the last time I drank anything? Without a way to see outside, there was no way to tell how long I was unconscious before waking in this container of horrors. The trickle of water all around me made my thirst worse. Water seeped from cracks and fissures above, but I couldn't risk drinking the runoff. Adding dysentery or a brain-eating amoeba to the mix would not help my situation.

I chuckled. Maybe I read one too many of the medical journals that came into the library.

The water along the floor soaked through the thin material of my shorts and pooled around my calves and arms where they pressed into shallow puddles. If I wanted out of here, I needed my hands.

Each twist of my wrists elicited pure agony, ripping and digging into the already raw flesh. Still, I continued to rotate both hands, hoping to stretch the fabric or snag it on the metal floor. As a distraction from the pain, I inspected my metal cage of death and kept working at the bindings.

Deep ridges, almost ripples, waved along the wall, and I felt the same pattern pressed against my back and shoulder blades. A container for shipping or trucking maybe. Which meant there was a door somewhere.

A single drop of water splashed onto my nose, tickling the skin as it rolled down, gaining momentum. Reaching up, I rubbed the tip to quell the insistent itch.

I stilled. Holy hell, I actually did it. Slowly raising my hand in front of my face, I turned it to inspect the damage in the faint light. Deep red lines covered in seeping blisters encircled my wrists, but I was free. A relieved sob rattled my chest, irritating my dry airway. A violent cough erupted, leaving me gasping for air.

Slick, cool metal pressed against my palms as I pushed to sit upright. My weak, slightly numb fingers fumbled with the knot securing my feet. I cried out in frustration at every failed attempt, which turned into a cheer when the binding fell to the floor. I rotated one ankle, then the other to encourage the flow of blood to my unfeeling toes.

My pulse raced, heart nearly in my throat as I shifted to stand. Tremors vibrated down my legs at my first attempt, sending me crashing back to the metal floor. Determined to get the fuck out of there, I used the couch as leverage, crawling until I sat on the edge of a worn cushion. Using the armrest as a makeshift crutch, I stood, the wave of dizziness almost sending me back to the floor.

But I didn't. Fingers dug into the sides, I held on until my vision sharpened. Still holding on, I took a moment to scan the long dark container. Doused in black, the end now in view didn't offer a single light to show what waited in those menacing shadows. I turned my focus to the dim light.

Steps hesitant, I eased toward the chair and side table.

The three-legged table wobbled as I approached, unsteady on the metal flooring. I squinted at the light and bent lower for a closer look.

A lantern, not a lamp like I expected. The smooth rounded metal felt cool along my skin as I wrapped three fingers around the handle and lifted it into the air. No cord held it in place. Battery operated, then, or maybe rechargeable.

I swung the lamp left to inspect the decaying leather chair where I first found my captor waiting and watching. Stuffing pushed through rips along the back while two springs jutted out, poking through the leather seat.

Using the lamp, I scoured the area around the chair, hoping for a bottle of water, Gatorade maybe—even better, wine. I shook my head. Clearly I'd reached the delusional part of dehydration.

Nothing. Not even an empty plastic bottle to collect rainwater.

Worry tightened my chest as my panic returned. He could return at any moment.

Get out.

Get out.

Get out.

Lantern in my grip, I stumbled forward, feeling my way down the length of the container with one hand on the metal wall. An army green cot with a dirty blanket and yellowed pillow stopped me halfway to the other side. A naked and bound woman's face contorted in pain stared up at me from the opened porn magazine.

Terror filled my veins, visions of what he might do when he came back flying through my groggy thoughts. I gagged, doubling over and hugging my stomach as I dry-heaved.

Crying out for help, I stumbled to the doors. The metal boomed under my pounding fist, and screeching pierced my ears as I scratched and clawed at the unmovable lever. Nails cracked and split as I wedged my fingertip into the seam that split the two doors.

My crackling scream of frustration echoed throughout the container as I staggered back. All my attempts failed.

Picking up the discarded lamp, I whirled around, using its weak light to look for another way out. A stack of wilting cardboard boxes stuffed in the corner made me pause. Maybe food or even water hid in those boxes.

The damp cardboard flap ripped as I tore into the first box, rummaging around with one hand while the other held the hovering lantern.

Clothes. Men's clothes.

Useless.

I shoved it away; it tumbled to the ground, the contents spilling along the floor, and tore into the next box.

Books, stacks of books. A mix of paperback and hardback. The unmistakable tag along the spine had me reaching for the library book. I held it up and flipped to the front. A red-stamped "SOLD" marked the title page. There was no way to remember this exact book or whom I sold it to, but a feeling of dread crept over me.

How close to death had I walked over the past several years? Had he watched my every move, waiting for the right moment, the right person to terrorize me further? Why didn't he end it all that night he murdered my parents? Why wait until now? Now when I had hope for a future and someone out there waiting for me?

Someone I loved.

The lamp, my only source of light to chase away the impenetrable darkness, flickered.

"No," I breathed and gave it a coaxing wiggle. It flared back to full force, but I knew my time was short.

Reaching into the box, I blindly felt around until my fingers brushed against something soft. Pinching whatever it was between two fingers, I lifted it out into the light.

A faded blue stuffed bunny stared back at me with its one button eye. Something white was wrapped around its neck. I moved it closer. Row after row of dingy white shoelaces encircled its elongated neck. Eyes wide, I dropped the sinister bunny back into the box.

Shoelaces.

He used shoelaces to strangle his victims. My parents.

The lamp in my trembling hand dimmed.

And dimmed.

Black surrounded me when it gave out completely.

I sucked in gulps of air, but it wasn't enough. The useless lantern clattered to the metal floor as I stumbled toward what I hoped was the door. I tripped, my shin nailing a box, sending me tumbling forward.

My teeth clattered at the jarring impact as my shoulder slammed the ground; a disgusting popping sound and intense pain immediately followed. I cried out, my voice barely a whisper as I screamed for help, for anyone to save me.

There was no difference between my eyes open or closed, only utter darkness.

No tears leaked from my dry, scratchy eyes as I sobbed in pain and terror. Each ragged breath sliced at my lungs, coming too quick and shallow.

Trapped, blind, and alone.

There was no way out.

Sadness washed over me at the realization that this was where I would die.

Alone.

Hopelessness dug in, sending me deeper and deeper into myself.

Even if Alec found me, it would be too late to save me.

28

ALEC

My pacing steps left a coating of water and grime along the tile. One side of the bullpen to the other, my pointed attention never leaving the man hunched over his computer, furiously typing. Every rational part of my brain knew Charlie worked as fast as he could to locate where Stark held Rae, yet still the urge to roar in his face for him to hurry the fuck up persisted.

My boots' rubber soles squeaked as I made another tight turn.

"It would help if you offered additional details to add to the search parameters," Charlie grumbled to his screen. His normally bright eyes were bloodshot, face pale from exhaustion.

"I heard you the first ten times," I snapped, pausing my steps. I scrubbed a hand over my face, the clammy palm scraping along rough scruff. "And same response as before. I'm thinking."

Only half the SWAT team stayed with me, the other half out hitting the streets, talking to the dealers on Charlie's list, hoping one knew where Stark liked to hide out. Some slept along the wall; others played on their phones as we all waited.

Four hours and nothing new.

Each glance at that damn ticking clock made my heart squeeze as thoughts of Rae scared or hurt with each wasted minute flickered through. Every time I attempted to focus on the search and determining additional parameters, Rae's face flashed in my mind, stealing my focus all over again.

"Stop thinking about her," Charlie said so quietly, I almost didn't hear him. "Don't you think I'm worried too? My thoughts keep getting darker every hour I can't find helpful information. Don't think about what she's going through, or how this guy has her. Just think about him. Get into Stark's head."

His words struck home. "How?"

"Think like him. You're fresh out of prison, but you don't go back to the place you used to deal knowing they would find you there. So where do you go?"

I rubbed at my jaw. "Someone like him would want isolated, safe, familiar. After being locked up with a cellmate for ten years, he would want space, but close to find Rae and pick up where he left off with his stalking routine." Interlacing my fingers behind my head, I blew out a breath. "So where would he have that? A place he knew no one could find or had found before. What about family?"

The keys clicked and clacked under his flying fingers. "His only family listed died when he was—" Charlie read down the screen. "—thirteen. Looks like her last known address...." He slumped back in the chair. "Demolished for a new upscale housing development six years ago. He can't be there."

"Fuck," I roared, smacking my hands against my thighs. "What are we missing?" The word clanged in my head. "Missing. Didn't you say Stark went missing from the children's home and was never located?" Charlie nodded, his full attention on me. "What if wherever they held him, hidden away, that's where he's keeping Rae? He knows the police didn't know the location then and assumes we don't know. It would be the perfect place to take someone you don't want found."

"Probable, but that doesn't offer any details to put into the search. I remember the file. There were no leads in his disappearance for me to go off."

Hands wrapped around the edge of the desk, I closed my eyes.

"Let's assume the mother wasn't the one abusing him. Who would that leave?"

"She wasn't married, so no husband. A boyfriend maybe." His chair creaked as he pitched forward, banging his fingertips along the keyboard once again. "I'll pull up her bills, see if he helped pay for any with a credit card or was listed on a bill.... Got him." Charlie stood so fast the chair rolled back a foot. "The boyfriend put the cable bill in his name." Bent at the waist, he squinted at the screen. His eyes widened and then snapped to me. "Holy fuck. I thought I recognized that name."

"What? Who?" I said, shaking his shoulder. "Where the fuck is he?"

"Dead. His mother's boyfriend, mostly likely Stark's main abuser, was murdered. And based on the timing and autopsy findings I pulled from the cold case files yesterday, I'd say he was Stark's first victim."

My hand slid from his shoulder, my entire body going slack. Grabbing the back of the chair, I wheeled it over and sank onto the foam seat. "Now what?"

"Now," Charlie said through clenched teeth, "I do what I'm good at. They might not have found Stark when he was a kid, but that was then, and you have me. We have a name, and now I do some digging."

I nodded, my knees bouncing with every pop of my feet against the floor. Around us, SWAT members waited, ready to leap into action the moment we found an address.

In the far corner, a hateful glare drew my wandering gaze. The detective who harassed Rae, the one I had removed from the case and requested Internal Affairs to investigate, looked as if he wanted to launch across the room and take a swing.

Leaning forward, I arched a challenging brow.

Bring it, fucker. I could use the stress release.

His face flushed red, but he didn't move from his spot in the corner. Much to my disappointment. I needed the fight to punch away this fear and anger festering inside me. I hated this, feeling fucking useless and out of control.

Charlie's grumbles snapped my gaze back to him and his bank of computers. Lines of code zipped across the monitors in the same quick rhythm as his fingers.

Gratitude washed over me as I watched him work.

"I'll tell them everything you did on this case," I muttered for only him to hear. "Everything you did in past cases too. You'd be an asset to the BSU team, and I'll make sure they know that."

His fingers paused for half a second, hovering over the black keys before starting back up again.

"Did you know my mother was murdered?"

Too exhausted to cover my shock, I sucked in a tight breath. "No I didn't. What happened?"

He continued working, not missing a beat, but the narrowing of his eyes said part of his mind wandered into memories.

"She was the first victim of many before they caught the guy responsible. Twenty victims before the cops pieced together the evidence and arrested the bastard. They created the BSU to help local officers stop killers before the death count rose to unsettling numbers, to help see the entire picture even with pieces missing. That's why I want to join. I want to stop other serial killers before they affect families, take more lives."

I nodded. What could I say to that?

"Ah, there you are, you sneaky little fucker," he whispered to the computer with a devilish grin.

The chair rolled backward, slamming into the far wall when I leapt to stand. The noise snapped everyone's attention our way. A dozen sets of eyes zeroed in on Charlie.

"The boyfriend was part owner in an unsuccessful junkyard. Everything was in some other fucker's name." That sinister smile grew. "But they can't hide from me. It's closed now, but the lot is still there."

"Address." The command was more of a grunt than a word.

With a few hard taps, Charlie stood to full height and turned. "On your phone. Let's go." I narrowed my eyes. "Don't give me that look. I'm coming with you. You're not the only one who wants her safe and this guy dead or behind bars. Plus," he said while pulling on a jacket with the letters FBI printed in bright yellow on the back, "I have a theory. A basic profile and plan in case he's there with Rae. It'll help you get her out of there alive."

"That's all I needed to hear." I smacked him on the back and turned toward the SWAT team. "Load up."

29

RAE

Nothing. I was nothing but a shell. Numbness settled into my soul, drifting away from my physical body hours ago. The pain in my shoulder seemed a distant memory as I sank deeper and deeper into despair.

Somewhere around me, metal groaned and screeched, followed by a string of curses, the voice sending a shiver down my spine. Yet I didn't move from my spot on the floor. Didn't run or hide or find something to use as a weapon.

Nothing. I was nothing.

Here, inside my cocoon of darkness, I was safe.

More gruff words reached my ears along with the pounding of boots that grew closer. A hard object slammed into my stomach, sending me rolling along the floor. The movement jolted my dislocated shoulder, pain and fire shooting down my arm and spine. I screamed, but nothing came out, only a push of air.

Fingers ripped into my hair and fisted. Out of energy and fight, I skidded along the metal floor, screws and sharp edges slicing into my exposed skin as he dragged me to the middle of the container and released me.

I crumpled to the floor and curled into a tight ball. The weight of his evil stare pressed into me, then vanished.

It was a trick. It had to be a trick. To get my hopes up, he left me alone again only to torture me. I curled further into myself and squeezed both eyes shut.

This was it. The end.

I wanted Alec. His fingers stroking through my hair, the commanding voice telling me it would be okay, and mostly so I could tell him I loved him. With all my heart, I loved him. I'd always loved him and never stopped all these years. More than anything I wanted him to know I died loving him.

My entire body trembled, the anticipation of what would come next so high my body physically quaked. Muscles burning, I held my tight ball, prepared for his next attack.

But it didn't come.

Only... voices. New voices. Shouts, commands, and the steady thrum of machinery hummed along the metal in a soothing vibration. Closer and closer those distant male shouts grew. My heart hammered as I waited for the mirage of hope to vanish.

Only it didn't.

The ridged metal vibrated under me in a slow beat. Steps, slow and steady, grew closer. A ragged voice tore through the darkness, a single word in a tortured voice stripping away the darkness.

"Sunshine."

I sucked in a breath. *Is this real? Is he really here with me?*

A soft touch ghosted along my arm, sliding up my neck and caressing my cheek.

"It's me. It's Alec." Peeking one lid open, I stared into the darkness. An enormous mass moved in the dim light. "You're safe. I have you."

The intense emotion in his voice broke through the dark haze, shattering the protective bubble I'd created for self-preservation. I shifted to see him only to hit my shoulder against his bent knee. A pitiful whimper crawled out my throat as I curled back into my protective cocoon.

Chapter 29

"You're hurt."

Even with his features doused in shadows, there was no mistaking the pure fury in his tight tone. That boiling anger didn't scare me. I was fucking grateful.

He found me.

But... something didn't add up. My dehydration-fogged brain couldn't put together what was off, but I knew deep in my gut something was.

"Come on," he whispered, lips brushing against my cheek. "Let's get you out of here before that bastard comes back."

That's it.

I clawed at Alec as he tried to pick me up.

He didn't leave.

He. Didn't. Leave.

That man was still here waiting for him.

"Rae, it's—"

His words cut off as his hands released me. I folded back to the floor. A flashlight rattled along the metal, shooting beams of bright light around the container until it rolled to a stop just feet away from where I lay. The shadows of two men danced along the wall. I watched in horror, not knowing who was who or who was winning.

I had to do something.

Bad arm tucked to my chest, I crawled toward the flashlight. Male grunts and cries of pain bleated through the container, sounding like an army of men instead of just the two. Fingers reaching, I stretched for the flashlight, only for it to roll just out of reach.

With a cry of frustration, I gripped the ridge of the metal floor and tugged my limp body forward. I nearly cried out in relief when two fingers wrapped around the cylinder handle. Rolling to my back, I swept the beam of light from one side of the container to the other, searching for Alec.

The light illuminated a man.

Alec.

Fist raised, he slammed it into the limp body pinned beneath his knees. Over and over that fist rose and fell. Dark drops rained around him with each punch, the man beneath him unmoving.

"Alec." My voice was a mere rasp. His raised fists stilled. "Stop. Please."

I wouldn't allow him to kill that man, not for me, even though I wanted him to. Even with everything that happened, I knew without a doubt Alec would hold that death as a validation of the monster he believed roamed inside him.

That red-coated hand hovered high, trembling. Hard eyes turned toward me, squinting in the bright light. It all became too much as the last of my energy reserves depleted.

The flashlight clattered to the floor, sending beams of light to rotate around the container as my arm dropped to the ground. Strong arms wrapped around my waist, hauling me upright.

"Shh," he murmured into my ear. "It's okay. I've got you. Where are you hurt?" Pain laced his tone mixed with tenderness and relief.

A tearless sob rattled my chest. "Shoulder," I rasped.

"You're bleeding," he whispered, stroking a finger along my sticky cheek. "Let's get you out of here." Alec's massive body shifted, moving to balance on the balls of his feet to help me stand. "Put your good arm around my neck, Sunshine."

I nodded, wrapping my sweat-slick arm around his neck and perching my chin along his shoulder. The discarded flashlight shone along the container floor, yet something was missing.

A dark puddle glistened in the light.

But where was—

A silent scream tore up my throat when a shadow just outside the beam of light shifted. My ragged nails sliced into Alec's back in warning at the glint of metal as it arched through the light, the knife's razor-sharp edge angled for Alec's back.

Without second-guessing myself, I pushed with everything I had, shoving my full weight into Alec and sending him toppling backward. As he tumbled to the side with a barked curse, I watched. Watched the tip of that knife, maybe the knife that was predestined for me, sink into my shoulder and slice through flesh and muscle.

Chapter 29

Pain like I'd never experienced flared along my torso, burning and excruciating.

I screamed. It crackled around the container, covered immediately by the resounding boom of a gun. High-pitched ringing vibrated in my ears, erasing any other sounds.

Sprawled across Alec's chest, I rested my cheek on his pec and sighed at the steady beat of his heart as it thumped against my skin.

A wet, sticky palm wrapped around my chin, tilting my face upward. Alec's nostrils flared with each breath, his lips moving, though I didn't hear a single word.

In fact, everything was silent except the ringing. And I was tired. So damn tired.

My attempt to pat his face ended up a hard slap. "You came," I thought I said out loud.

Behind Alec, movement drew my hazy gaze. Charlie stood in the open doorway of the container, gun held between two hands with several other men heavily armed pouring into the surrounding area.

Still not a sound.

I felt them move, the vibrations along the metal tickling my skin, yet I heard nothing.

One man kicked the flashlight, sending light dancing around the container again. It circled before slowing and stilling. I blinked at the beaten, bloody face it highlighted. Eyes open, that dead stare somehow felt fixed on me, like he might pop up, ready to torment me all over again.

I trembled. From my head to my feet, every part of my body shook.

Then he disappeared. The container rotated. My mind swam with the quick movement as Alec hauled me into the air. Held against a firm chest, I soared through the door. Each of Alec's steps sent shots of jarring pain through my shoulder, but it wasn't nearly as bad as before.

A heavy mist coated my face as we moved into the open air. I inhaled deep and tilted my face to the sky.

Free.

Really free. Not only from the container but from the horrors that had shadowed me for half my life. I wanted to leap from Alec's arms and dance in the rain, but I could barely muster the energy to blink, much less fight the man clutching me to his chest like a lifeline.

A wave of euphoria washed over me, relaxing my muscles. With a sigh, I let my head slump back, dangling over Alec's solid arm.

"Rae." Alec's desperate shout pierced through the dullness that crept over my thoughts. "Stay with me, Rae."

My limp head rolled and bobbed with each of his hurried steps. Above us, a bright spotlight shone, following us as we moved.

"The ambulance is at the entrance. They couldn't get back here because of the mud."

Charlie's voice was somewhat clear through the fog, yet I still couldn't feel my injuries or my entire body. That thought made me smile.

"She's still conscious, but barely," Alec said above me. "Why'd you have to be the hero, Rae?" I frowned at the anger in his tone. "Hold her dislocated arm. We need to move faster or she'll bleed out."

That didn't sound good.

A steady grip wrapped around my elbow, stabilizing my arm. That I felt. A scream scratched its way out my throat. Suddenly every cut, bruise, and bump flared to life.

"Fuck. Hold on, Sunshine. Hold on."

Alec's pleas continued as we moved. The pain turned to numbness, which slowly stole my awareness. One moment we were running, the next came loud arguing voices. Blinking at the harsh lights, I squinted to find a metal roof above where I lay.

Panic sliced through me, shooting my fight-or-flight instinct into gear. Something soft shifted beneath me as I shoved to a seated position, my eyes on the door just two feet away.

"Rae, calm down. You're safe. Sunshine, you're safe. I'm here." I turned, dry eyes wide, searching for the owner of that soothing voice. "You're on the way to the hospital. An ambulance. You're in an ambulance."

I nodded but stayed stiff.

Chapter 29

What if this was a dream, and I was still stuck back in that container waiting for... waiting to die?

"Water," I rasped. My cracked lips split with the small word.

"Not until we get—" an unfamiliar female voice started, but a bottle of water appeared in front of my face. "She can't have that before surgery. We have her connected to an IV to help with dehydration."

I turned pleading eyes to Alec, silently begging for the smallest of sips.

"A tiny one won't hurt." His words were soft as he smiled at me, but his commanding tone was a warning to the medic.

"Where's all that blood coming from?" Charlie's voice registered, but all I could focus on was the glorious water in Alec's shaking hand.

Twisting the cap, he held it to my lips and tilted the plastic bottle. The first splash of cool water disappeared on my dry tongue. I sipped tentatively before dipping my chin to slurp down the entire contents.

"That's enough."

My pleading eyes turned to a glare.

"Don't shoot the messenger," he grumbled. He turned to set the water down, but a wince pinched his features and a barked, pain-filled curse filled the ambulance.

"You're fucking kidding me." I whipped my head, the ambulance spinning with the fast move, toward Charlie's angry voice. "You dumb son of a bitch." He slammed a tattooed fist against the ambulance door. "You didn't tell us he got you too."

I turned back to Alec.

Features tight with pain and face so pale, unlike I'd ever seen him. Rolling beads of sweat slipped along his temples and down his clenched jaw. With a grunt, he slumped forward, his arm slamming to the gurney.

"It's fine. Take care of her first." His slurred words were barely understandable as he continued to drop forward. His lids drooped. The hand holding onto the bed slipped, sending him crashing to the ambulance floor.

I screamed. Charlie cursed. The medic beside my head shouted.

Desperate to be beside him, to help him, I fought against the hold someone had on my good shoulder, keeping me secured to the gurney.

"I'm sorry." Those two words registered half a second before warmth flooded my veins, making every tense muscle relax. I stopped fighting and slumped back against the stiff mattress. Blinks long and heavy, I stared at the shiny ceiling, unable to move as chaos erupted around me.

Tears leaked from the corners of both eyes as I listened to Charlie's panicked voice begging Alec to wake up and the deafening silence that followed.

30

RAE

A low insistent buzz, the murmuring of voices, and a beeping alarm pulled me from a deep sleep. Blinking against the weight keeping my lids closed, I fought the grogginess. A plain-tiled ceiling with a long florescent bulb hanging directly above me came into view as my vision cleared. Every muscle in my neck protested as I rolled my head to the side. Several machines blinked out of sync, the largest beeping in warning.

I curled my fingers, and thin cotton brushed beneath my fingertips. A white blanket lay along my legs where I rested in the high bed. Metal rails and the machines plus the baby blue gown I wore eased my worried thoughts.

A hospital.

A wince pinched my face, making the skin along my cheek burn, when the flimsy floral curtain ripped away. Full clear bag in hand, a young woman dressed in maroon scrubs stepped through the opening only to pause when our gazes met.

Her lips curled in a kind smile. "You're awake." My tongue stuck to the roof of my mouth, keeping me from responding. "I'll let the doctor and agent know." The way her eyes sparkled at the mention of the agent, I knew exactly which hottie she was referencing. "He's worn a rut in the waiting room while you were in surgery."

Surgery?

The word clanged in my head while she fiddled with the beeping machine and replaced the empty bag on the metal tree with the full one. Without another word, she turned and left, rolling the curtain back, sealing me back inside the makeshift room.

The desperate urge to pee sent me into motion. But putting weight onto the palm pressed against the thin mattress to help me sit up sent unbearable pain shooting up my arm. A silent cry swept past my dry lips as I fell back onto the bed.

What the fuck? Chest heaving from the pain and exertion that little move triggered, I focused on calming my heart rate before attempting to investigate what the hell happened. My right arm was secured in a sling against my chest. Raising the left sent bolts of pain along the back before I could get a look at the injury.

"Dislocated shoulder." I snapped my attention to the man who now stood inside the curtain. Dressed in blue scrubs and a long white lab coat, he barely paid me any attention as he scanned the chart in his hand. "You also have twenty-three stitches on that arm you're trying to rotate. Even more sutures on the inside holding your muscle together." He finally peered over the clipboard. "I'd appreciate it if you control your curiosity and keep still to not ruin the work I did to piece you back together."

Feeling reprimanded by the doctor, I sank deeper into the bed to hide from his withering stare.

"Take it easy, Doc." I released a relieved breath when Charlie stepped through the part in the curtain and paused beside the doctor. "She's had a rough twenty-four hours. Cut her some slack."

The doctor gave Charlie a side-eye glare before looking at me. "Now that you're awake, we'll move you to a room shortly." He turned and walked out, calling for a nurse while grumbling something under his breath.

With a feral grin, almost like he enjoyed getting under the arrogant doctor's skin, Charlie slowly slid the curtain back into place. It

Chapter 30

did nothing to diminish the sounds and voices of the hospital but helped foster the sense of some privacy, at least.

Charlie kept his blue eyes on me as he dragged a basic-looking chair to my bedside and fell into it. Mud caked his black pants; a bulletproof vest covered his chest. Leaning back in the chair, he closed his eyes and rubbed his lids with an exhausted groan.

"I don't know who I'm more pissed at, you or that dumb fucker Bronson."

My ears perked at the mention of Alec. Flashes of memories from the ambulance became clearer.

"Alec," I croaked. "Where's...? I need...." The burn in my throat stopped me from saying more.

"He's still in surgery," he replied, voice tight with worry. "The fucker took a blade to the lower back and didn't tell a soul. I'll kill him if he survives."

If.

I whimpered and shifted along the bed to sit up. I needed to get out, to get to him. He had to survive.

"Hey, hey," Charlie said in a soothing voice. "Sorry, I shouldn't have said that. He'll be fine. The doctors are doing everything they can. I'm just pissed, and...." He sighed, his hand slipping from where he held my knee. "You two scared the shit out of me. And I need a drink, a three-day nap, and a round with one of those nurses who keep eye-fucking me."

I huffed out a laugh and rolled my eyes as I settled back against the bed. "Cocky much?" I rasped.

His eyes brightened. "Always. It's why people like me so much."

We sat in silence for a few minutes before I gained the courage to ask the question burning inside me. I needed the truth, and Charlie would know.

"He said...." I tried to swallow down the building trepidation. "Said I'm...." His unblinking dead stare flashed in my mind. "Was his sister. Twin. Was it true?"

Tears welled in my eyes at the wash of pity that overcame Charlie's tired face. That was all the answer I needed. My chest shook with a sob.

"No," I cried. "Not true. It's a lie. It can't be true."

He stood and gripped each bed rail to hover over me.

"Calm down or that doctor will come back in here and sedate you. Calm down, Rae." I sniffled and nodded. "I'll tell you what I know if you promise me to stay calm and just listen." He gave me a hard stare before sitting back in the chair. "I validated it all. Even brought in the doctor who delivered you and him. It was true, the twin part. What else he told you while he had you"—his hands fisted at that—"I'm not sure. Alec can fill you in on all the details, but yes, it's true he was your brother."

"How?" I needed to know that much now. I couldn't wait another second without knowing why my mother never told me, why she and my father lied my entire life.

He blew out a breath and looked at the ceiling. "It's a long complicated story of a woman who was desperate for a baby and a woman who couldn't afford to care for two babies when one would already be a strain." Sympathy poured off him when he turned his face back to me. "You weren't stolen, you were gifted to Stephanie Chapin. To a woman who your birth mother knew would give you a good life."

"He hated me for it," I whispered, remembering his rants. "For leaving him."

Charlie's lips pursed into a tight line. "I assumed as much based on his background. His life was rough, Rae. I'm not excusing what he did to you or the other murders he committed, but I wouldn't wish his early life on my worst enemy."

I nodded, not sure how to take that bit of information.

"What—" I sighed and squeezed my eyes shut. "What was his name?"

"Jared Stark. He was a terrible man, Rae, messed up from years of abuse and drugs. Whatever he told you as to why he fixated on you, why he wanted to get back at you, were the thoughts of a psychopath. They won't make sense to anyone but him—hell, maybe not even to him. He looked for someone to blame for what happened to him, and probably right around that time, his mom let it slip that he had a sister. He wasn't right in the head, Rae."

I opened my mouth to ask the question burning the tip of my tongue, but he held up a hand, stopping me.

"Don't even think it. You're nothing like him, Rae, blood or no blood. I'm an excellent judge of character, and I know you're one of the kindest, sincerest women I've met. You're. Nothing. Like. Him."

I nodded and cleared my throat while trying to think of something to divert us from this topic. "So for my injuries, there's the shoulder, the cut—"

"Slice. Slice, Rae. You jumped in front of the knife. It cut through the length of your tricep. That doctor literally had to stich your arm back together."

"What else?" I asked before he gave more gruesome details.

"A cut along your cheek needed a few stitches. Other than that, lots of bruising, cuts, and scrapes. I think the nurse mentioned they administered a tetanus shot just in case."

"Smart. That place...." I looked at the ceiling to avoid his focused attention.

"Rae, I don't know what happened while we searched for you, but whatever happened, whatever he did or said, it's over."

Over. I considered that word. "What does that even mean? It's not over in my head. I can still feel"—my breathing picked up—"it all. The fear, knowing I was going to die."

"I know, and it'll take a long while for those memories to fade, but you're free, Rae."

"Free." I blew out a breath and fisted the blanket with my free hand. "Free."

"The police no longer consider you a suspect and have almost two dozen previously unsolved murders now solved. No more hiding from the world."

"What do I do now?" I asked in disbelief.

Charlie's lips parted into a wide smile. "Whatever you want to do. That's the beauty of freedom."

The same nurse from before popped her head through the split in floral fabric and smiled. "Your friend is out of surgery. It went well, and he's expected to make a full recovery." With a bashful grin, she dipped back behind the curtain.

Charlie and I let out a relieved sigh and smiled at each other.

"He loves you, you know that, right?" he said, settling back into the chair and propping his head on his raised palm. "He meant nothing he said back at the house. Which, really, Rae? You called the cops on us?"

I chuckled. "I needed time to get away. And yeah, I know, but I still want to hear it from him." Charlie's lids drifted closed. "And I have a lot I want to tell him too."

Closing my own eyes, I relaxed into the flat pillow.

Freedom.

Free from this town, from my self-imprisonment.

Free to live.

And I knew exactly who I wanted to start living my life with.

31

RAE

Chilled air crested over my bare arms, causing goose bumps to sprout as I slipped into Alec's recovery room. My steps faltered at the sight of him connected to various tubes and machines. Charlie gave my hip a gentle squeeze, a silent question if I was okay. I nodded and continued forward, moving toward the bed.

It was unnerving seeing Alec so vulnerable, lying completely still. Tears welled in my lower lids as I shuffled along the bedside, Charlie at my side, making sure I didn't fall and wheeling my IV tree. The doctor and nurses weren't thrilled at my decision to seek Alec out, but there was nothing they could do to stop me.

I had to see him no matter who tried to stand in my way. Charlie saw that determination and agreed to help me find Alec as long as I took it easy.

"Here," Charlie ordered as he dragged the lone chair in the room to Alec's bedside. "They said he might be out of it for a while. He lost a lot of blood, plus the time he was under anesthesia. He's also on heavy antibiotics to offset the bacteria from the liver nick."

Worry creased his forehead as he watched me sink carefully into the chair without the use of either arm. I couldn't even go to the bathroom on my own, which was mortifying considering I peed every thirty minutes with the fluids they pumped into my body through the IV.

A pinch and sting burned down the back of my arm as I reached toward Alec's massive hand lying on top of the white blanket. A sense of calm washed through me, chasing away the recent horrifying memories from the moment my fingers wrapped around one of his.

I gave that single digit a soft squeeze.

"He'll be okay, right?" I asked Charlie while searching every inch of Alec's pale, slack face. Even sedated, the man appeared menacing somehow, as if his fighting spirit raged behind the soft, relaxed features to free itself of the immobile body.

"The nurse said he should make a full recovery. That bastard is one lucky fucker that the knife only nicked his liver instead of impaling it in the center."

I grimaced at the thought. "Should? What do you mean he *should* make a full recovery?"

"You know him. Alec will probably do something stupid before he's fully recovered that will delay his healing." I huffed in agreement. One after another, I swept a single finger along the ridges of his cut knuckles. "You'll be there to help him though, right? Make sure he takes his meds, doesn't overdo it, and coddle his whiny ass?"

I smiled at that, only for it to slip as I stared at Alec.

"I don't know what he wants. All this has happened so fast. I know what I want, or rather who I want, but... it's complicated. We're complicated. He has to make a choice between me and what he's believed for a very long time. I want him to choose me, but... I mean, you know."

"I don't follow." Charlie stepped alongside me and placed a hand on the back of the chair. "Why is it complicated? I've seen you two. It's what everyone searches for in a relationship. It's real, Rae, the realest thing I've ever seen."

"Look at him, Charlie, and look at me." My hand slipped from the bed. "He can have anyone he wants. We had fun this past week, outside of the dead body and being captured, but what happens when we go back to real life? When he goes back to being this badass

Ranger and me a lonely librarian with a slight drinking problem? I had a twin brother who I never knew about and tried to kill me. Talk about family drama. No one wants that mixed in their family. He's everything, and I'm a no one." I hung my head, strands of greasy hair slipping over my shoulder and curtaining around my face. "I want him to choose me so much it hurts. As in my heart hurts at the thought of not being with him. But who am I to ask him to stay?"

Silence settled over the room, my confession hovering in the air between us.

"I'm disappointed in you, Rae." I snapped my face up to Charlie's. "I thought you were smarter than this. That you could see you mean everything to him. Complications are a fact of life. It's how you overcome them that shows the strength in the relationship. With what you masterminded for those women." My eyes widened. *Forgot about that part.* "Did you really think we wouldn't piece the details together? Your Hulk is the one who discovered the library connection."

"Charlie," I groaned and attempted to stand. A heavy hand pressed to the top of my head, keeping me in the chair. "You can't look into me, into them. They're safe, and if—"

"I'm not, Rae. But trust your heart and believe in Bronson. If you can do that, then nothing else matters."

"Am I interrupting something?" Both Charlie and I snapped our attention to the frowning Alec, whose narrowed eyes were on the hand still resting atop my head.

"Alec," I whimpered with the swell of emotions. "You're awake." Tears freely slid down both cheeks. Forgetting about everything but him, I reached to touch his face. The stitches tugged, stopping my hand halfway. With a grimace, I pulled my hand back and covered his with my own. "How do you feel?"

He gave me a blank stare. "Like I was stabbed."

A delusional chuckle tickled in my chest. "I know the feeling."

"What were you two talking about?" Alec asked as he shifted along the bed. "Fuck, this is worse than being shot."

"You've been shot before?" I gasped.

"Three times, Sunshine. Now stop avoiding the question."

I chewed on my lower lip, not excited about the idea of talking about either topic Charlie brought up.

"Little Rae here was about to tell me how she masterminded the escape and vanishing act of fifteen women and seven children. Weren't you?"

I cut a glare his way. "Was I now?"

"Yep," he popped the *p* for emphasis. The bastard smiled. "And as for me touching your girl, don't get all pissy or the heart monitor will go ballistic. She tried to stand up, but she's in no condition, so I kept her seated with a hand on her pretty little head."

Alec's gray eyes turned stormy at the last comment. As predicted, the beeping increased in speed and volume. If he didn't calm down, the doctors would come in and force me out.

Not yet. I needed more time.

"The library," I said, and both pairs of eyes turned to me. "The first woman, Megan, I met at the library. She came in to borrow a book for her and her daughter. I noticed the bruises the first time only on her. Months passed, she kept coming back, and I eventually noticed bruises on the little girl. Red marks on her wrists, and once in a cast. It took another couple months for me to gain the courage to say something. I asked if she had anywhere to go, any family who could take her in. And you know her response? I'll never forget it. She said, 'Nowhere he won't find me and take me back.' And I knew, I *knew* right then that I could do something, be someone for her and her daughter. Even with my crappy job, self-isolation, and little money, I had the power to change her life."

A single finger stroked over my knuckles, drawing my attention to our hands.

"I read enough suspense and thrillers over the years that the plan was fairly easy. The fact that no one noticed me anymore made it even better. I started with researching the best drug to knock someone out. That's when I discovered roofies."

"How in the hell did you score roofies?" Alec asked, his voice gruff as if the words hurt.

"The parolees and recently released visitors at the library," I whispered. "They wanted money, which I had, and had access to the drugs. So I made a plan. Bought her a disposable phone, made her a new ID—which was oddly easy thanks to some YouTube videos—and gave her enough cash to get out of the state and find a shelter. Some wore disguises and hopped a bus, and others had a friend drive them to a different town to catch a train. It varied depending on what resources they brought to the table.

"The night they left, they drugged their husbands or boyfriends, whichever, waited for them to pass out, and then left. And it worked. Time and time again. And it became my thing, my way of making a difference with no one ever knowing except the people who mattered. It wasn't much, but to them it was everything."

A mix of awe and disbelief settled over Alec's smiling face. "Your bracelet has something to do with all this, doesn't it?"

"Did you find it?" I gripped his hand as hard as I could. "It broke off my wrist when he took me." At his confirming nod, I released a heavy breath. "Great, good. Thank you. And yeah, it has everything to do with all this. After they leave town, I instruct them to never contact me or anyone they knew again. It's too dangerous. But I want to know when they're safe. So when they're settled in their new life, safe and living, I ask that they let me know they're okay."

"By sending you a charm." I nodded. "Rae." Alec sighed. "What you did was—"

"Illegal," I said, defeated. Releasing his hand, I sat back in the chair, putting distance between us. "I'm not asking you to choose—"

"I was going to say brave, stupid, amazing."

"But... but you have to turn me in. Those drugs alone—"

"Drugs?" Charlie chimed in as he stepped along Alec's bedside. "I don't recall any drugs." He narrowed his brows in concentration and looked at Alec. "Do you?"

A small smirk popped that adorable dimple. "Nope."

I gaped at the two. "Alec, that's not why you became a Ranger. I'm not above the law—"

His hand snapped out and grabbed my own. "You're right, you're not. But, Rae?" He glanced over my shoulder. "Give us a minute, would you?"

Charlie exited without a word, the door closing behind him with a soft click, leaving Alec and me alone.

"You're not mad?" I whispered in disbelief. The urge to crawl into the bed with him, to snuggle against that expansive chest and have those powerful arms wrapped around me, became too much to resist. I craved his comfort and protection.

"I'm... no, I'm not mad. I'm in awe of you, Sunshine, and obsessively in love with the strong, confident badass woman you are."

"Alec...." Overwhelming emotions clogged my throat, preventing me from saying more.

"I'm disappointed you didn't tell me the truth," he continued. "And I'm pissed that I'm the reason you didn't. I know you ran to prevent me from choosing between you and the law, and, Rae, I'm sorry I made you think... for it to even be a thought that I wouldn't choose you. All day, every day, I'll choose you." He groaned and pressed his head into the pillow in frustration. "I hate fucking doing this while lying here like a damn invalid. But it needs to be said now, before I lose you again. I'm sorry, Rae. I should've believed you when you said it had nothing to do with the case. I should've given you a safe space to tell me the truth, to give you time to open up. But I didn't, and instead I forced you away, which put your life in danger."

Those dark lashes fanned over his cheeks with long blinks. Desperation swirled in his gray eyes as he looked over to where I sat beside his hospital bed.

"I don't deserve your forgiveness. For leaving all those years ago and for yesterday. But if you do, if you give me another chance, I'll spend the rest of my life worshipping you the way you deserve. You're beautiful inside and out, Rae Chapin, and I don't want you to leave. I love you, Sunshine. I want you home, with me, where you've always belonged."

I bit my quivering lip and smiled. "I'll forgive you if you can figure out a way for me to be up there with you." I nodded toward the bed and gave a pointed look at my injured arms.

Deep wrinkles formed along his normally smooth forehead.

"Charlie," he yelled so loud my ears rang. Within seconds, the door swung open and his face appeared through the gap. "Help Rae onto the bed, would you?"

Charlie huffed and strode into the room. "I did not agree to become an accomplice to this terrible decision. You're both hurt." Alec answered with a blank stare. "Fine." Standing beside me, he held his hands over my waist, then hips and paused. "I'll need to touch her to help her up. Don't Hulk out on me."

"Only where necessary," Alec grumbled.

The side bar lowered with a hard shove and click. Hands on my waist, Charlie helped me onto the mattress before swinging my legs around. Alec scooted to the far side of the bed, careful of his many tubes and cords, giving me enough room to lie on my back. With a few pinched cords, hissed curses, and groans of pain, we settled beside each other.

Contentment flooded my veins, allowing my first full, calm breath since we left his home over a day ago.

Charlie frowned as he looked at us.

"May I go now?" he asked with his hands crossed over his chest.

I giggled at the annoyance written across his features. No, wait. I squinted to see better in the dim light. Was that annoyance or sadness? Whatever emotion it was, it vanished as he turned and left without a second glance back.

A soft sigh slipped past my lips as I relaxed against Alec.

"Did you really mean it?"

"Mean what, Sunshine?"

"That you don't want me to leave?" I swallowed hard and cleared my throat of the uncertainty that crept up.

"Not only do I not want you to leave, but I don't want to leave you. Come live with me." I sucked in a breath. "I know that sounds crazy, and you have a life here in Sweetcreek—"

"No," I cut in. "I don't have a life." My face scrunched with a cringe. "What I mean is, I don't want that life anymore. This town only reminds me of what I've lost, and now of him. I was lonely, Alec, and honestly, I've always waited for you, like I knew one day you'd come back for me. I want to make a new life, with you."

A new life.

Yes, a new life without pain and grief.

A new beginning with the only man I ever loved.

Keep reading for the epilogue and BONUS epilogue!

Be sure to read the other two books in the Protection Series! FREE with Kindle Unlimited.
Mine to Protect (Book 1)
Mine to Save (Book 2)

EPILOGUE
ALEC

I watched from the gym doorway as Rae hugged and showered Jasmin and Cale with love-soaked kisses. The three were exhausted from the two-day sleepover, having spent their time swimming in the heated pool, exploring the property, and staying up till all hours of the night giggling. Knowing they could have this time with their aunt in a safe, fun place—my place—pushed pride through my veins. The moment I saw them, I knew Rae would want to be a part of their lives any way she could.

Over the last eight months, the three slowly worked toward the budding relationship they now cherished. Their mother trusted us to take care of them, giving her a few days off to relax and allowing Rae to relish the joys of being an aunt and having family to spoil.

I loved seeing her this happy with the kids, especially since we wouldn't have a family of our own. I offered to research vasectomy reversals but she said no, shocking the hell out of me. She never said why, but I had a feeling it had something to do with her brother and also took into consideration my feelings toward my own DNA.

With one more kiss and hug, she opened the front door to walk the two kids to where their mom waited in her running car, ready to make the drive back to Sweetcreek. Seizing my chance, I shrugged off the doorframe and strode to the kitchen. As I passed the counter, I paused, elbow resting on the edge, and reread the handwritten note for the hundredth time since I wrote it days earlier.

Sunshine,
I knew from the beginning you were the one. Your smile, your heart stole any chance of another woman ever being a blip on my heart's radar. Every day we were apart, it was like a piece of me was missing. I didn't realize what it was until I saw you behind those bars. It hit me that you never left me, that my soul held out hope, waiting for me to find my way back to you. These past several months with you back in my life have been the best days of my life. I feel complete with you near. Every day I fight with the lie my father drilled into me, but you're worth that fight. All day I will fight with the uncertainty to have even a second by your side. You're it for me, Sunshine.
You always were and always will be.
No matter where you go, I'll go. I'll always be there with you and for you for the rest of your life, if you'll have me. I'm not perfect. We'll fight, and there will be times when I'm an ass and I'll make you cry. But I swear to you, I'll never hurt you, and I will always, always love and protect you.
If you'll have me.
I can't do this limbo anymore, Rae.
I want you—all of you.
Meet me outside if you're ready for all of me.

I released a breath and folded the note in a tight little square, just like I used to do. After writing her name on the front, I left it on the counter and made my way outside. The glow of the hanging Edison bulbs lit the path, shimmering off the rose petals covering the stones.

That was Sher Sher's idea. I wanted simple, just me and the beauty of the Texas night sky. She won that argument, and I had to admit it added a little something seeing the red and white petals sprinkled everywhere.

The pool area glowed from the various lanterns and lights strategically placed around the deck and pergola. A bottle of champagne sat on a bed of ice in a bucket on the metal table, two glasses beside it.

Shoving both hands into my Wranglers, I stood along the pool's edge and tipped my face up to the dark sky filled with blinking stars. A cold winter wind cut through the quiet of the night. I welcomed the chill over my heated skin. Trepidation of what I was about to ask of Rae tightened my chest.

Could I do it, be the man she deserved for the rest of her life? I wanted that, wanted to be that man, and for her, I would try. Every day I would wake up and be the husband she deserved. Loving her body and soul. Supporting her in whatever venture she took next.

Since we left Sweetcreek, leaving behind her way to connect and help abused women, Rae brainstormed the idea of an underground network of safe houses and secret communications. The planning and groundwork turned out to be a full-time job, which she loved pouring her heart and soul into. With my financial backing and other silent partners, in a few short months, Rae's idea would be a reality, possibly saving dozens of women and children a month from their abusive partners instead of the handful a year like she did when working on her own.

I was so fucking proud of her.

A soft gasp sent me whirling around. Rae stood at the edge of the pool deck, the note dangling between two fingers at her side. She wore black leggings that showcased her curves and a long gray sweater, and I took her in from head to toe and back up again.

Mine.

I nodded for her to join me beneath the lit pergola.

She stared at everything around us, from the rose petals covering the table to the champagne to me. Tears already lined her lower lids as she bit back a smile.

"Sunshine," I breathed.

"Yes," she blurted before slapping a hand over her mouth and closing her eyes. "Sorry. You were saying?"

Lacing both our hands together, I tugged her close. Her chin dug into my chest as she stared up at me. Long dark hair hung in loose curls down her back, tickling our combined hands.

"I meant it all. Every word." I pressed a soft kiss to her forehead. "I love you, Rae Chapin. And I promise you I'll love you with all I have until the day I die. You'll want for nothing, and you'll never have to wonder who's number one in my life. You're all I want. You as you. I know it'll be difficult, but everything worth fighting for always is. And we, us, are worth fighting for with all I have. Will you marry me, Rae, and make me the happiest fucking man in Texas?"

Tears freely fell down her bunched cheeks, her smile so wide I could barely see her eyes.

"I've dreamed of this, you know? Of my second chance with you actually happening and what it would be like, and this, what we've shared these past few months, was better than I ever imagined. I know this won't be easy, Alec. And you won't have to fight for us alone. I'll be there with you every step of the way. You're the one I want to spend my forever with. Yes, I'll marry you."

BONUS EPILOGUE
RAE

Spoilers from Mine to Save included in this bonus epilogue. If you haven't read Chandler and Ellie's story yet... you can find it here!

Not an inch of the pool's crystal clear water was visible through the layers of perfectly bloomed magnolias floating along the top. Tiny lights flickered and swayed along the pergola and cabana. Over fifty people attended the earlier ceremony and stuck around to help us celebrate our union. Servers walked among the crowd, delivering bites of scrumptious food and flutes of champagne, glasses of whiskey, and of course glasses of red and white wine.

I only wished my parents could see it, but a part of me knew they were watching from above, smiling.

"Sunshine."

I turned with the wide smile that was a permanent fixture on my face nowadays toward the man I loved. My husband. The off-white soft layers of my wedding dress swished around my legs with the movement.

Alec stood, a soft happy smile on his handsome face, beside a man I didn't recognize. Considering I didn't know most of the people who attended our wedding besides Charlie and Sherry, I wasn't surprised by the unknown face.

Alec clapped the man on the shoulder, shoving him forward an inch. The man shot my husband a glare with zero heat.

"Such a damn brute," he grumbled before turning his attention back to me. "Rae, it's nice to meet you. I'm Chandler Peters and this"—he slung an arm around the slim shoulders of the small woman beside him—"is my wife, Ellie Peters."

"It's nice to meet you both." I shook his extended hand and then hers. "I'm slightly obsessed with your hair," I admitted, unable to take my eyes off the soft pink strands.

"Don't get any ideas," Alec muttered into my ear as he slid an arm around my waist. Turning his attention back to his friend, he hugged me closer to his side. "Where's this baby of yours? I was hoping to meet my goddaughter."

"You're not her godfather," the woman, Ellie, laughed. She shook her head, sending her hair swinging along the tops of her shoulders. "No religious stuff, remember?"

I felt Alec tense against me. "Right, sorry."

She waved him off, dismissing the comment. "Candice is at home with a sitter." She sent a wicked smile up to her husband and winked. "We used the wedding as an excuse for some adult-only time. We haven't had much with his work and the baby."

"Speaking of his work, I heard you have a new member of the BSU team. He's a good one." Alec tilted his whiskey glass in Charlie's direction by the pool, though he was too busy with the swarm of women around him to notice. "But be sure to haze the shit out of him."

We all laughed, finally drawing Charlie's attention. He raised a dark brow and smiled. No doubt he knew we were laughing at his expense.

"Yeah, we're excited to have him start," Chandler agreed. "The cases are stacking up, and we don't have enough manpower to cover them all."

"Hey," Ellie said, drawing my attention away from the boys'

conversation. "Chandler told me what you're doing with the safe houses and helping women escape their abusers." I nodded. I didn't need to ask why she was interested since Alec had mentioned her past once or twice over the last several months. "I want in."

My grin broadened and my cheeks and eyes burned. "I'd love the help. Yes, please."

"How many houses do you have set up now?" Taking my elbow, she directed me toward one of the high-top tables scattered around the pool deck. On the way, I stopped a server and snagged a glass of white wine off their tray.

"Four," I said after taking a tentative sip. "I'm trying to locate more, but it's a lot. You offering to help is a godsend honestly. I'm in over my head because there's a waiting list now, and I hate the idea of someone...." I shook my head. "It's just a lot of pressure from every side."

We stood in comfortable silence for a minute before she spoke up, breaking the tranquility.

"I'm happy for him." She sighed and smiled at Alec. "For you too, but I know Alec. He deserved someone who would make him happy. And look at him. He hasn't stopped smiling. I wanted that for him as much as I wanted that for myself."

Her gaze turned distant, as if she was revisiting those memories.

"Why?" I asked.

"Because from the moment he stepped into Orin, I knew he was one of the good ones. I had little trust in anyone, yet this huge man walked into town, and I instantly knew I was safe with him. Our friendship grew from there, and I honestly think he was the first man I let my guard down with. And that opened the pathway for Chandler."

"I'm sorry you went through all that." I tentatively grasped her forearm and gave it a squeeze.

"I could say the same to you, Rae. Chandler told me your story." I followed her gaze to the two laughing men. "I'd say we both got exactly who and what we deserved. Wouldn't you?"

"I would, but so did they."

She turned, that soft pink hair swinging with the movement. After grasping a glass of wine off the tray of a passing server, she held it high.

"To all of us." She clinked her glass with mine, but I didn't take a sip. Instead I held her gaze and clinked her glass again.

"To those who don't stop fighting and dreaming until they find the happiest ever after they deserve."

Like me.

Read the other two books in the Protection Series now!
Mine to Protect (Book 1)
Mine to Save (Book 2)

Want more of our tatted hacker? Charlie's story will hit Kindles December 2021!

ALSO BY KENNEDY L. MITCHELL

Standalone:

Falling for the Chance

A Covert Affair

Finding Fate

Memories of Us

Protection Series: Interconnected Standalone

Mine to Protect

Mine to Save

Mine to Guard

More Than a Threat Series: A Bodyguard Romantic Suspense Connected Series

More Than a Threat

More Than a Risk

More Than a Hope (Coming June 2021)

Power Play Series: A Protector Romantic Suspense Connected Series

Power Games

Power Twist

Power Switch

Power Surge

Power Term

ABOUT THE AUTHOR

Kennedy L. Mitchell lives outside Dallas with her husband, son and two very large goldendoodles. She began writing in 2016 after a fight with her husband (You can read the fight almost verbatim in Falling for the Chance) and has no plans of stopping.

She would love to hear from you via any of the platforms below or her website www.kennedylmitchell.com You can also stay up to date on future releases through her newsletter or by joining her Facebook readers group - Kennedy's Book Boyfriend Support Group.

Thank you for reading.

Printed in Great Britain
by Amazon